"You shall be marked as captive so that all the world will know at a glance what you are."

He signaled to two of his men, who pinned her arms to her sides. She fought against them, her calm deserting her.

"What do you mean?" Annis's voice held a note of panic.

Haakon gritted his teeth. Did she think he'd be lenient because they had lain in each other'

"Cut her hair. Place a
her in the pigsty, whe
done." Haakon stared
him, whispered soft w
the lands to the south

He had liked her, lusted after her body, wanted to spend time with her, and all the while she'd wanted to betray him. He should have remembered the lessons of his youth—women were not to be trusted.

Taken by the Viking
Harlequin® Historical #898—May 2008

Author Note

When I was very young, my maternal grandfather gave the grandchildren an illustrated book of Scandinavian fairy tales so that we could learn about our heritage. Some of the tales caused nightmares, but one of my earliest memories includes looking at the wonderfully romantic picture of a dark-haired Viking on a white horse, holding the woman he had just kidnapped, as my mother read the story about how Sweden was founded. I have had a soft spot for Vikings ever since.

Thus, when I met my lovely editors for lunch and they casually suggested the Viking period, I struggled to maintain my poise, be very professional and not punch the air in excitement. On the way home from the lunch, I scribbled basic notes, wrote a premise, then held my breath. Would they see the possibilities? Luckily, they were very enthusiastic about my ideas, and I was given the go-ahead to write this book. Hopefully you will find this time period as exciting as I do and enjoy this tale. I certainly enjoyed writing it.

As ever, I do love reader feedback. You can contact me through my Web site, www.michellestyles.co.uk, my blog, www.michellestyles.blogspot.com or through the Harlequin Books office. If you are interested in my latest news and forthcoming releases, I have a newsletter that readers can subscribe to. You can find details about it on my Web site.

Taken by the Viking

Michelle Styles

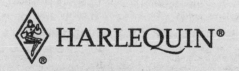

HARLEQUIN®

TORONTO • NEW YORK • LONDON
AMSTERDAM • PARIS • SYDNEY • HAMBURG
STOCKHOLM • ATHENS • TOKYO • MILAN • MADRID
PRAGUE • WARSAW • BUDAPEST • AUCKLAND

ISBN-13: 978-0-373-29498-5
ISBN-10:   0-373-29498-0

TAKEN BY THE VIKING

Available from Harlequin® Historical and
MICHELLE STYLES

The Gladiator's Honor #817
The Roman's Virgin Mistress #858
A Christmas Wedding Wager #878
Taken by the Viking #898

DON'T MISS THESE OTHER
NOVELS AVAILABLE NOW:

#895 WESTERN WEDDINGS
Jillian Hart, Kate Bridges and Charlene Sands
You are cordially invited to three weddings in the
Old West this May!
Three favorite authors, three blushing brides, three
heartwarming stories—just perfect for spring!

#896 NOTORIOUS RAKE, INNOCENT LADY—
Bronwyn Scott
Her virginity would be sold to the highest bidder! Determined
not to enter into an arranged marriage, Julia could see no way
out—unless she could seduce the notorious Black Rake....
Harlequin® Historical is loosening the laces with our newest,
hottest, sexiest miniseries, Undone!

#897 COOPER'S WOMAN—Carol Finch
A proper lady should have no dealings with a gunfighter who
has a shady past, yet Alexa is bent on becoming
Cooper's woman!
Carol Finch's thrilling Western adventure will have you on the
edge of your seat.

To my sister, Kate, *med elske*

Chapter One

8 June 793—Lindisfarne, Northumbria

Annis pressed her lips together, trying to keep her head from moving as her maid plaited her hair. What had she really hoped for? That her uncle, the Abbot of St Cuthbert's Priory, would give her money to fight her stepfather? His only suggested alternative had been the church. She could have a good position as long as she brought her dowry with her.

'My lady, it will take less time if you bend your head slightly this way.'

Annis regarded the wall of the guesthouse at St Cuthbert's, with its mural of Mary kneeling at the base of the cross, and concentrated harder.

It had been a mistake to come. Last night's conversation still rang in her ears. Her uncle refused to listen to her arguments. Why had she ever thought otherwise?

She'd leave the monastery and the island tomorrow at low tide when the causeway was passable, Annis decided. She would have to return home to Birdoswald on the River Irthing in the west of Northumbria. And face the future her way.

'Is this suitable, my lady?'

Her new maidservant, Mildreth, finished plaiting her hair and handed her a small mirror. Annis took a brief glance at herself. Her wayward tumble of brown curls had been tamed into two neat plaits on either side of her head. Annis considered her hair to be her best feature, perhaps her only noteworthy feature, but something with a will of its own. Mildreth knew what she was doing, she'd allow, but Annis refused to trust her.

Mildreth was her stepfather's creature. Had to be. Her stepfather had forced all her maids and retainers to be changed after her husband had died and she had returned to the family lands. There had been no excuse for her to stay with Selwyn's family. She had no child and her sister-in-law had always resented her. So she had returned, hoping for a better reception, and discovered her stepfather firmly in control of the family lands.

'Soon we will be preparing for your betrothal.'

'If God wills…' Annis placed the mirror back on the dressing table and forced her face to remain bland. She had no intention of marrying her stepfather's son, the odious Eadgar, with his damp hands and even damper manner. Neither did she intend on retiring to a convent as her uncle had suggested. There had to be another way.

'You will have to marry sometime. Eadgar is a fine—' Mildreth stopped and her face grew distressed. 'Mistress, I cannot lie. I have grown fond of you. Eadgar is a terror. All the maidservants fear him if they are caught alone with him. Please say nothing.'

Annis caught Mildreth's hand. A faint pink tinged the maid's cheeks, making her almost pretty. Annis felt happier than she had been in weeks. Her journey to Lindisfarne had not been in vain. She had discovered an ally of sorts.

'We share the same view of Eadgar.'

'They said you were kind, my lady, and you are.'

'It is far too soon to speak of remarriage in any case.' Annis straightened the neck of her gown. 'My husband is barely cold in his grave. There will be time enough to speak of marriage after I have finished mourning him. I came here seeking my uncle's advice and, having received it, I will return to my home.'

'As you say, my lady.'

A sudden fierce tolling of the bells resounded in the room, crowding out all thought or speech. Every fibre of Annis's being tensed.

'We are going to be attacked!' Mildreth wrung her hands. 'Murdered in our beds!'

Annis forced a breath from her lips. Despite the increasing shrillness of the bells, she had to stay calm. It could be anything. Blind panic would not serve.

'Attack? Really, Mildreth, you must not let your fears take hold. Who would dare attack this place?' She forced her voice to sound normal. Annis wasn't quite sure whom she was trying to convince, her maid or herself. 'The bells will be ringing for another reason. A pilgrim misjudged the tide and is stuck on the causeway.'

Mildreth gave a tremulous smile and ducked her head as the bells continued to peal. Annis offered up a small prayer that her words were correct. They had to be. Who would risk eternal damnation by attacking one of the most holy and learned sites in Northumbria, if not Europe?

The protection it offered was the reason her family chose to store the bulk of their coin with the monks rather than keeping it in locked chests on their estates. The vast majority of landowners in Northumbria used this simple but effective way of ensuring their coin was truly safe.

Then, as suddenly as the bells started, they stopped. The silence became deafening.

'It will be nothing.' Annis's voice sounded loud, echoing off the wooden walls. 'A ship might have been stranded and a monk panicked. My uncle says some of the newer monks can be excitable. Whatever it was, it is sure to have been solved.'

'As you say, my lady.'

Mildreth gave another nod, but her thin face bore a distinctly unhappy look to it. Annis reached out and touched her hand.

'All will be well, Mildreth. We are in God's place. He will look after us.'

'There have been portents,' Mildreth said and then dropped her voice to a whisper. 'One of the monks said he saw dragons flying across the moon. And strange fires in the night. Whirlwinds in the skies. Something to punish us for our wicked, sinful ways. They were speaking of it in the Abbot's scullery only yesterday.'

'Tales to frighten young maidservants, without a doubt.' Annis gave an uneasy laugh. 'By Michaelmas, after the harvest, no one will remember. It is the way of things.'

Annis rose and crossed quickly to the small window that overlooked the sea. Yesterday, she had admired the view of clear yellow sand and bright sparkling water, empty save for a few fishing boats. Today, an entirely different sight lay before her.

'I may have been wrong, Mildreth. The monastery has company.' Annis fought to keep the sound of rising panic out of her voice. She must not jump to conclusions. She was too impatient, her imagination too active, or so her uncle had told her several times this visit.

The early morning sunshine threw sparkles on the water but the sea was no longer empty. Three boats with serpents on their prows, round shields on their sides and red-and-white striped sails were in the shallow bay. One had drawn up on shore while the others followed closely behind.

As Annis watched, warriors disembarked from the first serpent ship, wading through the surf. They were dressed in trousers and chain mail, carrying their helmets and round shields. An air of wildness hung about them. No two were dressed alike. Heathens. Pagans. Raiders.

Annis leant out the window to get a better look. The leader had dark hair that touched his shoulders and several days' growth on his beard. An intricate design of a serpent and beast fighting covered his shield. The warriors behind him ranged from a wild man with flowing hair and beard to a slim, blonder version of the leader. The leader glanced up towards the window. His startling blue gaze held hers for a heartbeat. A brief smile touched his lips as he turned to greet the group hurrying from the monastery. Annis put her hand to her throat.

Had he seen her?

Her uncle stood at the front of the group in his white habit, taller than the rest, but not as tall as the barbarian leader, with an air of confidence and command. Annis gave a half-smile. She had been wrong to worry. Her uncle's skill as a politician was renowned throughout Northumbria and Mercia. She was certain he would have the measure of these heathen warriors in no time.

Her uncle held out his hand to be kissed in the traditional manner. The pagan warlord ignored it, and inclined his head before he handed her uncle a tablet.

The colour drained from her uncle's face and his hand shook.

What did these barbarians want?

Haakon Haroldson stared in disbelief at the fine-featured Abbot. He had shown the elderly man the tablet and the tablet was quite specific. He had made certain of that, taking the trouble to read it after Oeric the Scot's scribe had written the demand out. And he personally placed Oeric's seal on it.

The *felag* had come for gold coin lawfully owed them. If they could trade or provide some measure of protection while they were here, so much the better. But no one cheated them.

This summer's sea voyage was proving reasonably profitable. The new design for the boats had worked, skimming the ocean's surface, increasing their speed. The Scots desired the Vikens' thick fur pelts and amber beads.

There was simply this business to conclude. Then they sailed back home with honour.

'We have come here for the money Oeric the Scot owes us.'

The Abbot raised a brow. 'I am surprised at a Norseman speaking Latin.'

'We are traders. We learn the languages as they are needed.' Haakon kept his eyes fixed somewhere over the Abbot's shoulder. There was no need to give his life's history, not yet. Later, perhaps when their business dealings were complete and they were enjoying a cup of mead together. He held out his hands, palms upwards. 'We come in peace. We only want what is promised us.'

'How can I tell this tablet is genuine?'

'We would have hardly come here if it wasn't.'

'I have heard of raids by your sort against defenceless farms.'

'Other traders. Not us. We come to do business, not to make war.' Haakon permitted a smile to cross his features. 'Although we have been known to provide protection, should it be required.'

'This is God's chosen place. We have no need of protection here.'

Haakon was pleased neither his half-brother, Thrand, or, more importantly, his leading oarsman, Bjorn, understood Latin. It had been hard enough arguing with Bjorn that they should try for peaceful negotiations. There was much potential for good trading with Northumbria, but equally there were dangers. The Northumbrians were known to be skilful fighters. Haakon glanced at the large berserker standing next to him. There were many who might say that Bjorn's place was back on the boat, but he wanted him here, in case of trouble.

Beside him Bjorn stiffened and his nostrils flared. What

did his old friend sense? Were there Valkyries in the light breeze? Haakon dismissed the thought as fanciful.

'We have come in peace,' Haakon said again, keeping his voice steady.

The monks might look feeble, but he felt certain the monastery would be well guarded. How could it be otherwise? He had heard tales of its fabulous wealth and learning. Surely he and his men were not the first to have been tempted, but the Viken did not have enough men for a sustained assault. They had lost several to storms and sickness earlier in the summer. They would need each one to get the boats safely back home. It would be too risky a venture. They would settle this dispute diplomatically.

'If you have come in peace, then perhaps we should discuss this.' The Abbot bowed his silver head. 'No doubt once I have weighed the merits of the case, I can make a better assessment. May I?'

'There are few merits to weigh.'

'But I fear you have been sent here on a fool's errand. I do not know offhand if we store any money for Oeric the Scot.'

'That is not my problem. The Scot showed me the tablet in your hand, with your seal, saying you did.'

A monk with a pockmarked face, standing at the Abbot's side, tugged on his robe and then whispered in his ear. Haakon watched a frown appear on the Abbot's face.

'And you have this tablet?' The Abbot held out his hand, and then let it drop to his side. 'I thought not. Still, I will investigate it. It will take some time. You and your men are welcome to take on water and supplies.'

'I do have his mark.' Haakon gritted his teeth and crossed his arms. 'Oeric assured me that would be sufficient. We do not intend to be cheated out of our rightful gold.'

'You scum, you raiding scum. My uncle Oeric never cheated anyone!' the pockmarked monk shouted out. 'You cannot foul this holy place with your poisonous heathen lies.'

'You are right, cousin!' another shouted. 'These are the raiders who destroyed my father's farm last year.'

'We never—' Haakon began.

Before he could finish the sentence, the second monk rushed forward with an outstretched dagger, reaching Erik and stabbing him in the stomach before he could react. A red stain spread out over his leather jerkin.

'To me! To me!' Haakon shouted. 'We have been attacked!'

Annis leant out as far as she dared and tried to hear the exchange of words between her uncle and the handsome barbarian.

Her uncle, head held high, turned his back and began to walk away. Someone called out sharply in a foreign tongue. Her uncle stopped. A monk rushed forward, punched one of the barbarians in the stomach. How would her uncle punish the insubordination? Her uncle's guards rushed forward to protect the monk as the raiders drew their swords.

Annis felt as if she was watching underwater. Time slowed and each movement seemed to take an age. The guards charged, but were engaged immediately.

The wild man lifted his axe aloft, shouting in a barbaric tongue. The dark-haired man put out his hand to check him, but the man shrugged him off as he advanced towards her uncle, axe gleaming in the morning sun.

Her uncle did not move. There was a questioning look on his face. He held up his hands—in blessing or as a plea.

The barbarian paid no attention. He brought his axe down with a single savage blow.

Annis stifled a cry and turned her face from the horror, but the image of the axe falling, and blood spurting, staining the golden sand with its deep red as her uncle's head rolled, was imprinted on her brain. She did not dare look back as the noise from the beach swelled around her, screams and pleas for mercy combined with furious barbaric chanting.

The bells began pealing furiously again.

Her body became numb. Her hand covered her mouth and her insides churned. Her brain kept protesting that this could not be real. It had to be a nightmare. Such things did not happen here.

Annis wanted to sink to her knees and cry, but above all she wanted to wake up. She bit her lip, tasted blood and then she knew everything was real, horribly, terribly real. But her feet remained frozen. Annis knew if she glanced back, the golden sands would be stained red with blood.

'What is it, my lady? What has happened? Your face has gone pale. Tell me—what did you see?' Mildreth's voice cut through her paralysis.

'We need to hide. Quickly.' Annis clasped her hands together. 'Something terrible has happened on the beach. We are not safe. No one is safe.'

Annis swept the contents of her dressing table into a satchel as she tried to think clearly. There had been rumours of such creatures for several years, attacking farms and demanding tribute from towns near the coast, but she had never imagined any barbarian would attack here. The stories her uncle told were about robbery, rape and worse. He had considered them exaggerated, but she now knew they were too mild. This heathen horde was capable of anything. They had to leave. Now, before they were discovered.

'Hide?' Mildreth squeaked, her eyes growing round in her thin face. 'Hide where? Shall we go to the church? St Cuthbert in his tomb will protect us.'

'No.' The image of the axe falling on her uncle's head flashed before Annis. 'They did not respect God's representative. Why should they respect his holy place?'

Mildreth crossed herself and fell to her knees. 'Then we are doomed.'

'Never say that.' Annis grabbed Mildreth's arm and tried to right her, but the maid was having none of it. She kept to the ground and started to mutter her rosary. Annis passed a hand over her eyes. She had no desire to curl up into a ball. She wanted to live. There had to be a way to escape. 'We need to make it to the mainland. Raise the alarm.'

Mildreth's muttering increased in speed.

Annis risked another glance at the window. The beach now teemed with warriors, swords and axes drawn, advancing forwards. A loud thumping noise filled the room as the monsters began to beat their weapons against their shields.

There was a great crash as the gate to the courtyard fell open. It was only a matter of time.

Annis pressed her hands to her temples. She could not leave Mildreth. They had to move, to get out of here. She did not dare wait for any of her retainers. Either they had run off or were too busy fighting the barbarians to consider her.

They could not stay here in the guest house. The barbarians would be swarming all over it, searching for gold and silver. They would not hesitate to take captives. Annis's stomach churned as she remembered the stories from her uncle's dinner table two nights ago. She had thought then they were tales to frighten young children. Now she realised that they had not even begun to describe the terror.

Mildreth finished her rosary and stared straight ahead, white-faced with unfocused eyes. Annis knelt down and gathered Mildreth's ice-cold hands in hers.

'We will make our way to the pigsty. There will be nothing for the barbarians there. No one will look in. They will want treasure. Once they have gone, we will emerge safe and sound. Unharmed. Do you understand me?'

The maid gave a barely perceptible nod. Annis scooped the remaining items into a cloth. The mirror had belonged to her grandmother and the brooch to her aunt. Her own silver cross.

The work of an instant. She struggled to stay calm and think of each step clearly. They would go down the stairs, and out the back door, along to the kitchens and then to the pigsty. There was a good view of the causeway; when the tide was right, they'd walk across. 'We go. Now.'

Mildreth stood, took a trembling step and then collapsed in a heap. Annis clenched her hands in frustration.

'Leave me, mistress.' Tears streamed down Mildreth's face.

'Never. We will get through this, you and I.'

'May God, Mother Mary and all the saints bless you.' Mildreth's hand clenched Annis's.

A crash reverberated throughout the upstairs room. An axe hitting the door. Then the sound of shouting and running of feet as someone sought to prevent entry. Mildreth let out a loud whimper. Annis instinctively felt for her eating dagger on her belt. Small protection in the face of swords, but it was all she had to defend herself.

Silently Annis whispered a prayer to God.

Beads of sweat began to trickle down her face and neck.

'Block the door!' Annis tugged at the bed as Mildreth crouched unmoving. 'Help me now, Mildreth, if you value your life.'

Somewhere in the bowels of the building, a stair creaked.

He had planned today differently. They had come in peace, seeking trade, not war.

Haakon surveyed the battle or, rather, rout that was raging around him. Already flames licked many of the buildings. He knew Lindisfarne's reputation as a centre for learning, but it could not be helped. The Abbot should have had more control over his monks. He had lost a good warrior and a good friend for no reason when the crazed monk had attacked. Had the Abbot expected him not to react in the face of such unprovoked aggression?

'Bjorn was correct, Haakon,' Thrand called from a doorway. He appeared disheveled, but unhurt, and dragged a chest spilling over with gold chalices and bejewelled crucifixes. 'The church groans under the weight of gold and jewels. You have never seen the like. You were wise to say that we should come here to get the coin that the Scotsman owed us.'

'Burn the buildings. This is like any other raid, Thrand,' Haakon replied. 'Gather what you can. We shall feast well once we return to our lands.'

He refused to feel anything for these men. There would be no place in Valhalla for them or wherever their God sent warriors. These were no warriors. Children knew how to handle swords better. This priory was undefended.

'Watch your back!'

Several burly Priory guards advanced towards him, but Thrand reached them first, and they clashed swords. These knew what they were on about, Haakon thought as the swords clashed and clashed again. He sent one spinning to the ground and Thrand dispatched the rest.

'You could almost make a berserker in ferocity, Thrand.'

The younger man lifted his sword. 'Killing brings me no pleasure, Haakon. You know that. I differ from Bjorn in that respect.'

'Have you seen Bjorn?'

'Not since the fighting began. How stupid of those men to attack us with a puny dagger and not expect us to defend our honour.'

'I would have preferred that Bjorn waited for my orders.'

'You were the one who had him stand next to you.' Thrand gave a shrug. 'Bjorn is a dangerous man—to friend and foe alike when the blood madness hits.'

'He would never attack one of the *felag*. He has given his blood-oath.'

'So you say. There were rumours two summers ago about

Bjorn breaking an oath, but I never believed them.' Thrand gave the chest another shove. 'You are in charge of this expedition and I have no wish to challenge for the leadership. Bjorn is your responsibility.'

Haakon rubbed the back of his neck, silently acknowledging the truth of Thrand's words. Bjorn was a danger to everyone, and to himself. Now, all he had to do was to find Bjorn and bring him back from the madness that had engulfed him. They had sworn loyalty to each other, but he knew what Bjorn could do when he was engulfed in his blood-lust.

'Bjorn,' he called. 'Bjorn, the day is ours. It is time to divide the spoils.'

Annis crouched behind the makeshift pile of a bed, mattress, chests and the table. Her plaits had come loose as she frantically worked, and her hair now tumbled freely down her back.

Waiting, hoping. She scarcely dared breathed.

Thus far, there had been no other sound but the one creak of the stair. A false alarm or something more sinister?

Had the attacker left the building?

Wisps of smoke swirled in the air, making it difficult to breathe properly and stinging Annis's eyes. Her muscles complained from moving the furniture in front of the door. Mildreth had not helped with the building of the heap, but sat stony faced, rocking back and forth as she guarded Annis's meagre store of possessions.

Annis offered another prayer up to God, but she feared He was not listening. God had turned His face from them and left them to their fate as warning to the others. That is what her uncle would say if he had lived.

How could the death of her uncle and the other brothers please God? Her uncle had been revered by all. His piety was well known, and his wisdom respected. Now he was dead and his blood spilt on the golden sand.

She stared at the knife in her hands.

'I will protect you,' she whispered to Mildreth, who gave no sign of having heard her. 'I promise.'

The door to room jangled, rocked.

She froze. Her breath stuck in her throat. Would the attacker go away, seeking easier prey?

Then it crashed open with a sickening thump as if the bed and other things were but dry sticks.

A great beast of a man strode in. His axe dripped blood. His skins were splattered with many dark stains. Annis's blood turned cold. This was her uncle's killer.

Behind his helmet, his eyes glinted yellow. His teeth were drawn back in a snarl.

Help me! Annis sank farther back into the shadows.

The beast-man regarded the room, searching. The shutter flapped open and closed. His eyes narrowed, his attention caught.

Please let him think we escaped.

The beast-man gave a grunt and turned to go. Annis's heart leapt. Against all reason, they would be saved.

Go. Leave. Depart, she willed.

A whimper escaped Mildreth's lips. The beast started. Breathing heavily, he turned. This time he did not miss where Mildreth crouched.

An evil smile crossed his features and he lovingly stroked his axe.

'Bjorn, here I find you.' Haakon advanced into the narrow upstairs room. There had been quite a fight as the furniture lay scattered. 'There is nothing here. Whoever was here has departed—long ago.'

He froze. The berserker started to slowly advance towards a cowering woman. In the other corner, another woman with luminous eyes crouched amongst the shadows. She put her fingers to her lips as her eyes pleaded with him. Haakon's jaw tightened. There was no honour in killing defenceless women.

'We have everything we came for and more. Time to depart, Bjorn. Before the tide changes.' Haakon kept his voice steady. He had to bring Bjorn back from this madness.

No reaction from Bjorn. Just the slow, steady advance. Haakon willed the woman to move and save herself while he held Bjorn's attention. But she cowered on the ground like a scared rabbit.

'The gold has been secured, Bjorn Bjornson. Time to go.'

Bjorn swung his large head around and regarded Haakon as if he had never seen him before. His gaze appeared to become fastened on Haakon's sword. An unearthly light appeared in Bjorn's eyes.

Blood and spittle surrounded Bjorn's mouth as he advanced towards Haakon, swinging his axe.

Haakon stood still. Bjorn had to realise who he was. They had shared many adventures together. Bjorn had never before been this far gone in the madness of the berserker.

'Bjorn, it is I, Haakon, your Jaarl. Stay true to your oath. Come back to me.'

Something appeared in Bjorn's eyes. He checked the movement of his axe. Haakon gave an encouraging nod, beckoning him forward. He had done it.

Bjorn's eyes became fixated on Haakon's sword, blazing with an unholy light. Madness descended again as he licked his lips.

Bjorn lifted his axe. Haakon dodged to the right, raising his shield to meet the axe. He felt the reverberation go up his arm. Bjorn drew back and tried again.

'I am your shipmate, Bjorn.' Haakon held out his hands and kept his voice soft, like a woman crooning to her baby. 'We swore an oath on Thor and Odin. Our blood mingled. You are a member of the *felag*.'

But the berserker gave no sign. The scent of blood had driven him into a red fury. And the only thing he understood was killing. A great roar emerged from the depths of his being.

Haakon raised his shield again and heard it crack as Bjorn hit it with his axe.

Annis watched the barbarian warrior fight the other. His sword clashed with the axe several times. It made no sense that they should fight, but it was distracting the beast-man.

'Run, Mildreth, run now. The pigsty! I will meet you there!'

The maid needed no second urging. She darted behind the warrior. Mildreth's feet clipped his and he stumbled slightly. His shield crashed to the floor and his sword slipped from his grasp. He lay there, defenceless.

Annis knew she, too, should run, but her legs refused to move. She had to go. This was her best chance to escape. She should go now, but still the barbarian warrior lay there.

This warrior had saved Mildreth's life and probably hers. Now he was in mortal danger. And once he was dead, the beast-man would come after her.

The beast-man advanced towards where the warrior lay on the ground, breathing heavily. He stopped and gazed at the man. A slow smile spread over his face as his tongue licked his lips.

Annis forgot to breathe.

The beast-man's skins gaped open at the base of his throat as he lifted his axe for the final blow.

Chapter Two

Annis hurtled herself forward from her hiding place, her dagger curving upwards. She had this one chance, this one opening.

She had to do it.

The beast-man turned slightly at her approach. The knife slid easily into his throat. Blood spurted from his mouth as a look of surprise engulfed him. Her hand jolted from the impact and she felt her fingers slip from the knife.

Annis landed on the hard body of the fallen warrior. Instantly, she felt his arms go around and pull her body under his in one swift motion. Protecting her. A muttered curse was whispered in her ear as she struggled to breathe.

A great crash resounded in her ears as the beast-man toppled to the floor, narrowly missing them both.

As Annis lay there underneath the warrior, she noticed the tiny stone against her back and the long, hard length of him, their breath intermingling. She could see the dark stubble on his chin and the brilliance of his blue eyes. Everything in a heartbeat. Then the rush of air as he stood up.

A warm hand engulfed hers, pulling her to her feet. His blue eyes held a look of concern. Annis stood there, hanging on to the hand as she gazed at the fallen figure with blood silently pooling beneath him.

Her aim had been true!

She turned her head into the warrior's chain-mailed chest and rested it there, drawing strength from him. His strong arm encircled her. Distantly she could hear the roar of battle and crackle of fire, but closer she heard the thump of his heart. Gradually what she had done sank in.

She had killed. The beast-man was dead, dead by her hand!

Annis pushed against the warrior's chest and immediately his hands loosened. She staggered a few steps and sank down on an upturned bucket, trying to regain control of her body as shudders went through her.

The smoke-filled air stung her eyes and throat. She should go now, flee and try to get across the causeway, but when she stood, her legs refused to move. If she took another step, she'd sink to her knees.

'I was sick after my first time.' A low rumble of a voice filled the room. It was a comforting sort of noise, and flowed over her like fine linen.

Annis glanced over her shoulder at the warrior. Had he spoken? Surely she was hearing things. Such a man would not speak Latin. Heathen raiders such as he did not speak the language of the church. She had to be hearing things. Was that what killing people did? Made you hear voices in your mind? She put her hands to her ears and shook her head to clear it.

The warrior took off his helmet and his dark hair was plastered to his forehead. He was tall, powerfully built with broad shoulders. He ran a hand over the dark stubble on his face.

Annis started. The man she'd saved was the pagan warlord she had seen earlier, the one who had quarrelled with her uncle, the one who was responsible for the attack. She wanted to put her face in her hands and weep. She had saved her uncle's destroyer. If she had realised, she would have fled as

Mildreth had done. She regarded her hands, wondering what he would do now, what he was capable of.

'You saved my life,' he said in Latin with only the faintest trace of an accent—not unpleasant, just different. 'I, Haakon Haroldson, Jaarl of Viken, am in your debt.'

Annis blinked. She had not heard wrong. This raider spoke Latin as well as, if not better than, a Northumbrian noble.

'Is he dead?' she asked in Latin. Annis stared at the prone figure.

'I fear so.' Something like sorrow crossed his face. He bent down and turned the beast-man face up, muttered something and then closed the beast-man's unseeing eyes. 'Bjorn was a fierce fighter. We shall miss him. Great will be the celebrations in Valhalla tonight.'

'He tried to kill you. And you regret his death.' Annis stared incredulously at the warrior. 'How can that be?'

Haakon regarded the woman in front of him. Her dark hair flowed down her back. She was dressed in a simple dark green gown without ornaments, none of the jewellery so beloved of his stepmother or Queen Asa and the ladies of the Viken court. Her sea-green eyes were wide and he could see the trembling starting to set in. This woman had never killed before.

Was she real or one of the Valkyries—the warrior women who scavenged the battlefield for fighters worthy of Valhalla?

'He was a great warrior, a berserker.' Haakon looked at Bjorn's trusty axe.

How many times had he killed? How many men's lives had he saved with the unhesitating strokes of his axe?

It was unthinkable Bjorn should behave like this, to end his life by breaking his oath and deliberately attacking a member of the *felag,* his sworn leader. Haakon shook his head. No, Bjorn had to have been too far gone in his blood-lust. He had no idea of what he had attempted to do.

'A berserker?'

'He lived for fighting.' Haakon attempted to think of the Latin words to describe Bjorn, but decided there were none. 'He was a great warrior.'

She nodded, but her expression remained unconvinced.

Haakon regarded the fallen man. There were many among the fellowship who would seek to kill her for what she had done, demand her blood in retribution for killing a warrior such as Bjorn. He followed the warriors' code but her actions had saved his life. This was by far the bigger debt.

'You are under my protection, Valkyrie.' Haakon rubbed the back of his neck. 'Tell me what happened here. What did you do to provoke Bjorn?'

She shook her head, and started to back away. Her bottom touched the window ledge and she stopped. She held out her hands and her eyes grew big. 'I saved your life.'

Something inside Haakon twisted. She expected death. He was not so far gone that he would kill a woman in cold blood.

'That is why you are under my protection. No harm will come to you.' Haakon inclined his head. 'Bjorn was valuable to my people. You must understand this. No one thought he could be killed, least of all by a woman.'

'He was going to kill you, this…this berserker of yours, after my maid caused you to trip and fall. I did what I would have done for anyone.' Her voice rose slightly. She scrambled to bring together a few jewels and held them out. 'Let me go. Leave me here. Take these and go.'

Haakon stared at the slender woman in disbelief. He pushed the jewels away.

Did she realise the penalties? Did she not understand what was happening out there?

When he and his men had finished, no building would remain standing. They had not come seeking this fight, but they refused to turn away from a challenge. The next time, the people of this island might not be so eager to resist the legitimate demands of the Viken. No more would they tolerate those who lied, cheated and attempted to abuse their goodwill. The *felag* had come to trade, but had found a war.

Her body shook and the area around her mouth was pale. She reminded him of a highly strung horse. He wanted to tame her, to make her understand, so she would be able to live.

'Where are your warriors?'

'My warriors?'

'Yes, the men who would look after you. Such a prize as yourself would not be left unguarded.'

'All the men here are engaged in fighting you and your kind.'

He gestured towards the small window. 'Out there, it is a scene from the end of the world. You do not wish to be there.'

'You are not giving me the option?' Her green eyes blazed defiantly. 'It was not me or my people who started this fight. I will go now.'

She started to move past him, but Haakon reached out his hand and held her firmly, preventing her from moving. He could see her heart beating at the base of her throat.

'If I let you go, you will lose your life. There are others like my friend out there…on both sides.'

Annis angrily tore her arm away. 'I shall take my chances.'

'Trust me.'

'The Abbot was cut down, destroyed with one blow of this man's axe, and you stood by.' She choked back the words 'my uncle'. It would not do for him to discover who she was. 'I saw you. You were in charge of your warriors. He bid you welcome. You and you alone have brought death and destruction here.'

'Where were you?' He raised an eyebrow. 'I failed to notice any woman in the welcoming party. Perhaps your Latin is not as good as you would like to believe. We came in peace and were attacked. As I told the Abbot, we only wanted the gold due to us, the gold promised. It was a monk who attacked first.'

'I watched from the window. The Abbot was…was a good man.'

'His death was regrettable. As you have killed the man who struck him, perhaps you will consider it avenged.' Haakon ran his hand through his hair, making it stand up on end. 'We came wanting the coin owed for our fur and amber, and offering our services for protection. Good men fell today for no reason.'

'Yes, they did.' Annis's throat closed. She refused to cry in front of Haakon, this barbarian who had saved her. Later she'd mourn her uncle and the rest of those who had fallen. Now she had to plan a way of escaping him and alerting the lords of the nearby estates to the danger of these raiders.

The smell of smoke increased and the floorboards became warm underneath her feet. She heard the slight crackle of fire.

'We must move and get away from this place. My men have orders to set fire to all the buildings.'

'I would rather die than move.' Annis placed her hands on her knees and wondered how she could walk a few steps.

'You will die, if you do not do as you are told.' A faint, sardonic smile crossed his lips. 'And you lie.'

'How so?' She tilted her head. How dare this barbarian Jaarl provoke her with his insolent speech!

'You have already shown you have a great desire to live. You will come with me and I will get you to a place of safety.'

Annis swallowed hard. She had made one gigantic mistake today. She should have left Haakon to face his own man. But he was correct. She had to go. Her only hope was that she could somehow escape when they were outside. She would have to watch for her chance and be prepared to run and hide. She swallowed hard, hating him. 'I will do as you say…for now.'

'You will do as I say if you want to live to an old age.' His voice hardened. 'We go.'

Annis started to gather up her belongings. Her hand hovered over her mirror, now scratched.

'What are you doing?'

'Getting my things.'

'You will not need them.' Haakon bent and retrieved her dagger and cleaned it before he held out it to her. 'But you will need this.'

She regarded it with suspicion. Exactly what was he intending? He knew she had killed with it before. She could use it to escape. Before he could change his mind, she grasped the dagger and tucked it into her belt.

His hand closed around her wrist. 'Do I carry you or do you walk?'

'I walk.'

He went first down the stairs, his sword in front of them, stopping to check at corners. When they emerged, the sky was black, the air oozed smoke. The scene in front of them was what hell must look like. Annis regarded the piles of looted bounty that stood at various points with revulsion. Tapestries from her uncle's solarium, broken jewel-encrusted crosses and chests of gold. A pile of vellum and codex books burnt in the centre courtyard. A lump of tears formed in her throat and she used the back of her hand to wipe across her eyes. All that learning and knowledge gone. She wanted to rush in and pull the burning bibles from the fire, but Haakon's hand held her wrist firmly. There was no escape.

More than anything, the scene brought her predicament home to her. This was not some night fancy from which she'd awake to see the smiling face of her nurse. Everything on Lindisfarne had been wilfully and wantonly destroyed. The world had changed. Irrevocably.

Annis started when Haakon did not lead her towards the

boats or the others. Instead, he headed towards a small knoll
a little way away from the scenes of the destruction.

Here the air was clearer, although the sun shone red
through the haze of smoke. A few rocks provided a bit of
rough shelter and the cries and crashing were a distant blur
of noise. Overhead a seagull circled, oblivious to chaos and
confusion below.

Haakon's fingers loosened on Annis's wrist, freeing her.
She stood rubbing her wrist, not quite understanding why he
had brought her here. He walked around the rocks in silence,
then made a satisfied noise in the back of his throat.

'You will be safe here. Wait until my men and I have left
and then go across the causeway. Quickly. Never look back.
Return to your home.'

'Why are you doing this?'

'A life for a life.' He put his hand under her chin. 'Here we
say goodbye, Valkyrie.'

Annis blinked back the sudden hot tears. He was freeing
her. She had thought she was a captive and he had set her free.
She knew she should move away from him. His fingers were
no more than the gentlest of touches on her chin.

'Goodbye, Haakon Haroldson, Jaarl of Viken,' she whispered with her lips a mere breath away from his.

'You can do better than that.'

Without warning, he lowered his mouth to hers, covered
it. One brief meeting of lips, firm but gentle. Her body swayed
towards his, and his arms came around her, drawing her into
the hard, muscular planes of his body. The nature of the kiss
grew, intensified, becoming hot and searing like the flames
that engulfed Lindisfarne.

Her knees weakened and she held him tightly, her hands
clinging to his leather armour, savouring the feel of his
mouth roaming over hers. Then it was over, and he had put
her away. She stared at him, dazed as she watched his wide

chest heave as if he had run a race. She knew her breathing must match his. All this from one kiss. She struggled to take a normal breath, to stop her blood from feeling as if it were on fire.

'If all the Valkyries were like you, I would welcome Valhalla.' Haakon nodded and turned his back, without waiting for her reply. He wanted no hesitation. What he was doing was the right thing.

Haakon forced himself to march away from the woman.

It was the simplest way. She would be safe as long as she stayed there.

He and his men would be gone in a few hours' time. She could then live her life and he his. He had repaid his life-debt to her. They were even.

Annis's fingers explored her well-kissed mouth as she watched his tall, broad-shouldered figure disappear into the swirling darkness. Bent, no doubt, on some other mission of destruction.

Did he have to be so handsome? His kiss had been far more pleasant than Selwyn's kisses ever had been. Selwyn had always tried to dominate her, but Haakon's kiss had been gently persuasive. And her body responded.

But he was her enemy. And he had set her free, possibly saving her life. She was sorry that they had to meet like this.

Would it have better to remain in ignorance that such a man existed?

She sank down on the spiky sea-grass and drew her knees up to her chest. She was safe and free. Free to go back home and pick up the pieces of her life. After today, she longed for the safety and solid reassurance of Birdoswald's stone walls.

The waves hit the red-and-white sailed ships, signalling a change in the tide. The men looked tiny as they moved, carrying chests and crates to the boats. She caught the echoes of their laughter on the wind. How long would it be until they had departed and she could get across the causeway?

A scream rent the air.

The hair on the back of Annis's neck stood on end. She rushed to the edges of the rocks and looked out, with her dagger in her hand.

No one. A tern circled overhead, opened its beak and screeched again.

She sank down amongst the rocks again, holding her dagger out in front of her, listening. But there was nothing. There had to be nothing. All the while her mind kept returning the promise she had made to Mildreth. She had to hope Mildreth was safe in the pigsty and would wait for her.

She had promised to meet her there. She had to be there.

Annis knew she should wait until the Vikens departed, but the promise preyed on her. If she went to the back of the pigsty, no one would see her. She could rescue Mildreth and none would be the wiser.

She shielded her eyes and peered down at the boats again. The departure preparations continued a pace. Most of the Viken warriors would be there, not in the town, and the pigsty was situated by the kitchens. There was nothing for them there. No gold. No jewels. No books to burn, just the midden heap.

Her stomach clenched. She had to go. She had a duty to Mildreth.

Haakon's word rang loudly in her ears. She was safe here. She would come to no harm if she stayed still.

But what if he changed his mind? What if he returned for her? Could she really trust such a man? A heathen warlord?

She was not safe as long he knew where to find her. She had to leave.

First, she'd find her maid and fulfil her promise. She had never knowingly broken a promise to her maidservants in her life and she did not intend to begin now.

She would go as far as the pigsty and no farther. Mildreth had to be there. These Norsemen would be much more interested in plundering the treasury of one of the wealthiest monasteries in the Christendom than capturing reluctant pigs. They would be safe and could wait without fear of discovery.

Annis shuddered to think how many Northumbrian and Mercian families faced ruin because of today's work. How many had thought their treasure would be safe in the hands of the monks, as who would risk eternal damnation?

The sky was thick black with smoke and it appeared closer to midnight than midday. Annis picked her way down the hill, back into the carnage. St Cuthbert's church glowed orange. As she watched, a huge timber crashed on the centre aisle, sending a shower of sparks into the sky.

She stumbled and fell, knees first, into a puddle. Her hand closed around a small silver cross that lay in the shallow pool of mud. She tucked it into her belt next to her dagger. It had been a gift to her from her mother. Mildreth must have taken it with her when she ran and then dropped it in her confusion. It had to be a portent that she would find the maid safe and well. When she returned to Birdoswald, she would tell her mother the story. And they'd laugh together, agreeing it was indeed Providence that allowed her to find it.

Annis pinched the bridge of her nose, feeling the sting of smoke. She blinked back the tears. There was little point in thinking about what would happen when she got back to the mainland. She had to survive first.

She took three more breaths, waiting, but the Norseman had disappeared and no one appeared to be paying her any attention. In fact, no one was around her at all.

Annis straightened her gown. She gave a half-smile at the gesture. The dark green wool already bore too many stains and was ruined beyond repair. It was incredible that she should even think about her clothes. Even now, her nurse's many admonitions about how she had to behave—the proper Northumbrian lady, rather than a serf's daughter—guided her.

It was time. She had to move or for ever be a captive.

She slunk back into the shadows and started to edge her way along the side of a stone building. The smoke was thicker and even the stones radiated heat.

Miraculously no one challenged her and she soon made her way to the outbuildings. The fence was broken and the pigs had vanished, leaving trampled earth as a sign of their escape.

'Mildreth?' she called softly. 'It is Annis, your mistress. I am here. I have kept my promise.'

No answer. It was quiet, an all-enveloping quietness. So very different from the noise and confusion of the courtyard.

Annis concentrated her whole being, straining to hear the slightest noise. Mildreth had to be here. She had to have escaped. Surely God meant for them to escape. He had delivered them from the beast.

Then she saw the problem—the roof of the sty smouldered. Mildreth, if she made it this far, must have found a new place of refuge. But where? There had to be somewhere close. But could she afford to search for her? Annis, hating herself, decided no. She had to trust Mildreth would make it through and they would be reunited on the mainland.

She started to turn, but her eye was caught by a piece of light russet material in the corner of the sty. She put her hand to her mouth to stifle a scream and struggled to keep her balance.

Mildreth, Mildreth's body, trapped under a timber.

Annis hurried over. Her hand touched Mildreth's neck, but already the flesh cooled and her eyes stared up unseeing. All the air vanished from Annis's lungs. She crossed her hands about her chest and rocked back and forth, struggling as her mind recoiled from the sight in front of her.

'No!' was torn from the depths of her soul as she tried to

focus, tried to think. How long she stood there she didn't know, but gradually she realised she had to go. The fire had taken hold, jumping and crackling all around her. But it was impossible to leave Mildreth like this, face, unseeing, turned to the sky.

Annis closed Mildreth's eyes and whispered the last rites. There would be no way of knowing if Mildreth understood, but Annis fancied the body looked more peaceful. Then she placed a kiss on Mildreth's brow and stood up, wiping her hands against her gown.

Later, when she had time, she'd come back and make sure she was properly buried. She would also seek out Mildreth's relations and let them know what happened.

Annis's mouth twisted. So many wrongs to right. She had to get across the causeway, in safety. She would return to her former look-out, see if the ships had departed.

She covered her mouth and nose with the sleeve of her gown as the smoke began billowing again and the heat of the fire beat against her face.

In the semi-darkness, she stumbled, trying to keep to the shadows. She went first one way, realised she was lost, started heading the other as the stinging smoke blinded her.

She ran into what seemed like a wall, bounced off and started to run. A hand reached out and grabbed her arm.

He said something in their barbaric tongue.

'You had what you came for. There is nothing for you here,' Annis said, forcing her voice to remain firm. 'Leave this place immediately.'

The man paused and his grip eased. Annis risked a glimpse upwards. He appeared younger than Haakon, but had a look of him. He was regarding her with a quizzical expression.

She pulled her arm away and drew herself to her full height.

'Go. Now.' She pointed vaguely in the direction she had come from and hoped.

He started to go, a puzzled expression on his face.

Annis released a breath and willed him to step away farther. But he turned and placed a pinching grip on her shoulder. His face broke into a wide smile as he drew her closer.

Chapter Three

'Haakon Haroldson!' The scream welled up from within Annis as she fought against the hands. Haakon had warned her such things might happen, but she had chosen to ignore it. She should have listened. She was furious with her attacker and more furious with herself. She had thought she was doing the right thing, but she had blundered. It was too late for regrets.

The warrior grabbed her hair and twisted it around his hand, hurting her, imprisoning her. A sword gleamed in his other hand. Her heart stopped. Her limbs froze.

A nightmare. Worse than a nightmare as she was awake. She had had a chance to escape and had thrown it away on nothing. The thought tasted bitter.

Annis felt her body begin to sag. She forced it straight. She hadn't survived all that had gone before simply to die at this man's hands.

She kicked out with her boot and landed a blow on his shin, heard a muttered curse and his grasp on her hair loosened. With her hand she yanked the few remaining strands free. The warrior raised his hand. Annis ducked, whispered a prayer and prepared to flee.

Suddenly the young warrior was hurled backwards, and Haakon appeared, his face black like a thundercloud.

'Has he harmed you?' he demanded as he placed a gentle hand under her arm.

'No, no. I am unhurt.' She shook her head as her limbs began to tremble, to shake uncontrollably. She wrapped her arms about her waist but still the shivers kept on coming.

Haakon's eyes were like daggers, and he once again wore his helmet. Gone was the man who released her and in his place was the warlord she had first glimpsed.

Annis swallowed, forced her limbs to stay still as a wave of exhaustion hit. She wanted to sink to the ground and never get up. This nightmare had to end. She had to wake. Her life wasn't supposed to be like this. She had had it orderly, planned, and now there was nothing left. Nothing.

Another wave of aching tiredness washed through her body, leaving behind it a numbing cold. Later she'd think about the horror that happened here, but now all she wanted it to do was end. Her eyelids became heavier than lead and started to close. She sank down in the dirt, resting her chin against her knees, her back against his legs. She no longer cared. This man had kept her safe before.

Haakon resisted the urge to shake the woman and force her to stand.

He had shown her to a safe place, left her there. All she had to do was to wait until the Viken had gone and she could have returned to her people with nothing worse than a bad fright. But she had ignored him and had returned to the monastery. It was only Odin's luck that he had chanced upon Thrand and her before anything had happened to her.

Surely the woman had realised the danger she was in. His men had little regard for the women. Some of the men would make good captives, but the women they just used and discarded.

'The woman is under my protection, Thrand,' Haakon said as he shifted so that she was firmly against his legs. 'And I have no wish to send you to Valhalla before your time.'

'Your protection?' His brother gave a shrug and fingered his jaw. 'I found her wandering on her own. You should look after your women better.'

'Ivar said you were in trouble.' Haakon put his hands on his hips, allowed the remark to pass and feigned ignorance at the jibe his half-brother was trying to make. 'He feared you would need a steadying hand.'

'Nothing I could not handle. A Northumbrian monk objected to being taken prisoner.' Thrand bent down and picked up his sword. 'Next time, keep a better eye on your captives. There are many about with the blood-lust running high.'

'How many have we lost? I know about the beach, but here in the monastery?' Haakon ran a hand through his hair. In a battle such as this one, he would expect to see many men go to Valhalla. Without a doubt, the hardest thing he would have to do would be to inform their wives, sweethearts and families when they returned to Viken, so a rune stone could be raised to them.

'A few cuts and bruises. Perhaps six seriously injured.' Thrand stopped, brows coming together in concentration. 'Bjorn is missing, but you know how he behaves when the blood madness is on him. You are the only who he respects. He will appear before the gold is fully loaded, no doubt laden with treasure and his axe dripping with blood. By all the gods, this raid has been a success.'

'Bjorn is dead.' Haakon dropped his arms and dared Thrand to question him.

'Dead? How? These are no warriors! A boy with a wooden sword shows more fight.' Thrand's eyes widened. 'Bjorn was a match for any man. And have you forgotten what the sooth-sayer said—no man can kill him?'

'I had forgotten the prophecy when he attacked me. The

blood-lust was such that he did not recognise me. We encountered each other in the guest house, and I declined to visit Valhalla, even for him.'

Thrand let out a low whistle. 'And to think you were the one who argued that he must join this voyage. He belongs to a powerful clan.'

Haakon glanced down at the woman. She had her head tilted to one side and her brow was wrinkled as if she was trying to follow the exchange. Her dark hair curled about her temples and her dress bore the stains of the fight. But he refused to tell Thrand the truth. He had given his oath. There were many who would demand the woman's life as penalty for killing a berserker. But Haakon owed her *his* life. And he would keep her safe—whether she wanted to be or not.

'Then let them challenge me. I have my sword.' Haakon put his hand on his sword belt.

Thrand held his hands up. 'Your prowess as a swordsman is well known and there are legends about your sword, Leg-biter.'

'Leg-biter has served me well.'

'You do realise that the tales will only intensify now that you have slain Bjorn although the *wergild* will be great.'

Haakon allowed his brother's words to wash over him as he studied the woman before him.

What would Thrand say if he knew the truth? Would he offer up the woman to appease Bjorn's powerful relations?

'I was too busy defending my own skin to think on the amount I will owe Bjorn's family. Or what his friends might do to me afterwards. I do not believe he gave much thought to the amount he'd owe you or our mother.'

'I would ask much for you, my brother. You have done much for the family.' Thrand gave a slight shrug of his shoulders. 'I for one am pleased you killed Bjorn. If the family dislikes what you offer, they can always appeal to Thorkell.

He should do something for his kingship besides receive a portion of our goods.'

The words were lightly said, but an uneasy feeling passed over Haakon. An unease that he instantly dismissed as tiredness. He trusted his half-brother with his life.

'No doubt you are correct, Thrand.' Haakon leant forward. 'I never forget my obligations.'

Thrand flushed. 'And the woman. What will you do with her? You never answered. There will be some who wish to dispute your claim, particularly if she is discovered on her own again. You are lucky it was me and not another member of the *felag*.'

Haakon frowned as he regarded where the woman crouched at his feet. She had not moved since he had hit Thrand.

He had thought to leave her, safe and unharmed, by the rocks, her presence undetected by the rest of the Vikens. But Thrand had seen her, heard her speak in Latin. Thrand was not stupid. He would reach the same conclusion that Haakon had—this woman was high born and potentially worth a great deal of money. In this state, she would be prey for all the men.

It was a total victory for the men of Viken. His mouth twisted. A lone woman would be subjected to untold dangers. He would not do that even to his worst enemy. And this woman he had sworn to protect. No, she would have to come under his direct guard, and when they returned to Viken, he'd use his contacts with the court of Charlemagne and the Holy Roman Empire to send a ransom message to her family.

'It is for *me* to decide. She belongs to me now.'

'I apologise again, Haakon.' Thrand made a bow. 'I had no idea whom she belonged to.'

'You know now. And by the blood that we share, I challenge you to remember it. Do not covet those things that are mine.'

'I never have. Do not burden me with my mother's ambition.'

Thrand stiffened and stalked off towards the boats.

Haakon allowed him to walk away before he turned his attention to the woman, who had not moved from the spot on the ground. He reached forward and twitched the dagger from her belt. 'Mine, I believe.'

She struggled to an upright position and her eyes blazed. Her hand made an ineffectual grab at the blade, but Haakon calmly tucked it into his belt.

'What right have you? Give it back!'

'I told you that you would be safe if you stayed by the rocks. You chose to disobey me.'

'I had to find my maidservant….' She pushed her wild brown hair out of her eyes and held out her hands, beseeching him. 'You remember the woman who tripped you.'

'And did you find her?' Haakon allowed no softness to enter his voice. 'Where is she? Or has she been carried off by another?'

'She's dead.' A look of immense pain and sorrow crossed her face. 'The pigsty's roof collapsed on her.'

'I am sorry.'

'I told her to hide there. That she would be safe. And she wasn't… It was a mistake to come here, but I had to do my duty.' She put her hands on her face. 'Do you understand that? Will you let me go—as you did before?'

Haakon resisted the urge to sweep her into his arms.

'You are my captive now. Lindisfarne is not safe for you. It is not safe for anyone.'

She made no move, but simply stood looking at him. Her eyes wore a haunted expression. Despite the warm air, she shivered slightly, her body convulsing. Her lips held a bluish tinge, but she kept her body erect and did not collapse into a ball again.

Haakon undid his cloak and put it around her shoulders, fastening the trefoil brooch under her chin.

The heavy weight of the cloak pinned Annis down. She wanted to fling it off and run, but her encounter with the other warrior had made her wary. The cloak retained the warmth from his body. The heat rose, enveloping her, reminding her of the kiss they had shared earlier. His not-unpleasant scent filled her nostrils, surrounding her. Somehow, it felt intimate in a way she had not felt before. Her late husband would never have offered her his cloak.

Her hands fumbled with the catch. She had to give it back. She had no right to wear it. The brooch pricked her finger and she brought it to her mouth with a sudden exclamation of pain.

'Leave it on.' Haakon's voice allowed for no refusal.

What was she exactly? Captives were not given cloaks. She had glimpsed the groups of dispirited monks tied together. Her hands were free. There had been no humiliation…yet. She allowed her hands to fall to her sides.

'You wear a determined look on your face, Valkyrie.'

'Everything is going up in flames. I am a prisoner,' she said as a group of Norse warriors sauntered passed, carrying chalices, the remains of crosses and several bottles of mead. 'My life. My world. Nothing will ever be the same again.'

'The world constantly changes.' Haakon placed his hands on her shoulders. 'But you live. You will see the sun rise and set again.'

Annis knew she should pull away, but her body refused to move. In this unrecognisable world, Haakon represented something safe and solid. The warmth from his hands flooded through her body. His face was so close, if she lifted her lips but a fraction, she knew they would brush his. She closed her eyes, savouring the sensation. She longed to lay her head against his chest. Did it make her wicked? Her head pained her.

Then she forced her eyes open and stepped backwards. Her fingers worked the catch and the cloak fell away from her shoulders.

'I will be warm enough.' Annis kept her head proud and erect, met Haakon's eye. 'You will need it.'

'The cloak stays about your shoulder. It shows others in the *felag* whom you belong to. You will be unmolested both here and on the boat. I have no wish to rescue you another time.'

A shiver went through Annis. Belong to? Her mind had tried to avoid the word, but he had uttered it. She was his captive, his slave. Why had she saved his life? Surely it would have been better if she had escaped while he fought the beast. A little voice nagged at the back her mind—but look what happened to Mildreth. Do you wish to share her fate? And she knew that she wanted to live.

'I don't understand these words you use,' she said to distract her thoughts away from her captivity. If she could keep him talking, then maybe she could figure out a way to escape. '*Felag*—it means nothing to me.'

'Many of your words were foreign when I first began trading.' A slight smile came on his lips. 'You have yet to give me a name. Or shall I choose one for you? I knew you were high born from the instant you spoke in the upstairs room. What serf's daughter has Latin falling so readily off her tongue?'

Annis glanced down at the dirt. Her throat closed. She had no wish to lose her name. 'Annis,' she whispered. 'Annis of Birdoswald, near the River Irthing. My father was the Eorl of Birdoswald.'

'When it is safe, I will inform your people where you are, Annis of Birdoswald.'

Annis clenched her fists so tight they hurt. She knew what letting her people know meant. Haakon would ask for a ransom.

'When will you let them know?' There was nothing she could do about the demand. It happened in war. Selwyn had been ransomed twice—from a Scot's cave and later from

Mercia. It was expected. But much of her family's wealth was in the chests that the Norsemen now piled up.

Would they ransom her or would her family simply see it as a judgement from God? Her stepfather might use her capture as the final excuse he needed to secure Birdoswald for himself. But there again, he might retain a vestige of honour and duty.

'In good time, and from a position of strength.' His face was hard, and his eyes fierce.

Annis nodded. The raiders would not stay here. There were too few of them to hold this island in the face of attack from the Northumbrians. And it would not just be the Northumbrians, but the whole of Britain when the news got out. No, they not would stay. They would return to their northern lands and she would go with them, to await a ransom that would probably never come.

'What is a *felag*?' she asked to distract her mind from the gloomy path it was following.

'A *felag* is a fellowship of traders. We swore a binding blood-oath to each other before we embarked on this journey. All goods gained will be shared out according to the contribution each man made at the beginning of the journey.'

Each man would receive a veritable treasure from the sacking of Lindisfarne. Annis pressed her lips together and held back the angry words.

'Once we return to our homelands all accounts will be settled and your people will be notified.' He placed a hand on her shoulder.

'Accounts?'

'We came to trade—amber, fur and soapstone. Our season had been good until we encountered the Scotsman.' He gave a sudden smile. 'Now it is excellent. All of Northumbria will know what happened here and they will not be as quick to cheat us. We have earned their respect.'

'You will not find the rest of my country so easy. You attacked monks, men of God. Lindisfarne was a centre of learning. Northumbrians have long memories.'

A flash of unease passed through his blue eyes, but that was all. 'Your religion is not our religion. We worship the Aesir with Odin and Thor.'

'All Europe will recoil in horror. They will refuse to trade with you.'

'They will trade, Annis.' He wore a superior smile on his lips. 'They will trade because they want our goods—our furs and amber. And the next time they will be more honest in their dealings with the Norse. It is the way of things.'

Annis wrapped her arms about her waist as she silently watched the last few remaining sparks from the church fly into the air. She refused to cry. She hated these pagan warriors. If only Haakon had not taken her knife from her, she would stick it in him. Happily. She turned her face and examined the stains on her gown. That thought was a lie. She did not want to see this Viken warrior dead, despite what he had done here. He had saved her life—twice.

Dimly she realised Haakon was speaking again.

'You will keep on the cloak, and follow me if you value your life.'

'Where are you taking me?' Annis hated the way her voice quivered.

'You will be with the other prisoners, since you are so determined to join them.'

'Who else have you taken?' Annis thought of the gentle brothers and their community here. Most of their time had been devoted to illuminating the gospels. How long would they last in the hands of a pagan?

'Strong men, and the leaders of the community, if they are still alive. There were not many left. I will ask your pope in Rome for ransom.'

'I pray to God he pays it.'

'The wind begins to shift. We have what we came for. I must see to the ships.' He started off, then turned back. His eyebrow arched. 'If you value your life, keep the cloak on and do not try my patience. There are some who will see you as taking up space that could be better occupied by a chest of gold. You should be grateful, Annis of Birdoswald. You belong to me now. There are worse fates.'

'Yes, I know.'

'Thrand tells me you have found a woman.' Haakon's fellow Jaarl and old friend's voice broke into Haakon's concentration.

'And…' Haakon turned from where he was contemplating the chests of silver and gold coins. The main problem was how to transport so much back to Viken on the *Golden Serpent*. Never in his wildest dreams had he thought a raid would be that successful. And it was not even meant to have been a raid. The weight would have to be carefully distributed.

'We had an agreement—no women on this voyage. They do not fetch enough money. Yours will have to share the same fate as the others.'

Haakon gritted his teeth and drew himself up to his full height. He did not have to explain his actions to anyone. 'Circumstances have changed.'

'Thrand says that she is a kitchen wench. He discovered her by the kitchen spoils.'

'My half-brother says many things and some of them are true. But not this one.'

Why had Thrand not kept his mouth shut? He had no cause to go complaining to another Jaarl. The success of this voyage, even before today's raid, meant that Thrand would have enough money to buy an estate. Haakon's stepmother could finally depart. For far too long she had presided over the farm Haakon had inherited from his father, determined that she should be given prestige and favours, making little secret of her annoyance that he, and not her son, was the eldest.

'The woman Thrand is speaking of is the daughter of a Northumbrian lord. Think of her value.'

'Then you don't intend to bed her?'

'I had not given the matter much thought,' Haakon lied. He glanced back to where Annis stood, proud and defiant. A slight breeze whipped a strand of hair into her mouth. With impatient fingers she pushed it away. His blood stirred with the memory of the way her body had moved against his, softly arching. He would have her, but when he did she would participate fully. Not here amongst the rubble, but somewhere quiet where he could take his time and enjoy the delights of her body.

'Will the family pay the ransom?'

'I believe so. Trust me on this, old friend. The woman sails to Viken.'

Vikar stood stony faced with crossed arms, but Haakon held his gaze until Vikar's face relaxed and he broke into a wide smile. He leant forward and thumped Haakon on his back.

'Trust you? I would sail into the Midgard Serpent's lair with you and expect to return with my ship full of gold.'

Haakon experienced a sense of relief. With Vikar on his side, there would be few who would openly question his decision to hold Annis captive, rather than simply taking her and abandoning her. He would not welcome an open break with his fellow Jaarls, but he also knew where his duty lay. Annis deserved his protection.

Haakon started to reposition the chest of gold coins more centrally in the ship. Gradually he became aware Vikar was still standing there, regarding him with a quizzical expression. For what other reason had his fellow Jaarl sought him out?

'Tell me, though, Haakon, is there any truth to the other tale your half-brother spreads? Did you best Bjorn in a fair fight?'

'Bjorn is dead and I was the only warrior there when he died. I will pay the appropriate price to his family. But hear this and understand, Vikar—he raised his sword first. I am no oath-breaker.'

Vikar nodded, seemingly satisfied. 'Thorkell would expect no less.'

'I always fulfil my obligations, Vikar.'

Annis rested her head against the bulwark of the long ship. She and a dozen monks were all that she had seen—all that had survived? She did not want to think about the bustling place Lindisfarne had been. How many men. How many women. Her mind shied away from all that.

She should stand up and take a last view of Lindisfarne, but her legs refused to move. Maybe it was better this way. She had seen the smouldering remains of the buildings as she and the other prisoners had been marched down to the beach. One monk had tried to escape and had been dealt with summarily. After that, no one moved.

A welling up of noise filled the boat.

'Viken! Viken! Viken!'

'What are they shouting?' a monk asked in a hoarse whisper.

'Viken—it is where they are from,' Annis answered. Anything to keep her from thinking about the terrible events.

'Vikings? They come from no place. All they are, are heathen pirates. They despoiled God's holy place. Their souls will suffer eternal damnation,' another monk who had a pock-marked face proclaimed. Annis vaguely recognised him from her uncle's retinue—Aelfric. How had he survived when all the others perished? He raised a fist to the blackened sky, raining curses down on the raiders.

'It is in God's hands,' a third said and gave a gasp of pain.

Annis moved, knelt by his side and tried to raise the young man up. 'Is there anything I can do for you?'

His hand gripped hers. 'Forgive them, they know not what they do. Always remember Northumbria.'

He closed his eyes and a peaceful expression crossed his face.

Annis hunched farther down as the Viken began to clamber on board, laughing and joking. They appeared to be elated with today's work and she could think only of the countless lives that had been destroyed.

She recognised the backs of Haakon and his brother as they took up an oar very near her. The serpent ship began slide over the water, taking her away from Northumbria, from everything she had ever known.

A single tear trickled down her cheek. She allowed it to linger.

'Some day I will regain my freedom,' she vowed, clenching her fists. 'I shall not remain this Viken's slave for ever.'

Chapter Four

'Home at last!' Thrand said, as the *Golden Serpent* slid on to the sandy shore. 'I can't believe how much I missed it.'

'I cherish every day I spend here.' Haakon breathed deeply, savouring his first steps back on his land. All his muscles sighed as he was able to stretch for the first time since they had left Lindisfarne.

'No, you were the lucky one, the one who goes out adventuring, seeing new lands, meeting new people, gaining treasure.'

'But I never forget this fjord and the estate on the headland. It is what gives me a reason for living.' There was something special about his lands and the scent of pine trees that greeted him. This was home and he knew every inch of the ground. Through out the long years at Charlemagne's court, he had visited it often in his mind, reminding himself why he was a Norseman and not a subject of Charlemagne. 'If I could, I would remain here farming, but the harvests are too uncertain. My people come first. And so I have to leave to trade.'

'Adventure is a better description.'

'Now that you have experienced one voyage, Thrand, you can see that adventure is not always safe or pleasant.'

'But we have amassed a huge horde of gold and treasure, and

the voyage back was swift.' Thrand raised his hands above his head and gave a smile. 'Njordr the sea god was in a good mood.'

'The waves were swift and the winds favourable. We have made excellent time.'

Thrand's face sobered. 'But now we will have to endure my mother.'

'She expected me to perish.' Haakon stared at the wooden hall and its outbuildings. 'I am not sorry to disappoint her.'

'She cursed your name, and I hate to think what she said about me once she discovered that, despite everything, you had allowed me to go.' Thrand prodded a chest with the toe of his boot. 'I believe I will see to the unloading. You do the ceremony of welcome on your own. You are the Jaarl of this estate, after all.'

'If you wish. Your mother will have to be faced, Thrand, sooner or later.'

'As I said, I'd prefer later.' Thrand smiled and put his hands behind the back of his head. 'After she knows that I made a success of it, and returned back with gold. You know what she is like.'

'I do indeed.' Haakon nodded towards the great hall with its gabled roof. 'And if you wish to avoid Guthrun, I would begin unloading those chests—here comes the welcoming party.'

'Better you than me.' Thrand clapped him on the back and disappeared back down into the hold.

Haakon's mouth turned upwards in a bitter smile as his stepmother processed outwards from the hall, carrying the ritual horn of mead. Not a greying blond hair was out of place and she wore her best apron-dress over a linen shift. The large gold oval brooches his father had given her shone. Her eyes widened slightly and her hand trembled, spilling a bit of the mead, as she realised who was standing before her.

She had not expected to set eyes on him again, Haakon

thought with sudden insight. She had seen only the red-and-white sail, and had no idea who was on the ship.

'Guthrun, we have returned,' he said, accepting the horn and drinking deep from it as his dogs ran up, barking, to greet him. With his plumed tail wagging and his white eye-patch looking more roguish than ever, Floki was in the lead, determined to be the first dog to welcome his master. Haakon bent down to pat his favourite elkhound, who responded by turning over and baring his stomach.

'I expected you would—one way or another. The gods favour you, Haakon Haroldson.' Guthrun gave an exaggerated shrug. 'You are back earlier than expected. Did it go badly for you? Have your masts broken? I told you the voyage was ill starred.'

Haakon retained a grip on his temper. He had no wish for disharmony in front of his men. 'I am pleased to return to the northern lands and my home with my honour intact and the hold of my ship groaning with gold.'

'Have you brought your half-brother back alive?' she asked in a deceptively quiet voice, with her eyes hooded.

'Thrand survived and prospered as I predicted.' Haakon handed the drinking horn back to her. He wiped the back of his hand against his mouth, remembering how she had screamed and torn her hair when she was informed that Thrand was going. 'He served me well, and the skalds will some day sing of his fighting prowess.'

Guthrun nodded, seeming to accept the statement. 'And the other members of the *felag*? Have they returned as well?'

'We lost Bjorn.' Haakon kept his voice quiet and even. There was no need to recount the story in any great detail. She would learn soon enough.

'His family will be upset.' Her pale eyes flickered with something. Regret? Fear? But it was so brief Haakon wondered if he had imagined it. 'He was renowned as a fighter. How did he die?'

'He was in the blood-lust, and failed to recognise me. We fought.' Haakon stared toward where Annis and the rest of the Northumbrians were disembarking. 'There can be no question of oath-breaking when a man is in the grip of berserker madness. He lost his senses.'

'It is a shame that he reached such a sorry end.' Guthrun bowed her head, the perfect embodiment of a Viken lady, but Haakon knew she hid her knives well. She had not forgiven his father for having a child before her son. He would have thrown her out two years ago when his father died, but she had inherited part of the estate and until now, he lacked the gold to purchase it. 'You will have to pay compensation. I hope you can afford it. The harvest has been less than last year.'

'This voyage will provide the gold and silver required.'

With a struggle Guthrun controlled her face but Haakon was not fooled. He knew what drove his stepmother—luxury, money and her son. She rubbed forefinger and thumb together. 'How much is my son's share? He is your brother, Haakon Haroldson, and entitled to more than an ordinary member of the *felag*.'

'We have succeeded beyond our wildest expectations. Thrand will be able to afford his own estate and retainers.'

'You see I was correct to urge you to take Thrand on this expedition.' Guthrun's smile increased as she waggled her fingers at her son where he was busy supervising the unloading. 'He undoubtedly played a big part in its success.'

'Odin and Thor were with us on this voyage, providing gold, silver and captives.' Haakon gestured towards where the group of dispirited monks and Annis stood. The once-pristine white robes of the monks were now stained and mud-splattered. Alone among the group, Annis stood with her head held proud, no longer bowed but challenging with furious eyes. Through out the journey, she had never complained, but had regarded all around her in stony silence. 'It will take several days to unload and divide the spoils. Then we make our sacrifices to the Aesir and feast.'

'That woman is wearing your cloak,' Guthrun observed.

'Yes, she is under my protection,' Haakon replied in a mild tone. 'She is the daughter of a Northumbrian nobleman.'

Guthrun made an irritated noise in the back of her throat. 'I expect her to work. This farm has no place for idlers and slackers, even if they are concubines.'

'She is not my concubine.'

A thin smile appeared on Guthrun's lips. 'Thank you. Until you marry, I will continue to look after the house as I have always done.'

'Until the ransom arrives for all the captives, they will work for their shelter and food.' Haakon kept his voice smooth.

'And you have no fear of their god?' Guthrun turned her head to the side. 'He is said to possess a powerful magic.'

'If their god had not intended them to be here, he would have protected them.' Haakon turned towards the group and began to address them in Latin. 'Your God has seen fit to deliver you to the Norse. Worship whom you please. It is of little interest to me. I shall ask your pope in Rome for ransom. Obey my stepmother, Guthrun, and stewards as you would me.'

The monks were led away, leaving Annis standing alone. The sea breeze whipped her hair back from her face and moulded her gown to her form. Her steady gaze challenged Haakon.

'It is intriguing that a mere woman acts in this way,' Guthrun said. 'Maybe she is, in truth, your concubine. No captive will dictate how my house is run, however high born she is. She has a fierce air about her. I have no wish for her to intimidate my maids. How do I know what these people are like?'

Haakon frowned. Was this a ploy by Guthrun or was she truly afraid? He knew what Annis was capable of. He remembered his first sighting of her with her hair flowing down her back and the intent expression on her face as she had come to his aid without fear for her own life.

'She will not harm you, Stepmother. I give you my word on it.' He turned towards Annis. 'My stepmother seeks reassurance that you will not harm her.'

'Harm her?' Annis held out her hands and her eyes widened. 'Why should I do that? Where would I go? My home is on the other side of the water. I have no weapons.'

'You agree to conduct yourself. Or will you speak sweet promises that mean nothing again?'

He stared at her until she dropped her eyes, looking away, admitting defeat.

'While I am here, I will abide by your rules.' Her voice choked and she paused, closed her eyes tightly before continuing. 'What choice do I have? You are the master here. I will give no trouble on my honour as a Northumbrian.'

'You are right—you have no choice.' He turned to Guthrun, whose smile had become increasingly fixed through out the exchange. 'You will have no problems. She has given her word as a woman of noble birth.'

'Thank you, Haakon.' Guthrun inclined her head. 'I will see my son now. He needs his mother and her counsel.'

'He unloads the cargo. When he has finished his task, he will find you. Settle Annis in with the women. She can do some light work while she is here, waiting for the ransom.'

'When the woman is housed, I expect to see my son.'

Annis's brows had drawn together and Haakon wondered how much Norse she understood. Her bottom lip stuck out, looking like the colour of ripe strawberries, and he wondered what it would taste like. Would it hold a faintly salty tang from the sea water or would it be as sweet as the last time they kissed? Heat coursed through him.

Annoyed, he damped down the thoughts. Now was not the

time. He had no intention of bedding her. It would compli-
cate matters. He had a rule of not bringing his mistresses into
the house. Instead, he played at Thorkell's court or when he
was away in another country. A night or two of passion, then
the thrill of the chase wore away.

And what would it be like with Annis? He refused to bend
his rule to find out.

'Guthrun will give you orders.' The words came out
harshly. 'Obey her or you will have to deal with me.'

'In everything?' She tilted her head to one side as if
puzzled.

'Until I decide otherwise.'

Annis ground her teeth as she followed Haakon's stepmother into the long, low wooden building. It would have
been easier if she had been put in a dungeon, treated as if she
were a captive rather than a slave. There she could have
devised ways to escape. Here, she was surrounded by
everyday objects, reminded that the chances her stepfather
would send the ransom were slim.

The primitiveness of the house and hall shocked her. In
Birdoswald, they lived in stone buildings, so old that it was
said that the Roman Legion built them. There, the hearth was
at one end of the room, rather than in the middle as it was
here. And they had separate living quarters, not simply raised
areas on the edge of the hall.

'Too fine.' Guthrun leant forward and rubbed the wool of
Annis's dress. 'You work here.'

To Annis's surprise, she found Guthrun's words relatively
easy to understand. It was a bit like hearing Northumbrian
spoken with a very bad accent.

'Work holds no fear. Nothing could hold fear after what I
have endured.'

Guthrun raised her eyebrows. She clapped her hands and

gave orders to a plump, well-endowed blonde with tiny, pig-like eyes who wore an ingratiating smile. 'Tove, see to her. My son awaits.'

She said some rapid words to Tove, who gave a smirking smile and an exaggerated curtsy. Guthrun then departed, leaving Annis alone with the maidservant. Instantly the woman's countenance changed, becoming craftier, and a good deal less fawning.

Tove went to a chest, unlocked it and pulled a plain linen tunic and apron-dress out. She shoved them into Annis's hands. 'Change.'

A lump formed in Annis's throat. She had always had help dressing and undressing. No longer. She looked about for a screen to change behind, but there was nothing. Her fingers fumbled with the catch on Haakon's brooch, and Tove made a clicking noise in the back of her throat. She came over, undid the brooch with impatient fingers and nearly snatched the cloak off Annis's shoulders.

Tove clicked her fingers. 'The rest. And no head covering. You are a captive.'

The silver cross tumbled to the floor, and Tove bent to retrieve it.

'Not yours any more,' she said and put it on top of the cloak.

Annis's hand reached out for the cross, quick words sprung to her lips, but then she saw the carved wooden animals on the chest. This was not home. She cursed her bad luck, and forced her hand back down by her side.

Tove slammed the lid down, locked it with a click and pocketed the key. The cross had gone. Annis stared at the carved chest. She no longer had anything to remind herself of home, except for her memories.

Annis shivered slightly. But she rapidly changed the rest of her clothes. The linen scratched against her skin.

Tove led the way to the small kitchen area where a fire burnt in the middle of the room. A kettle filled with soup bubbled on the fire, and several maids were engaged in kneading bread. Two of the largest cats she had ever seen lounged in front of the fire, looking far more like dogs or half-tamed mountain cats. Rather than being chased away as they would be back home, the serving girls seemed to welcome the cats, pausing to give them strokes as they went about their business. Three other women were busy with spinning and weaving. Tove called out and several of the women snickered.

Tove gave Annis's shoulder a shove and pointed to a sack of barley and then to the large quern and mimicked grinding barley. Annis's heart sank. She had never had to do such a thing before—such things were done by the meanest servants. Annis clenched her teeth. She took a handful from the sack and placed it on the grinding stone.

After several passes with the stone, Annis saw the grain turn into a coarse flour. This wasn't as hard as she first feared. She gave a triumphant smile and placed the stone down.

Tove said something else. The entire room burst out laughing. Tove pointed to the sack. Annis's mouth dropped open. She was expected to grind the entire sack.

She put in some more barley and started to grind, faster this time. Her shoulders protested at the unaccustomed exercise. She would do this! She would grind the sack of barley.

She ground faster and faster, forcing the pace, and then suddenly the quern tipped over, spilling the flour everywhere, much to the intense amusement of Tove and her friends. Annis wanted to sink down on her knees and cry, but instead she forced herself to try to pick the flour up with her hands. It flowed everywhere. A cat jumped into the middle of the dust and began washing its whiskers as the roars grew louder.

A young woman with long teeth said something in rapid Norse, waving her hands and shaking her head.

'I can do it myself. I made the mess,' Annis said in Latin and then in Northumbrian.

'Let me help.'

The woman removed the cat, took a brush and rapidly swept the flour into a pile. She scooped it up into another dish. Annis bit her lip and nodded her thanks.

'Empty the quern often or else…' The woman gestured with her hands, mimicking what could happen. 'This has happened to me before—several times.'

Annis felt a lump grow in her throat. She touched the woman's hand. 'Thank you.'

'Ingrid.' The woman held up a finger and then said something in very rapid Norse.

Annis put her hand to her chest and took time with her words. 'Annis. I am called Annis. If you speak slowly, I can understand.'

'I am Ingrid,' the woman said, a smile breaking over her face and making it pretty and less like a startled hare. 'Tove makes mischief. She seeks to share a Jaarl's bed and perhaps have his child as that would make her future.'

'What does that have to do with me?'

'They are wondering if you share Lord Haakon's bed where you come from, and is this why he brought you here? The Jaarl has never brought a woman here before.'

Annis felt her face flame. 'No. I am a captive, not a concubine.'

'They wondered. Many would like to share his bed. He is reputed to be a kind and considerate lover.'

Annis felt her cheeks burn even more as she remembered the kiss they had shared. She should have known that he was an expert in these matters. Perhaps he was like Selwyn with many mistresses, changing them as often as he changed his cloaks. 'He is more interested in the ransom that he expects to get.'

'If that is true, then Tove will be very happy.' Ingrid leant closer. 'But you will admit—he does have strong arms, and a pleasing face.'

'Yes, I will give him that.'

The entire room burst out laughing.

Ingrid came over to Annis and took the grinding stone from her again. She poured some barley into the bottom bowl and showed Annis how to do the grinding properly. 'Like so, yes? Tove always makes the new serving girls grind the barley. Never teaches, but I help.'

A wave of relief washed over as tears pricked Annis's eyes. She had not expected kindness. Somehow it made her feel less alone. She had made a friend. It had been before Selwyn died that she had had a friend.

'Can you tell me why cats are allowed in the hall?'

'Do you not have cats in the kitchen back where you come from?'

Annis shook her head.

Ingrid reached down and picked the black-and-white one up, cradling it in her arms. 'This is Kisa, and the grey is Fress. They are beloved of the goddess Freya, and help to keep the mice down.'

Annis tried the unfamiliar names out and tentatively reached out a finger. Kisa responded immediately by purring and lifting her head backwards. 'They are the largest cats I have ever seen.'

'Kisa likes you. She is very picky about the people she lets stroke her. Cats can tell about people, you know.' Ingrid gave a decisive nod. 'I will like you as well, I think.'

Annis started to grind the barley again this time, following Ingrid's instructions as Kisa settled at her feet.

Annis wiped the sweat from her brow. The sack, which had been full, sagged with only a few handfuls of grain left at the bottom. Two days of grinding barley had been hard work, but she was nearing the end. The only compensation was that she was exhausted at the end of the day and fell asleep next to Ingrid as soon as her eyes closed. No dreams of burning buildings or strong warriors, only blessed oblivion.

She lifted the grinding stone and started to work again.

'Ow.' The blister on her right hand tore open and every movement was like fire. Annis resisted the temptation to cry. Of everything that had happened to her, it was this blister that truly hurt. Such a stupid thing to cry over. The monks were undoubtedly suffering far worse, yet this morning she could hear the sound of their chanting as they went about the work of the farm. She used the corner of her apron-dress to wipe away a tear.

'What is wrong?' Ingrid asked, hurrying over from where she was making bread.

'I held the stone wrong.'

'Let me see your hands,' Ingrid said, coming over.

Reluctantly Annis held out her hands. The red blister shone against her skin. 'It is nothing as I said.'

Ingrid touched the blister. 'Your hands are soft. You did not do this sort of work before.'

'They will soon harden.'

'Haakon waits for a large ransom, yes?'

'Yes.' Annis forced the word from her lips.

'Does he know that you are being forced to do this work?'

'I presume so.' Annis felt pain at the back of her head echoing down to the base of her spine. She had no doubt that Haakon knew what she was doing and had ordered it, taking some sort of delight in humiliating her. 'If I had some of my special ointment, I could soothe my hands.'

'Where do you find this ointment?' Ingrid stumbled over the last word.

'I make it from herbs and tallow. A simple recipe to make, if you have the correct ingredients.'

'That is a good thing.' Ingrid smiled. 'Do you know much about herbs and medicines?'

'Yes, I do.'

'You are wasted here in the kitchen.'

Annis started to reply, but Ingrid had gone. Annis shrugged. She put her hand on the grinding stone and winced. Then she gritted her teeth. She would do this. She would not think about what her sister-in-law or her mother might be doing; instead she would recite the various medicines and herbs she knew. Anything to keep her mind occupied and away from the pounding pain.

She gave the quern another twist as hard as she could, ignoring the ache that shot up her arm. The grinding stone started to tip. Her hand went out the catch the heavy stone, but other, stronger hands were there, lifting it back up on to the table.

The air crackled with something that had not been there before. Slowly she turned.

Haakon stood next her with a large dog sitting at his side, wagging its plumed tail. How and when he had arrived she did not know—she had been concentrating that hard on the grinding. But he was here, looking most unlike the warrior she remembered from Lindisfarne.

He had bathed and his dark hair still bore shimmering droplets of water. Rather than his chain mail, he wore a soft blue fine-wool shirt over a pair of tightly fitting trousers. His feet were covered in butter-yellow leather boots. He exuded a vitality that filled the entire room.

'Is there something you require, my lord?' Annis asked.

She kept her voice cold and formal. She had no doubt who was responsible for her present difficulty. He would see that such chores would not break her spirit.

'Ingrid came to find me. She said you complained.'

'I am doing the job I was given—grinding barley.' Annis

concentrated on the grinding stone. 'I may be slow, but the barley is being ground.'

'You are a woman of many talents.' His low voice contained a hint of laughter, irritating Annis. She certainly took no pleasure in being a captive. 'What do you think, Floki?'

The dog tilted his head and barked.

'There, you see, Floki agrees with me.' Haakon reached down and gave the dog a titbit from one of the dishes.

'I would have hardly been able to run my husband's estate if I did not know how to grind wheat or barley.' Annis gritted her teeth and hid her hands under her apron-dress. She kept her head held high, meeting his eyes, daring him to say differently.

He appeared to accept the statement. 'And you find my language easy to understand. Ingrid said that you and she speak.'

'I am a quick learner.' Annis lifted a shoulder.

She reached for the hated stone. If she went back to work, maybe he would go away and she could concentrate on her task rather than how broad his shoulders were or how well his trousers moulded to his legs.

'That makes life easier.' Haakon's hand caught hers and stilled her movement. The grip was firm, unhesitating. 'I wish to speak to you away from the kitchen. My business with you is not for the large-eared gossips who inhabit this place.'

Annis stepped away from the table and tried to ignore the smirking faces of the other maidservants.

But what good would it do?

Haakon led the way to a small, private alcove, outside the main hall. A bench stood at one side, but Haakon stood regarding her, his face unyielding and stern.

'Why did the monks allow you to speak on their behalf?' he asked, breaking the silence. 'They all have tongues.'

'Nobody asked me to say anything. I decided to speak.' The anger grew within Annis. 'Someone had to.'

'And they let you. Not one murmured a protest. Why?'

'My uncle was the Abbot.' Annis felt a light breeze push a strand of hair into her mouth. Instead of sea salt, it tasted faintly of wood smoke. She stared out at the bay where the serpent boats were pulled high on to the shore, the waves slightly lapping against the hulls. 'The rule of the monastery is strong. They were fearful.'

'And you are not.'

'When the occasion demands…' Annis ignored how tight her stomach felt. She knew whatever punishment he decided, she would speak again. Somebody had to give voice to the monks' situation.

'That explains much.' Haakon's face was inscrutable. 'My stepmother was not best pleased.'

'Have you sent the ransom demands?'

'They will be sent on the next ship that leaves for the Holy Roman Empire. I have contacts in Charlemagne's court.'

Annis gave a nod. No doubt Haakon would use this as an excuse to increase her ransom. She wanted to tell him that her stepfather would never pay to save her. He would deem it justification for taking control of all the lands around Birdoswald.

But the words refused to come. If she said them, then her tiniest spark of hope, the thing that kept her going at night, would be gone. Her home would be lost to her for ever.

'I look forward to the answer.' She pressed her palms into the folds of her gown to hide their sudden trembling.

'You seem very sure.'

'I am.'

It was a white lie. He would discover his mistake soon enough. In the meantime, she might be able to help the monks. The Church, she was positive, would provide the money. She had heard of cases before. The Church disliked Christians being slaves to pagans, but she felt that it only extended to its sworn people.

Maybe she should have made her vows as her uncle wanted her to. But she would have been paying lip-service to them. She had no real vocation. She desired a home, children and a husband who wanted her for herself and not for the property she'd bring. It would have been a lie to take those vows.

Haakon said nothing in reply as his fingers traced the outlines of the carved wooden pillar. It was as if they were caught in a contest, a battle of wills. Each was waiting for the other to speak. To lose. She was more aware than ever of his form, his strength.

'Annis! Annis, where have you got to? The barley has to be finished! Annis!' Tove's shrill voice sounded, breaking the spell. 'Annis! You will be punished.'

'I need to get back to my work. Tove calls.' Annis lifted her chin and stared directly into his eyes. 'Something I will try to do much more cheerfully from now on.'

'Does Guthrun know that you are grinding, doing menial tasks?' His eyes burned into her soul.

'Tove rules the kitchen.' Annis gave a careful shrug. She had to be fair. She had not seen the woman since she started working in the kitchen. She had no idea if Guthrun knew what Tove was doing or not. But she was not one to bear tales. 'I do what is asked of me.'

His hand shot out and grabbed her wrist, turning her hand over. 'You are unaccustomed to such work. Your palm is heavily blistered.'

Annis snatched her hand away. His touch sent strange tingles up her arm. 'I am not used to being a captive either. The monks suffer far worse.'

Haakon's eyes hardened to blazing blue points, but he made no attempt to recapture her hands.

'The monks understand hard labour. Not one of them was born into the nobility. You are a lady. It is different.' He rubbed his thumb across his lips. 'Ingrid tells me that you can make ointment to soften hands, to heal blisters.'

'I know of one,' Annis replied carefully. Exactly what had Ingrid told him?

'Then make it.'

'I do not have the necessary herbs.'

'Are they exotic? Or don't you know what is required?' His voice held no warmth.

Annis paused. She had to be careful. She had no wish to sound overly proud, and what if the ointment did not work? But to be given the chance! Anything was better than grinding barley. Quickly Annis listed the herbs she required, counting each one off on her fingertips and ending with lavender.

He nodded and his eyes took on a speculative but impressed expression. Annis struggled to contain her growing hope. Would he give her permission to try?

'Intriguing.' He wiped his hands against his trousers. 'Return to your work.'

'But…but…you will speak to Guthrun. About the ointment. It would take but a little time.'

'Back to work, Annis. Do your appointed tasks.'

'Is that an order?' Annis asked, dismayed. She had been so certain.

His face became stern. 'Do not try my patience any further.'

'And your word is law.'

A blue flame flickered in his eyes. 'Yes, and you would do well to remember that.'

Chapter Five

'The Jaarl requested these be delivered to the kitchen.'

Annis started to hear the soft Northumbrian burr, instead of the Viken tones. Aelfric, the only monk close to her uncle to survive, stood in the doorway to the kitchen. In his hands he carried a variety of dried herbs which he placed on the table. He pursed his lips in disapproval as Kisa came and gave the herbs a very cat-like sniff. Annis lifted the cat off the table.

'Did he give any reason?' Ingrid asked, turning the dried herbs over. 'What does he expect us to do with them? Add them to the meat?'

'For the *lady* Annis.' Aelfric's emphasis was unmistakable.

Annis regarded the herbs. Everything she had told Haakon was there. 'They are to make an ointment to cure blisters. I told Haakon about it and he remembered.'

'Haakon remembers everything,' Ingrid said. 'Whenever he has been away, he inspects the entire estate. His eyes notice everything and woe betide to anyone who has forgotten to carry out his orders. He cares about his people. He constantly looks for ways to improve their condition.'

'There is no lavender, my lady,' Aelfric said in Latin. 'I believe the Viken want it for the horses.

'Thank you, Aelfric, for bringing the herbs to me so swiftly,' she said. A great wave of homesickness washed over her. 'And how do you fare, you and your brother monks?'

'We are well, my lady.' The monk dipped his head, and Annis could see the shaved tonsure beginning to grow out. In a few weeks' time, he would resemble an ordinary man, instead of a monk.

'All of you?'

'We survive and get enough food,' he answered in Latin. 'The work is no harder than what most were used to at the abbey—although the soil is poor.'

A thousand questions sprung to Annis's lips, but she was aware that Tove watched with narrowed eyes and thinned lips.

'I look forward to the day we all see home again,' she replied in Northumbrian so that the women could understand they spoke of inconsequential things. Tove pursed her lips and turned back to her work.

'I do as well, my lady.' He bowed his head, made the sign of the cross and left.

'Can you really make an ointment to heal cracks and blisters in hands from these dried plants?' Tove asked, with her nose in the air.

'Given a bit of fat, I can do.' Annis moved the herbs off to one side. She wanted to begin straight away, but undoubtedly Tove had another sack of grain for her to grind.

'The Jaarl Haakon sent these.'

'Yes.' Annis touched the herbs and released their scent.

'What are you waiting for?' Tove said. 'Make it then. Now. My hands are rough. I would like them to be smooth.'

Annis hesitated. The great hall teemed with men playing with dice and drinking from horns. Haakon's broad back was to her. His laughter floated out across the hall. She bit her lip.

He was busy, surrounded by his men. She could go away, return to the kitchen. She straightened her shoulders. That would be the coward's way. He deserved her thanks.

At her approach, he turned, lifted an eyebrow. 'Yes? Is there another problem?'

'I wanted to thank you.' She twisted the end of the apron-dress around her hand. Thanking him in her mind and in person in front of his men were two very different things. She forced her chin to rise and met his gaze.

'Thank me?' He put his hand under her elbow and led her away from the group to a quiet corner of the hall. 'What do you want to thank me for?'

'Ever since Tove learnt yesterday that I have some skill with herbs, she has had me mixing ointments and potions.' Annis gave a brief smile.

'And your hands?'

'They heal.' Annis held out her palms for his inspection. The angry redness had gone. 'Soon, they will be well.'

'But what does this have to do with me?' Haakon tilted his head to one side; his eyes watched her mouth.

'You sent the herbs,' Annis explained. 'You gave me the opportunity.'

'I sent the herbs because a woman with blistered hands is no use to me.'

'Nevertheless, I am grateful.' Annis's throat became tight.

'Good.' He nodded and then returned to his men. Laughter rose from the group. Annis winced. They were probably making fun of her. She knew the sort of crude jokes Selwyn and his retainers had indulged in. Haakon would not be different. Men were all alike. She'd endure. She'd forget his kiss and his kindness. She wanted nothing to do with him.

'I hope you have chosen the warrior that you want to serve,' Tove said with a smirk on her face as she adjusted her apron-dress to reveal more of her figure. Instead of helping with the peas, she spent her time looking at the silver platters and adjusting her hairstyle and neckline. But she appeared to have a sixth sense about when Guthrun might poke her nose through the door. Always, when Guthrun appeared, Tove had her head bent, being industrious. Guthrun would sigh and tell the other women to be more like Tove.

'What do you mean, Tove?' Annis asked, not bothering to keep the scepticism from her voice.

'These men have been without female companionship.' Tove smacked her lips and gave a suggestive twist to her hips as she sauntered up and down the kitchen area.

'I have not given it much thought.' Annis kept her eyes cast downward. She hoped that when the time came, she could melt into the shadows. Over the past few days, she had managed to convince herself that her attraction to Haakon was an aberration. Now that she was beginning to find her feet in her new situation, the strange hold he had over her would vanish. She did not even want to begin to think about entangled bodies or stolen kisses. Her hands trembled and she hid them under her apron.

'It is a case of choose or be chosen,' Tove said to general laughter. 'A matter of the utmost simplicity—you serve mead or ale to the warrior you want, standing near to him. He grabs you.'

Annis knew she should have expected this. It had been no different in Northumbria. Only there, she sat at the high table, removed from the activity, but Selwyn had taken part. Through out their marriage, she endured the parade of flesh— forced to watch as Selwyn would pick out the woman most suited to his tastes that evening—to know her only attraction to her husband was her dowry and the prestige her family brought.

'And, yes, we know who you would choose, Tove!'

Laughter filled the kitchen.

'Do you indeed, Ingrid? I wonder.' Tove tapped her finger to her mouth, a glint coming into her eye. 'I gave up on Haakon months ago. He still has feelings for Thorkell's queen, Asa. Men buzz around her like bees near a dish of honey.'

'That is just gossip, Tove,' Ingrid said quickly, looking over her shoulder. 'How can you repeat such tales!'

'But it is said they were once very close when he went to send Birka to fetch her. And you know she had a hand in Vikar's divorce.' Tove patted her hair. 'In any case, there are other Jaarls than him in Thorkell's kingdom.'

'But none as good looking,' one of Tove's friends said with a sigh.

'I think I prefer the look of Vikar as Ivar has a scar on his face, even if Ivar lost his wife six months ago.' Tove made a little pirouette, causing her dress to swirl about her legs and to reveal her ankles. 'There are few men who withstand my ankles. Skalds have written poetry to them.'

'One skald and he was cross-eyed,' someone called out to general laughter.

Tove's face burnt and she put her hands on her hips. 'Who said that!'

The air of the kitchen suddenly crackled with tension as everyone hurriedly bent over their tasks.

'Ingrid, it was you!'

Annis set down her bowl of peas as Kisa jumped on to her lap. If it came to a fight, then she would not hesitate. She knew who she'd defend.

'What is that supposed to mean, Tove?' Ingrid asked as she popped two more peas into the bowl.

Annis looked from Tove to Ingrid. Tove wore a superior expression on her face. 'You overheard the verses, but then we all know that you have lusted after Thrand since you first arrived.'

Ingrid's face grew bright red. She mumbled to her hands, 'He has a pleasant smile and manner.'

'You had better not let his mother catch you saying such things. She has great plans for him—a Jaarl's daughter with a large dowry.' Tove gave a derisive laugh and leant forward so that her face was level with Ingrid's. 'It must be why she assigned you to the kitchens, instead of serving at the tables. Your days of being fostered are numbered, Ingrid.'

Annis waited until Tove had been called away by Guthrun before she whispered to Ingrid, 'Is it true?'

'Thrand and I were friendly before he left on the expedition.' Ingrid picked up a squirming Fress, burying her face in the grey fur. 'I have no idea what he feels about me now. He has not been near me since he returned. He has not even enquired about Fress or Kisa. And he was the one who found them as kittens.'

'By Thrand, you mean Haakon's brother?'

'Yes, he holds part of the estate, but hopes to buy his own farm, away from here. He and Haakon do not always agree. He used to confide in me.' Ingrid patted her hair. 'I think he is very handsome and kind. He sometimes pulls a string for Kisa or Fress to chase.'

'I will do the work in the kitchen for you, if you wish.' Annis reached over and squeezed her friend's hand. Ingrid deserved better than Thrand, but if he was her choice, she wanted to help.

'Would you?' Ingrid's eyes lit up. 'Do you really mean it? I would have thought you would want to serve the mead at the table.'

'I have no desire to do such a thing,' Annis said decisively. 'I doubt anyone will notice. They will be too busy eating and drinking to notice who is serving. And it was only Tove issuing the orders, after all.'

Ingrid shifted from one foot to the other. 'If you are sure…'

Annis made little shooing motions. 'Go, get yourself ready, and hopefully all will turn out like you want it to. Thrand will remember you.'

Ingrid flashed a happy smile and left the room, her hips swaying.

Annis pressed her fingertips together. She would be safe here in the kitchen. Everyone would forget about her. Maybe when the feast was in full flow, she'd attempt to find a means of escape for herself and the monks.

The cool water from the bucket near the barns refreshed Annis's face. She hated to think how long she had worked with the feast preparations nearing completion. All she wanted to do was lay down and rest, but tonight loomed large.

'Making yourself ready for the feast?' Haakon's low voice sounded behind her. 'The store of dried herbs appears to have been heavily depleted. Not all for beauty aids, I trust. Doubtless, though, my men will appreciate the results.'

She spun round. Haakon was standing but a foot from her, watching with a speculative glint in his eye. His dog nudged his head forward, demanding attention. Annis gave the dog a quick stroke and tried to think of an appropriate response. He made it seem as if she desired the attention of his men. He took a step closer, and she could see the individual lashes of his eyes.

'It is hot and work in the kitchen is hard,' Annis replied carefully. Every nerve in her body tingled with awareness of his nearness as she remembered the kiss they had shared. Silently she cursed Tove's gossip for stirring the memory.

'No other reason?'

'What else would there be?' Annis stared directly into his

blue eyes. Let him say it. Let him accuse her of behaving in a seductive fashion. She had behaved perfectly properly.

'After the victorious ships' figureheads have been paraded and blessed by the priests of Odin and Thor, you and your fellow captives will be shown along with the rest of the captured bounty.'

'I had expected it.' Annis hated the tightness of her voice. It sounded as if she was about to burst into tears. She refused to.

'The chief skald will declaim the story of the *felag*'s voyage. He will include my fight with Bjorn.'

'Am I to be mentioned?'

'No, it will be told my way.' Haakon's eyes were hard. 'What happened in that room remains between you and me.'

Annis's head ached with a dull pain. She wanted to believe he was doing this solely for his own glory, but her heart whispered that he was protecting her. She had seen the esteem Bjorn was held in, and knew the sorrow that many had expressed at his death. They accepted Haakon's killing of Bjorn because he was their leader. They would want revenge if they knew the truth.

'Thank you for warning me. I shall keep my face impassive.'

A quick smile flitted across his face. 'I knew you would understand, Valkyrie.'

'It makes sense.' Annis hugged his use of 'Valkyrie' to her. 'What happens after that?'

'It depends.' His voice held a husky note and she felt drawn into his blue eyes.

His lashes were lighter than his dark brown hair, she thought idly, and his lips firm. Her body started to sway towards him as her mouth became parched.

Floki pushed his wet nose under her palm again. She blinked and regained control of her body. The moment had vanished. She shook her head. Tove and her stories.

'I am not sure I understand.' Her voice sounded thick to her ears.

She concentrated on stroking Floki's ears to hide her confusion.

'It is a matter for you. The feasting will go on all night and well into tomorrow and the next day.'

Haakon gave a low whistle and Floki rushed to his master's side.

The noise from the feast echoed through out the kitchen. The sounds of laughter and banging of feet against the packed earth sounded almost as bad as the war cries that still echoed through her dreams. Her prediction proved accurate. Guthrun and Tove were both too busy to notice who was serving the mead. She had been able to stay back in the kitchen, refilling the jugs of mead and platters of food.

'Annis,' Ingrid called. 'Annis, I need help.'

Annis started and put a hand to her head. She concentrated on drawing a deep breath. 'What is it, Ingrid?'

'This is embarrassing, but someone asked to speak to me in private, and the warriors are crying out for more mead. Can you be a love and take the jug around? I will return shortly.'

Annis was tempted to refuse, but she saw the look on Ingrid's face—flushed and excited. She might not like Thrand, but her new friend appeared pleased.

What harm could it do?

'Yes, I will do this for you, Ingrid. Take your time.'

Ingrid gave Annis's hand a squeeze. 'You are a true friend.'

Annis picked up her jug and went through the door into the long hall. The hall had been transformed. Long tables edged the sides of the room. Tapestries hung on the wooden walls, pelts were scattered on the wooden benches and torches glowed; in the centre of the room a fire smouldered. The high table stood at the end opposite to the kitchen.

Annis glanced towards the table and her breath caught in her throat. Haakon appeared even more magnificent with the torchlight making his hair midnight black, and a wealth of gold about his neck and forearms. He wore a richly embroidered red tunic, with a matching red cape. It was exotic, but as fine as anything she had seen in Northumbria.

Her mouth went dry as her blood began to race. She wanted to hate him, but her eyes kept returning time and again to his long fingers and the way they curled around the drinking horn. It was as if she had been drinking jugs of mead. She swallowed hard and concentrated on walking across the uneven floor.

Every now and then, she stopped to refill drinking horns. When she reached the high table, Guthrun raised her eyebrows, but held out her drinking horn along with Thrand's.

Annis tilted her head. She had been wrong. Ingrid was not meeting Thrand—he sat drinking with Haakon and the other Jaarls. His eyes were slightly unfocussed. He was regaling the table with a story about the raid.

'At last, Annis, we see you,' Haakon's voice rumbled. 'I was beginning to be concerned. You disappeared after the captives were displayed. Perhaps you thought to escape, but the boats are well guarded and so you have returned.'

'There were chores that required my attention.' Annis started to fill the drinking horns. She tried to concentrate on the act of pouring, but her mind kept returning to Haakon and his hands.

'Stupid girl, you allowed the mead to run all over the table,' Guthrun cried.

Annis started and lifted the jug, but not before a few drops had spilled over the drinking horn.

'There is no harm in it. No doubt the little Northumbrian has never seen Viken warriors in their full glory before,' one of the warriors called with too much ribald laughter.

'Do you want to make it worse for yourself?' Tove whispered in her ear. She pushed herself forward and began to fill the other drinking horns. 'This is where I serve.'

Annis nodded and carefully kept her eyes downcast as she poured the remaining mead into the drinking horns farther down the tables.

'That is a very pretty piece,' Vikar said, leaning over to Haakon as Annis walked away. 'I can see now why you refused to give her up.'

'I told you she was a high-value captive, a noblewoman,' Haakon replied and tore his mind away from the way Annis's hips swayed as she balanced the jug against her side and neatly stepped around the dogs who lay at the warriors' feet. The memory of how her body had felt against his came flooding back. There was passion in this woman, he felt sure of it. It was simply waiting to be unlocked.

'Since when has that ever stopped anyone?' Vikar drained his horn and held it to be refilled. 'My cousin Sigrid was held captive and came home with two babes in arms. It is expected. And then it is up to her lord to decide what to do. If he had taken better care of her in the first place, the woman's charms would not be available.'

'Something worth considering.' Haakon stroked his chin. Vikar was right. If Annis had been properly guarded, he would never have taken her. 'She would have perished on that island.'

'And if you are not interested in her in that way,' Vikar continued, 'there are several others who might be, who would be willing to advance her ransom. Me, for example.'

'She is not for sale.' Haakon banged his fist down on the table. 'I have my principles.'

'It was only a suggestion, but if I were you, I would make sure others know of your intentions. An enormous amount of ale and mead has been drunk, and the men will be looking for…companionship.'

'They are welcome to it…as long as no one touches my captive.'

'If that is the case, can I beg acquaintance of the little blonde? She has been giving me the eye all night, and I think her bosom might be just the place to rest my head.'

Annis rested her jug on the table. Exactly how much did these warriors intend drinking? They had already drained ten barrels of mead and ale. And the cries rang out for more, but still Ingrid had not returned.

She heaved a sigh, filled the jug with the little that remained in the barrel and started to head back to the hall. A stamping circle dance had begun around the central fire.

As she re-entered the torchlit room, several warriors blocked her path. She could smell the honey-sweet scent of mead on their breath, and at least two swayed.

'Carry your jug, little Northumbrian?' one asked as he suggestively ran his hand down her arm. 'Or shall we dance? I can tell you are a good dancer.'

Annis flinched. She should have expected this. She had heard the talk. Somehow, she hoped that she would be spared with so many other willing women in the household. She smiled and shook her head, trying to move forward. 'When I need help, I will ask for it.'

But the warrior took no notice and his hand went around her waist. 'I can give you all the help you require.'

'I doubt it.' Annis spun away as the calls from the other men increased. A circle had formed around her and the warrior. She had to fight back, to escape, but how?

The circle started to press closer as more and more helpful comments were shouted out. The warrior put his hand about her waist, drawing her close. Annis turned her head away and his lips brushed her hair. Angrily Annis jerked her face away, and hit at the hand with her jug. 'You leave me be.'

'You are a spirited one. Just how I like my women to be.' The man wiped the spit from his mouth and started to reach for her again.

'When the lady says no, she means no, Godfred,' Haakon said.

Annis spun around to see Haakon advancing towards them. The man started to back away from her, holding up his hands.

'Why are you here, Annis?' Haakon's eyes glittered dangerously.

'I was attempting to return to the kitchen,' Annis said, lifting up the jug. 'I have run out of mead.'

'And were delayed.' Haakon pursed his lips. 'Yes, I saw.'

'What happened was not my fault.'

'You merely appeared and lust overtook these men.' Haakon's voice dripped with sarcasm as he lifted one eyebrow.

How dare he imply that she welcomed the advances! These men were drunk! She was not a wanton!

'I have no idea why this happened.' Annis pushed an errant strand of hair behind her ear and tried to straighten her crumpled apron-dress.

'We shall have to disagree on that.'

'You may think what you like, but I know what happened. Now if you will excuse me…' Annis started to move forward. All the muscles in her legs were trembling. She wanted to go back to the kitchen and sit.

'Sometimes you presume much,' Haakon growled in her ear.

Annis drew a single breath before he reached for her, pulled her into his arms and his mouth lowered on to hers. This time, the kiss was not gentle but bruising. It sought to overpower and show who was in charge. And Annis, to her horror, felt her body respond to the hard, dark kiss invading her mouth as he ran his fingers through her hair. The warmth spread to the inner reaches of her body, filling her.

It did not matter that they were surrounded by the men. She knew she should defend herself, but her hands were clinging to his tunic instead. She wanted the kiss to continue. She wanted to explore his mouth, his tongue, to taste him.

His mouth lifted and he released her. She stumbled backwards, landing on the hard-packed dirt as laughter erupted.

Haakon said a few sharp words and the laughter stopped.

'What did you say to them?' Annis asked through tingling lips as she ignored his hand and stood up on her own.

'I thought Northumbrian was the same as Norse.'

'Not all words.'

'I told them you were my captive.' His chin lifted arrogantly. 'And that they should remember who holds sway here.'

'I am no such thing,' Annis replied through gritted teeth, despising him and the small thrill that still ran through her body.

'Would you prefer one of the other warriors?' He snapped his fingers. 'I was obviously under the mistaken impression that you disliked the attention.'

'I did. I do.' Anger at him, at herself for reacting to the kiss, filled her. She should have more self-control. She had to remember what he was and who was responsible for taking her captive. She could not react to his kisses in that way. 'If you will allow me to return to my duties…*my lord*.'

He ran his hand lightly along her shoulder. Annis resisted the impulse to purr. She stepped away and wrapped both arms about her waist, struggling to banish the sudden ache from her body.

'You not need fear, Annis. I have never forced a woman and no one has ever complained that my coupling was rough.'

'I was not afraid of that.' Annis lifted her chin. She had not found Selwyn particularly attractive, with his rough manner and vulgar laugh. In many ways she'd been grateful when he found other company, but she had not feared him. She knew her value to him. Now, Haakon's kisses made her think she had missed something. Her treacherous body wanted more, much more.

'Then what are you afraid of?'

'You are my enemy. You kidnapped me.'

His brows drew together. 'You were told to stay by the rocks out of sight until the ships left, but chose to go back into the priory. You disobeyed me.'

'I told you why.'

A smile crossed his features. 'Then we are at an impasse. Should you desire to further our acquaintance, you will know where to find me.'

'I believe your presence is required at the high table. Your stepmother is frantically trying to catch your attention.'

Haakon glanced towards the high table. His eyes narrowed. 'It would never do to upset my stepmother's plans for the feast. We have tarried here too long. Perhaps I should have thrown you over my shoulder and taken you to my chamber. I regret I will not be able to take up the invitation your lips issued just then when we kissed.'

'My lips never did.'

'Ah, but we both know the truth, don't we, Annis?'

Annis hated the way her cheeks burned; by the time she had thought up a suitable riposte, Haakon had vanished.

Chapter Six

Eventually the torches spluttered and died. Soft laughter filled the hall along with the sounds of bedding being unrolled as people found places to sleep. Annis returned to the narrow pallet she had shared for the last few nights. Neither Ingrid nor Tove had returned and Annis was able to stretch out a bit, lying with her hands behind her head and toes pointed.

Every time she closed her eyes, the memory of Haakon's fierce kiss welled up within her. Here in the dark she knew her body desired the touch of his mouth against hers again, his hands on her skin. She screwed her eyes up tight and forced her mind to think of home and her old life.

How could she desire a man who had destroyed her world?

When finally the grey light of dawn appeared, Annis crossed the hall, not bothering to fumble about for her apron-dress. A masculine laugh came from Haakon's chambers, followed by a female one sounding very much like Tove's. Annis froze, her heart sinking. She clenched her teeth. It did not matter. She was not interested in him. Two of the elk-hounds lifted their heads, but did not move from where they lay by the embers.

She lifted the latch and slipped outside, before her nerve failed. Annis drew a deep cleansing breath, enjoying the feel of the cool air. For the first time since that dreadful day, she felt free.

Freedom. To breathe. To think.

The yard was still. The cows, goats and sheep stood like silent sentinels. The waves gently lapped the hulls of the boats where they lay pulled up on the shore.

A shiver passed over Annis. Even without their fierce serpent figureheads, the boats held a certain menace and foreboding. But they were lifeless, unguarded.

No one was awake to guide her movements. She could to wander where she willed for a short time. She made a wry face—anywhere except to where she wanted to go—home. It lay on the other side of the sea, a sea that she had no hope of navigating.

Escape by sea was not an option. And dark stands of pine and larch rose on three sides behind the hall, breathing danger.

Haakon was right—she did want to live. She wanted to live on her own terms and not be dictated to. Someday, she'd have her freedom back.

Leaving behind the boats, she skirted around the great hall, and down a small hill towards the lake that supplied the fresh water. Its silver-mirrored surface matched the grey-tinged pink of the sky. A tiny smoke curl came from a hut nestled on the shore.

Annis wandered through the sweet meadow grass towards the lake. She was about two hundred paces from the shore when she became aware that the surface was not still, but broken by the head of a swimmer.

As she drew back into the shadow of a birch tree and watched, the swimmer rose from the lake. Water streamed off his head, his bare shoulders and torso.

Haakon. Haakon was out here, not in the hall or in his private chamber. Annis stared as a wave of happiness washed over her.

His chest was far more muscular than Annis had imagined. It tapered down to his narrow hips and sculpted legs. Droplets of water clung to his skin, making it shine in the grey light.

Warm heat infused through out her body. She had to stay where she was or otherwise she would be seen. He would know that she had watched him. She retreated farther into the shadow of the birch, but found it impossible to tear her eyes away from his form, from the way his muscles rippled as he pulled his clothes on.

Had he seen her? Annis offered up a quick prayer.

A twig cracked as he ambled away towards the barns, never once having glanced in her direction. Annis allowed a sigh to escape from her lips and rested her cheek against the smooth bark of the birch.

She had thought to escape the heat of the house, but now found her body burning. The thought of returning to the hall was repugnant. There she'd have to lie awake and listen to the sounds of other people taking their pleasure when her hands ached to touch his skin and wipe the droplets of water off.

She pressed her palms against her thighs, banishing the thought.

What was wrong with her? Before the raid, she would never have imagined such a thing about any man, but, after last night's kiss, she found her brain full of him and these longings. She loathed him and all he represented. Had to.

She waited until all sound had vanished, then she walked quickly and purposefully back towards the hall.

The courtyard was no longer silent or empty. Several warriors moved gingerly as if their heads pained them while the hens pecked at the cracks in the stones searching for bits of grain.

Annis had nearly reached the great hall when she encountered Aelfric. The monk's face reddened and then paled as she came close. He put what appeared to be a loaf of bread and a jug of wine into his robe and then turned to face her with a superior expression on his face.

'Is there any reason why you are here?' Annis asked, fearing that one of the monks had taken ill. She fancied his pockmarked cheek flushed.

'I wanted to see if you needed…needed any…any more herbs for your ointment, but you obviously had other duties this morning.'

'I have all that I need,' Annis answered as she regarded the monk, trying to remember what she knew of him. He was young and came from a good family. Her uncle had had high hopes for him. She bit her lip. She had to keep from jumping to conclusions. His visit to the kitchen could be entirely innocent. 'Is there anything I can help you with?'

'I heard of the kiss you shared with the Jaarl last evening.' Aelfric's eyes narrowed and his face contorted. 'Consorting with a heathen! And such a one!'

'If you heard of it, then you will know that I had no choice.' Annis crossed her arms, but forced her voice to remain even.

'A true Christian…' the monk began, adopting a pious posture, but his eyes glittered with malice.

'You are not my confessor, Aelfric, kindly remember that.'

Annis prepared to sweep by, head held high. Aelfric reached out and grabbed her upper arm.

'Proud, arrogant woman, you are blind.'

'If my uncle remained alive, you would not dare speak to me like that!' Annis shook off his hand.

'Someone has to!' Aelfric shouted and then continued in a more conciliatory tone, 'Annis, as someone who is concerned about immortal souls, I feel it is my duty. All this will be over one day and you will go back to your life in Northumbria. I know Eadgar has made an offer. Your uncle spoke to me of his hopes for this as we were fostered together. He is a good man.'

'Northumbria and Birdoswald are never far from my thoughts.'

Annis closed her eyes. She had nearly forgotten about Eadgar. He had as much substance as a vaguely remembered nightmare. It was a good thing about being captive—Eadgar would have found another to marry before she returned to Northumbria. He had to. Then a small voice insisted it was not the only good thing. Annis hastily silenced the voice.

'You looked pained, my lady. We shall talk at another time. In the meantime I will pray for you.'

Annis opened her eyes and saw Aelfric moving silently off towards the outlying buildings. She hugged her arms about her waist. She had to concentrate on the things that were important—getting home and back to her life.

'Annis.' Haakon's deep voice flowed over her.

She jumped. Haakon stood in the door of the barn. The fine white linen of his shirt clung to his chest; his dark hair still gleamed from the lake. She swallowed hard and tried to banish the image of Haakon's naked body rising from the waters.

'Is there something you desire?' Her voice sounded unnatural. She pressed her hands to her eyes, tried again, strove for an even voice. 'How pleasant to see you, Haakon.'

'What were you discussing with that monk?' Haakon's eyes were blue ice.

'He asked me if I needed more herbs,' Annis said quickly. She was certain Aelfric had lied to her, but she refused to betray a fellow Northumbrian. And all Aelfric had really done was express concern for her immortal soul.

'So early in the morning?' Haakon lifted an eyebrow.

'It would appear a number of people are early risers today.' Annis strove for a light laugh. With difficulty she held back the words asking Haakon where he had spent the night.

'You certainly are one.'

Had he seen her? At the lake? Annis dismissed the thought as fanciful. She had been hidden. 'I found it difficult to sleep, went for a short walk to the fjord. I trust there is no harm in that.'

'None whatsoever.' Haakon tilted his head to one side, as his eyes travelled down her form. 'I merely commented.'

Annis moved her weight from one foot to the other, and wished she had taken the time to find her apron-dress. Her shift was too thin.

'Did you find sleep difficult as well?' Her cheeks burnt. 'The sleeping quarters were crowded.'

'I gave my private chamber up to Vikar. He had more need of it than me. I spent the night in the hut by the lake.'

Vikar! One of the other Jaarls had been in Haakon's chamber. Annis swallowed hard. The laugh she had heard had definitely been his. Relief bubbled through stronger than before. It should make no difference but it did.

'Is the hut comfortable?'

'Have you seen it?'

'Only from a distance.' Annis controlled her voice. He must not suspect she had seen him, spied on him. 'I had wondered at its use. I must remember to ask Ingrid about it.'

'Bathing. It is my private bath hut. Do you like sweat-baths, Annis?'

Annis glanced at the hard-packed earth in the yard. 'I have never tried one. We don't have them in Northumbria.'

'You must try it some time. It is a pleasurable experience.'

Annis glanced up, and found her gaze trapped. With a great effort she tore her eyes away. She had to control her body, or she'd become worse than Tove.

'I need to get about my duties. Ingrid will be looking for me.' Her breath was coming far too quickly as Aelfric's admonitions rang in her ears. She was wicked to even think such thoughts, watching naked men and then wondering what it would like to bathe with them.

'As you wish.' He made no move to go, but simply remained where he was, regarding her.

She forced her legs to move away from him, away from the temptation he represented. Quickly retrieving her apron-dress from her pallet, she went into the kitchen. There, Ingrid stood, stirring a pot of porridge. She covered her mouth with her hand and gave a great yawn.

'I looked for you earlier,' she said. 'A monk came to enquire about your health.'

'I went out for a walk. I found it difficult to sleep. The hall was very noisy.' The words flowed much more smoothly this time. Annis drew a breath. She had recovered.

'It is like that at feasts. Too many people, crowding together.' Ingrid gave a wide smile. 'And here I was hoping you had discovered a nice warrior to warm your bed.'

Annis could feel her cheeks begin to tinge pink and hoped that Ingrid would think it was from the heat of the fire. 'Not in the hall. But who was the man that you went off with? I saw Thrand at the high table.'

'I have given up on Thrand. He is uncouth and has no idea about the ways of the world. There is someone else…a man who has seen the world and is gentle. He cares about what happens to me.'

A great shout went up, followed a long, low blast of a horn, echoing through out the kitchen before Annis could question Ingrid further. Annis cocked her head. 'What's that?'

'The signal that a sail has been spotted.'

'Is it a friend or a foe?' Annis put her hand on the table to keep her knees from buckling. All too clearly she remembered what had happened the last time that ships arrived.

'We will know when they land.' Ingrid reached over and covered Annis's hand. 'I would not worry. The Jaarl and his men are here. You would have to be madder than a berserker to attack this stronghold.'

* * *

Haakon used his hand to guard his eyes from the sun's glare. Despite the distance, he could just make out the figurehead of the boat as it cut through the fjord. A snarling bear, the symbol of the Bjornsons, Bjorn's family, rode high and proud.

Haakon frowned as he gave Floki an absentminded pat. The ship should not be here. It was too early for them to have heard of Bjorn's death or, indeed, the return of the *felag*. It would take several more days for the message boat he had sent up the coast to reach them.

'Trouble?' Thrand asked, coming to stand beside him as he tightened his sword belt about his middle.

'Potentially. The Bjornson figurehead rides high and proud.' Haakon ran his hand through his hair as he turned over the possibilities in his mind. Whatever the captain of the ship had intended, he would have nearly the full strength of the *felag* to contend with. Haakon wondered what the excuse for visiting would be. The Bjornsons were far from their usual trading routes to the east. 'I had hoped to meet Bjorn's family at Thorkell's court when we were on neutral ground, but it appears the gods have decided differently.'

Thrand gave a soft whistle. 'And do you think they will take the news well? Will they be satisfied with the size of the *wergild*? You know the family's reputation.'

'I know of three blood-feuds they are involved in, but it was an unprovoked attack that became a fight to the death. I have no wish to take up my place at Odin's table for some time to come.' Haakon put his hand on his sword. All too clearly he remembered what happened to several lesser Jaarls two years ago when the Bjornson clan came calling and found one of their members slain. 'Bjorn's clan holds no fear for me. I will make a fair offer, but not here. It is for Thorkell, with help from the assembly of nobles if he desires, to weigh the facts of the case and give a judgement on the amount of gold and silver I owe. It is why he is high king. He wants an end to blood-feuds and I agree. They do no good and place Viken against Viken, weakening us and making us vulnerable to our enemies.'

'You will never get rid of blood-feuds, Haakon. Too much honour is involved.'

'Honour can be met in other ways, Thrand. Remember that.'

'I will summon the members of the *felag* to stand behind you.' Thrand grabbed Haakon's elbow, his voice eager, his eyes spoiling for a fight. 'The brotherhood has not been formally disbanded. Sigfrid and the rest of the Bjornson clan will have to see that an attack on one is an attack on us all.'

'I believe I can handle Bjorn's brother on my own.' Haakon could see the wisdom in Thrand's words, but neither did he want it said that he relied on others. He had no doubt of his ability to face down Bjorn's brothers in a fair fight, if it came to it. But it wouldn't. Sigfrid was prudent, a man who preferred to have the odds with him, rather than against him. 'My sword arm is healthy and my eyesight keen.'

'But we would not want to lose you.' Thrand's face took on a pleading expression. 'You are a man who cheats death, and finds us much gold. The men will stand behind you. You only need say the word. We know what happened when Bjorn died.'

Haakon clasped Thrand's forearm and then regarded the white crests of the waves banging against the boat as it came into land. Cheating death was a good way to put it. Haakon regretted that Thrand did not know the full extent of how it had happened, but now, more than ever, he had to keep it a secret until Annis had left these lands. He refused to allow any of the Bjornsons to claim her.

'They are coming ashore now. Stand here with me, Thrand. Let us greet them warrior to warrior.'

'Until the death.'

Bjorn's elder brother leapt into the sea and waded across to where the group stood waiting. He took off his helmet and held it out before him. His huge hands were turned palm upwards and his sword was sheathed. 'I have come in peace, Haakon Haroldson.'

'And I receive you in peace.' Haakon grasped Sigfrid's forearm. He made sure his grip was firm and unhesitating. To do any less would be a sign of weakness. 'How are you here so quickly? The messengers sailed yesterday. We only arrived back a few days ago and have not yet completed the welcome feast. The *felag* stands together. Our oath remains unbroken.'

Sigfrid stood with his feet apart. The breeze whipped his shaggy blond hair, giving him the same bear-like appearance as his brother. There were rumours that the Bjornson clan was founded by a giant. Haakon was inclined to discount them, but the entire family was known for its fierce devotion to fighting. He motioned for quiet.

'Six nights ago, we saw portents in the skies.' Sigfrid gestured to the north. 'Strange lights that appeared to be ships sailing across the blackened sea. Then Thor appeared with his thunder chariot and lightning bolts. The women of the clan were frightened as the stew burnt and my prize cow's milk curdled. Our soothsayer said that it was an omen and we needed to head with all speed to your estate.'

'Is this the same soothsayer who said that no man could kill Bjorn?' Thrand murmured in Haakon's ear.

'Why should these portents cause you to make haste here?' Haakon asked. Silently he counted the twenty warriors who had appeared on the deck, handpicked men. Sigfrid had not intended a social call on his stepmother.

Sigfrid shifted uneasily, twisting his helmet in his hands. 'There were lights in the sky. The soothsayer interpreted it as a huge battle, and that a mighty warrior had fallen. As the soothsayer had already told us Bjorn was not destined to die by a man's hand, I thought of you. You must have had some misfortune. It could be no other. I came in peace.'

'I am grateful for your concern. Your soothsayer has achieved great renown in recent times.' Haakon inclined his head. If blood was spilt on this visit, he wanted to say to Thorkell that he was not the man who broke the peace. 'But as you can see, I am in good health and have returned from the journey unscathed.'

'Sigfrid, you need to learn.' Thrand rocked back on his heels. 'Soothsayers are not what they used to be. After a time, like raw meat, they go off and stink to the heavens.'

Haakon studiously ignored Thrand. He had seen portents used like this in the past, as a justification for attacking or occupying an estate. But as Sigfrid had not arrived with shields hanging from his boat, he could not accuse him of that…yet.

'Our soothsayer has a certain reputation.' Sigfrid plucked a hair from his cloak. 'All the women of my clan begged me to listen to him. Ill would have come to me if I did not follow the advice.'

'Why me? There were many other great warriors in the *felag*.'

'After my brother, you are the greatest fighter in Viken.' Sigfrid made a bow. 'Your lands are some of the best. If you were dead…they would need protecting from plunder. You left your stepmother without any to guard her. She needs a strong arm to help defend this land against raiders.'

Haakon allowed a wry smile to cross his lips. Simple half-truths. What Sigrid meant was that he wanted to be in a position to claim the lands, most likely through marrying Guthrun. As Viken law decreed, Guthrun stood to inherit the estate should he and Thrand die without issue. In many ways, Sigfrid deserved the acid-tongued witch. There again, he would have had to fight to regain control of his lands and the outcome would have been by no means certain. A clever trap, but he had arrived home too early for it to be sprung.

He glanced at Thrand and saw his face pale. He, too, did not need a soothsayer to explain Sigfrid's intended future for both of them.

'Your soothsayer misread the omens. My health is good and I intend to keep it that way. My time has not yet to come to join the throng at Odin's feasting table.'

'And despite my mother's predictions, I came back as well.' Thrand's voice was a bit shrill. 'The gods blessed the voyage.'

'And returned so early in the year.' Sigfrid's knuckles were white where he gripped the helmet. 'The soothsayer is obviously not as accurate as I thought she was. Her prediction was so clear, so very clear. You will forgive my concern, I trust.'

'I trust the next time you will be more circumspect in your interpretation.' Haakon put his hand on his sword belt. 'My people guard my lands well. While your intentions were no doubt honourable, they might have been mistaken. Tragic mistakes have happened in the past.'

'I only sought to protect you and your land. I am willing to swear it on Odin and Thor.' Sigrid stared at the growing group of warriors. 'Might I enquire where my brother is? He did go on this voyage, despite the omens.'

Haakon felt the weight of responsibility. He had to find the correct way to tell Sigfrid of Bjorn's death, and to tell it in such a way that a blood-feud did not immediately erupt between the two families. He had seen enough men die this season. If only they had met at Thorkell's court, then the appropriate number of gold rings could have been offered.

Haakon put his hand on Sigfrid's shoulder and led him a little way away from the group. Thrand followed, giving his brother a nod and showing that his grip was tight on his sword. Haakon inclined his head. He was pleased that Thrand had matured into a steadfast warrior. He would not dishonour him by asking him to leave. The words said now might affect his future as well.

'The soothsayer did not lie,' Haakon said as they stared out into the fjord. 'She only read the runes wrong. There was a huge battle and a mighty warrior did die.'

Sigfrid's shoulders slumped and his face became etched with grief. Haakon moved forward, but the warrior held up a hand. Haakon halted. 'Tell me that my brother died with his face to the enemy.'

'Bjorn died fighting. Fighting me—a battle to the death.'

'Fighting you? But I don't understand. Bjorn would never formally challenge for the leadership of the *felag*. He was content to fight—the bigger the battle, the better. He had no desire to lead. And surely you are not implying my brother was an oath-breaker.'

'Bjorn was far gone in his berserker madness,' Thrand broke in. He pushed his way forward. 'Forgive me, Sigfrid, but I feel you need to know the truth and my brother might honeycoat his words in an attempt to lessen your grief. Haakon had gone to find him. We were burning the buildings and Haakon wanted to ensure his safety. You know there was the earlier prediction about Bjorn perishing in fire.'

Sigfrid gave a nod and stroked his beard. 'Continue.'

'There is not much to tell. Bjorn did not recognise him. They fought and Bjorn lost. It was a tragedy.'

The warrior appeared to age several years. He shook his head. 'But the soothsayer said—'

'The soothsayer was wrong, Sigfrid.' Haakon made a cutting motion with his hand. 'In the end Bjorn was as mortal as you or I. No doubt the Valkyries gathered him up and he now sits at Odin's right hand in Valhalla.'

'This news is hard to credit, but it must be true.'

Sigfrid wiped a tear from his eye as once again he turned to face the sea. A seagull screamed in the quiet. Sigfrid's shoulders shook. Haakon allowed him time. The loss of a brother was a great blow. He knew how close Bjorn and

Sigfrid had been. The last thing Bjorn had done before the *felag* left was to send a message stick to his brother.

'Bjorn was an excellent brother to me. Honest, loyal and without a fault in his body. We expected much from this voyage of his. Our harvests have not been good these past three years.'

'We burnt his body, but I have saved his shield and arm rings as is the custom.'

'And the compensation?'

'It is too soon to speak of such things.' Haakon put his arm around Sigfrid's shoulder. 'Thorkell will determine the proper price. Come and break bread with me. See, Guthrun comes with a warrior's welcome.'

He motioned towards Guthrun, who came forward with a drinking horn of mead in her hand. The other women of the house spread out behind her, each carrying a drinking horn. At the end strode Annis. Her head was held high and, unlike the other women, she wore no kerchief, but allowed her hair to flow free. Haakon's palms itched at the memory of how it had slid through his fingers. He started. He had not expected such a strong reaction to merely catching sight of her. He was worse than an untried boy in the midst of his first calf-love.

'And who is the woman on the end?' Sigfrid asked. 'She does not have a Viken look about her.'

'She's a Northumbrian noblewoman that Haakon captured,' Thrand said. 'Haakon expects a large ransom for her and the monks.'

'How many of them did you bring back?' Sigfrid licked his lips and rubbed his hands together as if he had seen a plump chicken or a prize milking cow. 'They make them comely in Northumbria. How much do you want for her? She looks as if she could warm beds.'

'There were no other noblewomen on the island,' Haakon said in an even voice. The anger surged through him. 'She is not for sale.'

'I would have thought silver in your hand was worth more than a promise of gold,' Sigfrid said with a sly look.

'She is not for sale and remains under my protection. You may tell your men that as well.'

'Your word is law here….' Sigfrid made a mocking bow. 'But she is a tempting piece…if you change your mind.'

'You are here and welcome to enjoy my hospitality, Sigfrid.' Haakon forced his fingers to ease from his sword. 'If you wish to mourn your brother, I am sure none will take offence if you depart. I can assure you that he was treated with all honour due a member of the *felag*.'

Sigfrid accepted the drinking horn from Guthrun, who gave a tight-lipped smile. 'We shall stay for a little while to take on water. It would not do to misuse your hospitality, but I wish to hear of your exploits.'

'We shall be honoured to have you stay with us and join in the feasting. There is much to celebrate.' Haakon caught Thrand's arm and said in an undertone, 'I want you and the rest of the *felag* to keep your tempers. Do not be provoked. I want no cause for grievances.'

'I understand.' Thrand gave the briefest of nods. 'Sigfrid wants something. He did not expect to find you in residence. I do not believe his story about a soothsayer. He came here for some purpose. I know Sigfrid from old. He expects to gain something.'

'And I intend to see he leaves here without obtaining it.'

The wind whipped Annis's apron-dress, moulding it around her calves. She had stood here as long as she dared after the other women had gone back to the hall, along with the latest arrivals. Their leader had the look of the beast-man, but with hands that could crush a skull. She had fought against her fear, had remained upright, but she dreaded returning to the hall with them.

'Annis.' Firm fingers held her elbow. She turned. The breeze ruffled Haakon's hair, and his face held an intent look.

She forced a breath from her lips. 'Haakon.'

'The men who have arrived are from Bjorn's clan.'

'They resemble him.' Her hand had trembled when she had to offer the drinking horn, but she had no intention of confiding that. The images of Bjorn falling played on her brain. She was convinced they knew who had killed him from the expression in their eyes.

'I have told Sigfrid of his brother's death, and the manner in which it happened. The same tale as the skald's song.'

'But—' Annis started.

'You will keep silent if you value your life, Annis. Know you are under my protection.'

'Your captive,' Annis corrected.

'There are worse things than being my captive, Annis.'

A chill coursed through her body. He released her elbow and she stumbled backwards, cradling it with her other hand.

'I will go now.'

'And, Annis, a white dress stands out clearly against the background of dark trees.'

She swallowed hard, her body freezing in the act of turning. He had seen her. He had known she was watching him, but had done nothing, said nothing, in the courtyard. A shiver ran down her spine. What would she have done if he had come to her then? Would she have melted in his arms?

'I think I should go back to the kitchens now. I will be needed there.'

'It would be sensible, Annis, to remain with the others.'

'That was my intention.'

'It is gratifying to see you can learn.'

Annis tried to concentrate on her spindle. She had joined the other women in the great hall after her encounter with

Haakon. She did not need more than his veiled warning. Several warriors were in the hall as well, playing with dice a game that she vaguely recognised. The blank stares from the other clan caused her blood to run cold. She bent her head and tried to concentrate on creating smooth thread.

'You cheated!' Thrand shouted, standing up. 'It was my turn, and you cheated!'

The Bjornson warrior stood, and they tumbled to the floor. Annis watched in horror as they rolled over and over towards the fire. She wanted to scream, but her muscles were frozen.

There was a faint sizzle and a sickening smell as the pair reached the fire.

'He's holding Thrand down!' Guthrun shouted. 'Quickly! Do something!'

Another warrior reached the pair, pulled them apart.

'I'll get the butter,' Ingrid said and started towards the kitchen.

'No, my ointment is better,' Annis said decisively, catching on to Ingrid's sleeve. 'Butter can lead to scarring, but my ointment helps keeps the skin soft. I often used it…back home. Let me fetch it.'

Ingrid shifted from one foot to the other as Tove and Guthrun's wails filled the hall.

'It is the scarring I am frightened about.' Ingrid put her hand to her mouth as her face crumpled. 'The smell is dreadful. Do something quickly.'

'He will need something stronger than butter on his burn if he is to avoid scarring.' Annis did not wait for an answer. She rushed out and grabbed the ointment.

The hall still rang with shouts and cries and one of the benches was upturned. Tove and Guthrun had covered their faces with their apron-dresses. A variety of men held the Bjornson warrior, while another group stood around the prostrate body of Thrand.

Annis marched straight to where Thrand lay. Half his face

was red raw and one eye was closed. She elbowed the crowd of warriors away and knelt down at his side. 'Let me see. I might be able to help.'

'What is going on here?' Haakon asked, striding through the crowd. 'Why is my hall filled with all this wailing? I could hear it from the fjord where I was bidding Vikar and Ivar goodbye. It is nosier than a stallion fight and half as interesting.'

'Thrand had a disagreement with one of the Bjorn clan over *tafl*. He thought he had captured Thrand's king, but it was Thrand's move. The Bjornson cheated,' one of the warriors said as Thrand struggled into a sitting position.

Haakon winced to look at him. Thrand was lucky to be awake. He had seen other warriors die as a result of such burns. The very best he could hope for was that Thrand would be able to see out of one eye. His days as a warrior were probably over. It was all too much of a coincidence. Sigfrid had planned this fight. But for what purpose?

The other warrior fought against the hands restraining him, calling Thrand a liar and a thief, calling curses down on this hall and all the miserable scum who resided there.

'Enough!' Haakon roared and the entire hall fell silent except for Guthrun's sobs. 'Take him off to Sigfrid. He can deal with his own man. This dispute is childish and now a man is injured. You had best hope that he recovers.'

The man was led away, grumbling and muttering curses under his breath.

Haakon's fingers drummed against his thigh. 'I believe I warned to you to hold your temper.'

'You did, but what harm could a game like *tafl* do, particularly after all that we have been through?' Thrand attempted a smile, but it turned into a grimace and he spoke out the side of his mouth. One of his eyes had closed and his long hair was singed on that side.

'All too much.' He put a hand on Thrand's good shoulder. 'Next time, heed my advice. It is not given lightly.'

'You can tell me about it later.' Thrand eased himself back down. He put his hand to his burns as if he were holding on the skin. 'For now, all I want is the pain to go away.'

'I believe I have something that can help. I have seen it work time and again at Birdoswald.'

Haakon glanced down and saw Annis crouched at Thrand's side, a small jar in her hand. It touched him that she was there, willing to help, but then he damped the emotion down as he saw several more of Sigfrid's men loitering. He could not afford to allow Sigfrid to know he had any feelings for the woman.

'Why are you here, Annis? I would think there is enough in the kitchen to occupy you.'

'I have some small experience with such things. Some small skill that my grandmother passed on to me. She had it from her grandmother, who was a Celt.' Annis prised Thrand's hands away from his face and regarded the injuries. They were bad, but she had seen worse last year when the kitchen burned down and Selwyn's cook had caught fire, trying to save his precious store of salt. She would not think about Haakon's tone of voice and how different it was from the one he had used by the lake. She had to concentrate on what was at hand—saving Thrand from permanent damage. She could do this. The cook had recovered with only faint white scarring on his hands and face. 'This ointment has done wonders in the past. I see no reason for the herbs not to work.'

She bit her lip and waited for Haakon to say something. He had to trust her. She might not like Thrand, but neither would she want him to be in the pain he was. Above all things, she wanted to use her skill. She took pride in her craft, even if it meant curing Viken.

'Will he need anything else?'

'He will need rest and quiet for a few days, until his skin

has begun to heal. The ointment will help and then I will put on a dressing of honey and then cover it with linen. There is a chance he might be only very lightly scarred.' Annis ticked the points off on her fingers. There had to be something more. She had to think calmly and carefully. It was easy to make a mistake if one panicked, she remembered her grandmother saying on occasion. 'Possibly something like mead for the pain.'

Thrand gave a moan. 'My face! My face! I shall be hideous.'

'The women all love a wounded warrior, Thrand. It will give your face character. Isn't that right, Annis?'

'Yes, indeed.' Annis tried to keep her voice light, but all she could think about was the network of scars on Haakon's back. 'Please let me put the ointment on. It may sting a little, but it can help.'

'I can do without your jests, brother. I am in pain.'

'It might be wise to listen to others for a change, Thrand.' Haakon gave a nod, signalling for Annis to begin. 'Very well, Annis, I will follow your advice. But I shall hold you responsible for his welfare.'

Annis's hand trembled slightly as she scooped the first bit of ointment. 'What do you mean?'

'If you are certain you can heal him with this, I expect you to watch over him. I will allow you to use the storage area off the kitchen for your nursing. It will be much more private than here. I want my brother to recover.'

'It will work.' Annis slathered the ointment on. Her fingers moved with more assured strokes. 'Much better than butter.'

Thrand gave a soft cry and closed his eyes, leaning back on the hard-packed earth.

Haakon stood with his feet apart, watching Annis. Her hair curled around her neck, highlighting the slender column of her throat. Such grit, so much determination within her. She had shown no hesitation in her actions. He found a grudging admiration for her growing within him. She was unlike any other woman he had ever met. And Haakon was not sure if this was a good or a bad thing.

'Haakon, what are you doing?' Guthrun said sharply, grabbing at his elbow and lowering her voice to a shrill whisper. 'I can look after my son. I will call for the soothsayer. She can read the omens and tell us what has to be done. How best the gods can be appeased.'

'You do that—in the meantime, let the Northumbrian work.' Haakon pinched the skin on the bridge of his nose. 'Her methods show much common sense, something that has been singularly lacking in this episode. We have no other healer here.'

'I knew you were an unfeeling brute.' Guthrun wiped her eyes with the corner of her apron-dress. 'Have you no consideration for a mother's feelings? I had no idea this would happen when I suggested *tafl*. A board game! I wanted to prevent trouble, not cause it.'

He pointed towards the other end of the hall where Sigfrid's men and a few from the *felag* milled around. The atmosphere had been jovial, but now something sinister lingered. If he was not careful, full-scale warfare would erupt. It troubled him that Sigfrid's man had chosen his half-brother to pick a quarrel with. The insult was clear and unmistakable.

How long before it was something that he could not ignore? How long until they directly attacked him? His eyes fell on Annis's softly curling hair. Or would they try to strike at another target? Force him to attack and then claim that he had used unreasonable force. He should have seen this coming. He had underestimated Sigfrid today.

'You will attend to our guests' needs. I would hate it to be said that we did not keep a good house.' Then he continued on a gentler note, relenting at the sight of her stricken face. She appeared genuinely upset, but he could not rid himself of the feeling that she had something to do with Sigfrid's unexpected appearance. However, he knew that, for all her faults, her devotion towards Thrand had never been questioned. She would never put him in harm's way. 'You can do little good here, Guthrun, wringing your hands and sobbing. If there is any change, I will notify you.'

Guthrun glanced towards the group of warriors at the end of the hall and back to her son, clearly torn between a mother's love and the duty she had as the hostess.

'Go, Mother. I don't need your fussing. It is only a burn.' Thrand pointed his finger. 'The ointment the Northumbrian has put on has already taken some of the sting away.'

Haakon saw Annis's eyes regarding him, pleading with him to be allowed to continue.

'You may be right, but if anything happens to my son…' Guthrun's long claws dug into Haakon's arm and pulled his ear closer to her lips '…I shall hold that witch responsible. I will demand the right to punish her.'

'Nothing will happen to him. I give you my solemn pledge on that.' Haakon straightened and plucked Guthrun's fingers off his sleeve one by one.

'You brought my son home safely, with plenty of gold to spare, and you rule this place.' She plucked at the aprondress, straightening it. 'What is a weak woman like me to do? I shall have to trust you.'

'Naturally.'

Annis saw the rest of the group begin to move away. The sound of conversation and the rattle of knucklebones resounded throughout the hall once again. She slathered more ointment on Thrand's face, concentrating on smoothing it in, not on Haakon's direct gaze.

'Do you know why this fight started?'

'It happened very quickly. I believe my half-brother should learn better control of his temper.' Haakon's voice was guarded.

Annis finished her ministrations and sat back on her heels.

'This could have been much worse. A little bit farther to the right, and he would have lost an eye, but as it is, I think he will recover.'

'I want you to sit with him.' Haakon put a hand on her shoulder. 'That way you both will be safe.'

'Safe?' Annis put her hand to her throat. 'No one has threatened me.'

'I am not entirely sure this was an accident, Annis, and I want someone to watch over him. Sigfrid was much taken with you and has made two offers, increasing the amount each time.'

Annis put her hand to her throat. She would not cry. She refused to cry. Haakon looked at her with a raised eyebrow, waiting for her answer.

What did he expect her to say—that she wanted to become that shaggy beast's concubine? Or did he want her to say the truth—that she craved Haakon's touch? Wanted against all reason to feel his mouth against hers again? She could never admit that. She wiped her hands on the corner of her apron-dress and then rose to stand next to Haakon.

'You said that you had sent word to Charlemagne.' She forced her words to sound calm and unhurried.

'And so I have.' Haakon made a bow. 'I told Sigfrid the same thing. I cannot possibly consider his offer until I know what your people are willing to pay for your safe return.'

Somehow, his words did not make her feel any easier. Annis swallowed hard. Lately it seemed she had been abandoned by fate.

Chapter Seven

⁓⁓⁓⁓⁓

'Your man attacked my brother,' Haakon said without preamble as Sigfrid came to stand next to him by the lake.

Floki and the other two elkhounds raised their heads. Floki gave a low growl in the back of his throat, but Haakon motioned for the dog to be silent. Floki obeyed and put his nose under his paws. The barest hint of a summer breeze blew and the lake's water was a smooth surface, hiding the treacherous depths in the middle. An omen or merely a refection?

He had summoned Sigfrid here, rather than confronting him in the hall where men would be forced to take sides and tempers would run high. He wanted to avoid a blood-feud if possible. Dead men served no purpose.

'I had heard.' Sigfrid stood with his feet apart, his giant hands flexing and unflexing as if he wished for a neck to wring. 'A terrible business.'

'He abused the hospitality of this hall.'

'What was I supposed to do?' Sigfrid reddened and then held up his hands in a great shrug. 'I was with you bidding farewell to Vikar and Ivar. How was I to know that my man would take exception to being called a cheat? Surely Thrand bears some of the blame. He should choose his words with more care. But he is young. Wisdom comes with age.'

'Your man held my brother's face in the fire, burning him. He has marked him for life.' Haakon skimmed a stone across the lake and waited for the reply. The ripples from the stone spread out across the surface, marring it.

'He was a little over-zealous. My brother's death remains an unhealed wound. I understand there is fault on both sides. It was an accident.'

Sigfrid stood still, his legs slightly apart, a bantam cock spoiling for a fight. But Haakon did not intend to rise to the bait. He was no longer twenty with something to prove. He had learnt the hard way. Patience. He had to wait and watch for the opening.

'Easy words, but the fact remains your man injured the brother of a Jaarl. Thrand could be blinded for life. I will expect compensation.' Haakon sent another stone skimming five times before it sank.

'I understand your concubine is looking after him, cradling him in her soft arms. Surely she will be the one to pay if Thrand dies.'

'You leave her to me. And she is a high-value captive, not a concubine.'

'My mistake.' A faint smile touched Sigfrid's mouth.

Haakon kept a check on his temper, controlling his features. But Sigfrid already had a small, knowing smile on his face—he had seen the barb hit home. And now Annis might be drawn into whatever web Sigfrid was weaving. After the incident in the hall, Haakon knew Sigfrid's intentions were far from honourable. 'We are discussing the act that caused the injury.'

'As you wish…' Sigfrid bowed his head. 'But my man must be given time to recover. His honour was insulted. From the way he tells it, the honour of the whole clan. This must be taken into any accounting.'

'I fear grief overwhelms your natural sense of caution, Sigfrid.' Haakon threw his final stone into the lake and turned to face Sigfrid. Now was the time to lance the boil, to have Sigfrid openly challenge him or depart in peace. 'You are vastly outnumbered, Sigfrid. Even with the departure of Vikar and Ivar, my men are here. They are loyal to me. We sailed together and gained much gold. Has your family not experienced enough loss? Bjorn's wife and concubines will want to know of his death. He leaves a young son to inherit.'

Haakon waited. Across the lake, a bird called, a long, mournful cry. What would Sigfrid decide? Would he see that an attack was doomed to failure? Or would he take the gamble?

Sigfrid blinked. He picked up a stone, tossing it into the lake.

'You are right. Hilde does need to know. Suitable arrangements will have to be made to mourn Bjorn properly. The wind is favourable. I regret that I will be unable to partake of your feast tonight. You will give my apologies to your lovely and gracious stepmother.'

'Thorkell will settle this affair between us.'

'I will hear his judgement and then I will determine my course of action. He may need to call the nobles of the Storting to help him decide.' Sigfrid slammed his fists together and stuck his chin out.

'You will ask him to assemble the Jaarls?'

'I will think on it. I make no decision yet. First I must mourn my brother.'

'That is your decision. I trust, when the time comes, that you will make the prudent choice as you have always done thus far.' Haakon put his hand on his sword belt, so that Sigfrid would be in no doubt. He was prepared to use force to defend what was rightfully his.

'My men and I will depart in peace.' Sigfrid hooked his thumbs around his belt. 'But it is not over between us, Haakon Haroldson.'

Haakon inclined his head.

'I hope the next time we meet that peace remains.'

'And how is your patient faring? Is he obeying your orders?'

Annis paused, then laid aside the knife she had been using to chop herbs. A tingle of excitement went through her. Haakon had sought her out. Inwardly, she smiled. She had to stop building fortresses out of clouds. He had come to see his brother.

'Sleep has finally overtaken the pain. It is a great healer,' she said without lifting her head. 'Hopefully he will be able to sleep most of the night.'

'And will he recover? Fully recover? My brother is an active man with large appetites, a proud warrior.'

'These things take time.' Annis flicked her eyes upwards and caught the full force of Haakon in his finery. Like yesterday, he wore the heavily embroidered tunic and cape. The trefoil brooch emphasised the width of his shoulders. All too clearly she remembered how they looked naked and unadorned when he rose from the lake. She hurriedly looked down at her hands. She had sworn not to think about such things. And these feelings were growing, not decreasing as she thought they would.

'Hopefully, the scarring will not be as bad as his mother fears.'

'I do believe he rolled away from the worst,' Annis answered, forcing her mind back to Thrand's condition and away from Haakon's shoulders. 'Ingrid said that it looked as though his opponent was trying to get Thrand's face actually in the coals, but you know how excitable people can get in the heat of battle. People can sometimes think they see things.'

'I do indeed.'

Annis expected Haakon to say some polite, meaningless phrase and leave, but he continued to stand at the foot of the table, not saying a word, simply looking at her. In his hands, he carried a game board with intricately carved stone pieces arranged on it. He did not put it down, but there was a question in his eyes, almost as if he was waiting for her to invite him. Her heart started to beat faster.

Annis pressed her hands against the solid surface of the table. It was real and strong, not like the flimsy daydreams she had had. She had to take charge of the situation, rather than drowning in his deep blue eyes. She had to keep her self-respect. Aelfric was right. She had given in to her desire far too easily when Haakon had kissed her in the hall. She could see that now.

'I would have thought your presence was required in the hall….' She gave a purposeful nod towards the door but he did not take the hint.

'The skalds are reciting poetry about Thor and how his hammer was stolen. I have heard the story many times, but Guthrun wanted to hear it again. She sheds tears over Thrand. I swear she looked about ready to cut Sigfrid's heart out. It was well he departed when he did.'

'You decided to leave the hall?' Annis tilted her head.

'After the healths are drunk and the rings of peace exchanged, I can do as I wish.' Haakon gave a shrug. 'My men do not need to see me to know that this is my house and must be respected. I wanted time alone.'

'As you did the other night,' Annis said, then immediately wished she hadn't mentioned it as the now-familiar warmth started developing in her body. She made it sound like it was something she wanted to repeat, when she didn't. Not in the least.

Haakon's eyes lit up. 'I was thinking about a game or two of *tafl*. It helps me to focus my mind. I need to tease out the tangle of why Sigfrid appeared.'

'Why did he travel by boat? Did he intend to raid?' Annis

tapped her finger against her mouth. 'Is that the sort of thing you were thinking?'

She fancied he looked at her with a new sort of respect.

'We don't travel by boat simply to raid.' Haakon gave a short laugh. 'All of our trade and communication is done by the water. Our land is blessed with wide fjords and a long coast line.'

'But I was sure I saw horses—horses with manes the colour of straw.'

'I use my horses for hunting and short journeys. The sea is our road. After the farm, there are impenetrable woods and then high, lonely mountain passes where trolls live. People have been known to go out there and never return.'

'You could be a skald, telling tall tales. Trolls, indeed.' Annis gave a light laugh, but a shiver ran through her. It was not trolls who worried her but bears and wolves. Her father had been injured in an encounter with a wolf. The injury had taken ages to heal, and it had been then she had first discovered her talent.

'I thank you for that, even though you may not realise the compliment. When I was a boy, I used to lie awake at night and make stories. It helped me get through many a lonely time at Charlemagne's court.' Haakon made a bow. 'My responsibilities lead me in other directions.'

Annis tried to concentrate on mixing the next part of the ointment, but Haakon stood regarding her without moving. She was uncertain with Haakon in this mood. She had been able to hate him when he was a warrior, but when he approached her like an equal, she found herself dangerously attracted to him. She wanted him to stay. She wanted to learn more about him and his past. A queer bubbly sort of feeling filled her as if she had drunk several goblets of mead in quick succession.

He gave a slight nod, but did not move. Neither did he look

disappointed. He placed the board on the table. 'Perhaps I can find another player as Thrand is asleep.'

Annis's heart started to race and, rather than decreasing, the curious light-headed feeling seemed to be growing within her. She wondered briefly if the Viken *tafl* differed from the Northumbrian game of the same name. That was a board game where one opponent tried to capture the other's king. Sometimes her father had called it fox and geese. She forced her lungs to fill with air. 'I have not played your game, but when my father was alive, I used to play our version of *tafl* with him. Or sometimes we would play Nine Men's Morris.'

'If I set out the pieces, you will hopefully be able to pick up the game quickly.' He proceeded rapidly to explain the game and Annis saw that it was, indeed, similar to that which she had played with her father as Haakon's long fingers laid out the blue and white pieces.

They played the first game in near silence, Annis concentrating on moving her counters and protecting her king rather than on the way his skilful fingers moved. It was all too easy to imagine them stroking her, holding her. She shook her head to clear it. She had to pay attention. Rapidly she took several of his counters. Haakon raised an eyebrow, and a tiny smile appeared on his lips.

'You are a more difficult opponent than I first anticipated,' Haakon remarked as he finally took Annis's king.

'I told you that I had played before. In both your version and the Northumbrian, the king occupies the centre square and his men are arranged around him.'

'I can see that I shall have to have my wits about me when we play, Valkyrie.'

'As will I,' she replied, keeping her eyes trained firmly on the stone pieces. A warm tingling coursed through her. He was only talking about the game. He had to be.

For the length of the match, as it ebbed and flowed with

neither gaining advantage, Annis found she could pretend that she was free and that they were playing as equals. She wondered what if… And then dismissed the thought as pure fantasy. There was no meeting place for them. Haakon was only interested in the ransom, and once that failed to materialise she'd be sold on. There was no room in her life for 'what ifs'. She bit her lip. 'What are you thinking about with a furrowed brow? You have picked up that white piece three times and put it back down without moving.'

'Things…'

She hastily moved a piece and Haakon countered. Annis took a look at the board and then permitted a smile to cross her lips. He had left the hint of a gap. She moved another piece, and he followed, straight into her trap.

'Your king is mine, Haakon Haroldson!'

'How…how did you do that?' Haakon stared at the board and then back at her. His smile widened and his eyes grew dark. 'That will teach me.'

'Teach you what?' Her voice sounded thick and unnaturally low.

'Teach me to pay attention to the game at hand, rather than being distracted by rose-coloured lips and the way they purse when you are concentrating.'

Annis's hand knocked the king down on the ground. She bent to pick it up and her fingers touched Haakon's. She drew back as if she had been burnt.

'Now who is trying to distract?'

'But you are a distraction and a very lovely one at that.' Haakon came and stood behind her. So close she could feel the heat of his body, rising up to meet her, calling to her. Annis wanted to lean her head and encounter his chest, but she forced her body to stay still, remembering the words of the monk. She had already betrayed Northumbria once through that kiss. She had no intention of doing so again.

'It is all right. In a short while I will be gone.' She turned and looked at him over her shoulder.

A muscle jumped in his cheek and he moved away from her. His eyes blazed a brilliant blue. He reached and touched her shoulder, pushing away the strap of her apron-dress. 'I had not forgotten. I remember *everything* about our encounters. What a pity we were not wagering.'

'Can captives wager?'

Annis tried to keep the excitement out of her voice. Her breath caught. Could she wager for her freedom with her body? And what if she lost? She forced herself to remain where she was, not to say the words making the offer.

'It depends,' he whispered, and he reached out to touch her hair, a butterfly caress, but one that made something deep within her stir.

Annis's lips ached. She could feel all her resolutions draining away from her. She wanted him. She wanted to taste his mouth again.

A moan came from where Thrand lay and she could hear his hands moving against the cloth. Immediately she went to him. She peered under the linen bandages and sat back on her heels.

'Thrand is restless. He will need more ointment or he will start clawing his face and undo the good.'

'He needs you more than I do.' Haakon put a hand on her shoulder. 'We will continue our game at a later date. I can take a hint.'

'I wasn't aware I had given you a hint.'

His lips curved upwards, transforming his face into a soft boyishness. 'Sometimes it is from the gods. Now you must attend your patient. I have found it instructive to play *tafl* with you, Annis. And next time, we will play for something pleasurable.'

Annis's heart turned over as he strode out the door without a backward glance. She stood there watching, remembering his touch. Angrily she shook her head. She refused to have feelings for this man. She turned back towards Thrand, concentrating on lifting the bandages without tearing his skin.

'Annis,' Aelfric said in Latin, coming into the kitchen very early the next morning, before the household had properly begun to stir. Kisa and Fress wound themselves around Aelfric, who gave a series of loud sneezes. 'I have just heard. Last night you attended one of the Viken! How could you? He is a pagan. They even allow these creatures in their houses and everyone knows they are the devil's creatures. Look at their size. Unnatural.'

He gave an exaggerated shudder.

'He was a man in pain, Aelfric.' Annis picked up the cats, moved them out of Aelfric's way. It had taken a while, but she had managed to get Thrand off to sleep. She had then dozed by the kitchen fire, rather than risking going back to her pallet. Today she decided not to venture on to the lake, half-afraid of what she might discover and half-afraid that Haakon would not be there. Instead she had done simple tasks. 'I would have thought you of all people would have understood that we have a duty to help those in pain, regardless of their religion.'

Aelfric's face became cold and stern as he drew himself up to his full height. The overly smug look was back on his face. He held up his hand and started ticking off his points. 'He remains a Viken and they sacked Lindisfarne without regard to its inhabitants. They are pagan animals who live by a different code.'

'Their lifestyle is certainly different,' Annis replied cautiously. She bridled at the description of Haakon as an animal. He wasn't that. It was far more complicated.

'Do you find it easy to pray with your cross?'

'My cross?' Annis tilted her head and stared at the monk.

'Guthrun took it away when we arrived. It is far too valuable for a hostage to have.'

Aelfric tapped the side of his nose and winked. 'Sometimes if you look, you can find.'

'I have no time for riddles, Aelfric.' Annis removed Kisa from the table. 'There is work to be done. Speaking in Latin might make some-one think you and I have something to hide. Speak Northumbrian.'

He put his clammy hand over hers, but continued to speak in Latin. 'All I am trying to do is make sure you remember where you have come from, and why you are here.'

'Are you asking me if I have forgotten that?' Annis stood up and pressed her palms into the table. She knew Haakon was different. She believed him when he said that they had not intended to sack Lindisfarne. She had gone over and over the scene in her head. 'I remember that day with every breath I take. I was there. I lived through it. It is the reason I am here, that we are all here.'

Aelfric turned bright red and shifted from one leg to the other as he pulled slightly at his tunic. 'You gave every appearance…'

'Appearance can be deceptive, Aelfric.' Annis crossed arms. 'Like you, I miss Northumbria with every breath I take. I too long to be there, to be free once again and to live my life the way I want to. I have no great liking for being a captive.'

A strange light came into Aelfric's eyes. He dropped his voice to a hoarse whisper and leant forward. 'I have a scheme.'

'A plan for what?'

He motioned to her to be quiet and glanced over his shoulder. Seeing that Thrand was asleep, he continued, 'I overheard two of the Viken talking yesterday. Their king knew nothing of the planned raid. He may be sympathetic. It is why the Viken are going directly to Charlemagne's court.'

'I don't believe the raid was planned.' Annis's mouth grew

dry. It could not have been. Haakon had been furious that day.
He blamed the monks.

Aelfric's face became purple and his eyes bulged out.

'You are asking me to believe that those greedy heathens did
not see us as a ripe plum for the picking?' His voice broke with
emotion. 'No, any nonsense about seeking payment was just an
excuse. My uncle always paid everything. He never cheated any
true Christian. He had no time for such pagans as the Viken.'

Annis's hand trembled as she remembered how a monk
had rushed forward. It seemed incredible that Aelfric had
survived that first assault, but he must have hidden in the confusion and panic. A cowardly action followed by much more
cowardice. 'Your family caused this?'

'No! It was Haakon and his men. They are to blame. You
were not at the beach. I was! And it was only through the grace
of God that I survived. One of the monks fell on me and then
I lay as if I were dead. Later when I tried to escape, I was
captured. I moved when the toe of a Viken hit my backside.'

Annis turned to the fire, wrapped her arms about her waist,
trying to get warm. She wanted to do bodily harm to Aelfric.
In his arrogance, he was as much to blame for the tragedy as
the Viken. He might be correct that they would have raided,
but she was inclined to believe Haakon when he said that they
only came to get the gold legitimately owed them. And
Haakon did say that the monks had confronted them, accusing
them of stealing, the very thing that Aelfric now proudly proclaimed that he played his part in.

She tried to remember the sequence of events. Two monks
had rushed forward. Attacked.

If Aelfric's cousin had checked his movement, would her
uncle, Mildreth and the rest still be alive? Or would Haakon
and the rest of the *felag* have attacked anyway? She was no
longer sure what she wanted to believe.

When she had control of her temper, she turned back. 'I see.'

'You see what?' Aelfric's face grew red and his nostrils flared. 'There is nothing to see. The pagans had no right to expect payment. They are heathens.'

'But discussing the rights or wrongs of the raid will not get either of us released.' Annis curled her fingers around the waistband of her apron-dress. If she was not careful, her temper would get the better of her, and she'd attack him. He surely bore some responsibility for the destruction.

'Ah, but you are only a woman.' Aelfric waggled a finger. 'I should not expect you to grasp the significance. You should be guided by men. I wonder your first husband neglected to teach you that.'

Annis gritted her teeth and used every ounce of self-control not to throw something at him. He was a holy man. She started to count, but found it did not do any good. 'Perhaps you can explain it to me, so I can understand. In small simplistic words that a *woman* might comprehend.'

'Their king may be an ally,' Aelfric said. 'He will not wish to anger Charlemagne. If we could reach him, we would be immediately freed. He will have no wish to have the whole of Christendom ranged against him.'

'And just how are you planning to do this, Aelfric?' Annis crossed her arms as what little respect she had for the man vanished. 'Have you forgotten that none of us knows how to pilot their boats?'

Aelfric looked over his shoulder and dropped his voice. 'You wouldn't have to. It is a ruse, all these ships. Their king's court is no more than a few days' journey to the south. I plan to leave today when the Viken are busy with their gaming and drinking. I will go overland.'

'There are wild animals in the woods, and mountains to cross. It is why the Viken use the sea for transport. You will not make it and you will have put everyone who stays behind in danger.'

'Who told you that? A Viken?' Aelfric curled his lip. 'You cannot trust these people, Annis. I will go south, heading for the gap between the two mountains. It is simple. There is a road. I have seen it with my own eyes.'

'And how far does this road go? Or does it vanish after the next farm? Or become a track for deer in the middle of a dark wood?'

'I have no idea, but it is there for me to take. You can join me on the journey.'

'I think what you are planning is foolhardy. Do the other monks know?'

'They are weak-livered and believe that God and the Pope will deliver them without them ever having to lift a finger.' Aelfric rolled his eyes heavenwards. 'I am done with them.'

'It may go ill for the others,' Annis replied. She could understand Aelfric's desire to escape, but he should not attempt things alone. 'Not all are like you.'

'God will provide.' Aelfric grabbed her elbow. 'Now, are you with me? Will you come?'

'I think you are making a mistake, Aelfric. You cannot simply abandon people.' Annis pulled her arm away and rubbed it. 'I will stay here. Should any ask, I will let them think you acted alone.'

'I should have known better than to talk to you.' His eyes grew crafty. 'If you speak of this, things could go ill for you. I will tell them that it was your idea and that you urged me to do this.'

Annis drew a breath. 'Then you would lie.'

'It is you who call it that.'

'You seek to lecture me on the way I live my life and you are willing to sacrifice your brothers. It is here our association ends.'

'I will pray for you, my sister, when I return to civilisation. I came here, hoping for a bite to eat, and all I got was a harsh word.' Aelfric turned his back and started to walk towards the door with hunched shoulders.

Annis felt an instant of remorse. He was in a foreign land and friendless. She, too, knew what it was like to long to escape. His plan would come to nothing before he reached the end of the first field. He would realise the folly of leaving the others behind.

'Aelfric,' she called out and he stopped. She ran to the cupboard and pulled out a loaf of bread. 'Here, take this. It might help you…on your journey.'

Chapter Eight

Annis reached down and allowed the cool lake water to trickle through her fingers. Aelfric made her angry. The last thing she needed or wanted was to be worrying about him. She had been relieved when Ingrid appeared and said she looked flustered, suggesting a walk by the lake as a remedy.

She breathed deeply, watching a curl of smoke rise from the hut beside the lake. Who had bathed this time? She shielded her eyes, but no one swam. A vague disappointment filled her. She took off her shoes and allowed the lake to lap her toes.

'I wondered when you would return.'

Annis spun around and discovered Haakon facing her. His fine linen shirt clung to his chest in places, moulding to the hard muscles that she knew were underneath, as if he'd just pulled it on after a swim. 'The lake has much to recommend it.'

He threw back his head and a deep booming laugh echoed out over the lake. 'Does nothing disconcert you, Annis?'

'Some things,' she admitted as she watched two ducks glide past, seemingly untroubled by the people on the shore. Serene, but paddling furiously underneath. Annis knew she had to resemble them—insides burning, but with a cool exterior.

'Are you going to confide in me? Or do I have to discover them on my own?'

'You will have to find out.'

'Will I?' He put his hands on her shoulders. His blue eyes swallowed her. 'Why are you here, Annis?'

She had to say something, something that did not have to do with the droplet of water that had pooled at the base of his throat and the shape of his lips.

'The kitchen was too hot. Ingrid is looking after Thrand now. I had no wish to disturb them.'

'Indeed, I did not realise that Ingrid and my brother were close.'

Annis gave a shrug and rose on her tip-toes, trying to see farther out into the lake. She could almost see the steam rising from his body. 'Would I be out here for any other reason?'

'I could think of several.' He stared off into the lake before giving her a wry smile. 'I have learnt to underestimate you at my peril.'

'I am telling the truth. The air was far too confining in the kitchen.'

'And does the heat bother you—now?'

Annis ran a hand through her hair. How to answer? Anything she said would be a lie. She found it far warmer to be standing next to him. 'I can breathe.'

'But you remain uncomfortable.'

Without waiting for an answer, he scooped her up and marched towards the lake.

'Haakon! What are you doing?' Annis kicked her legs and flailed her arms, but he kept on wading out into the lake. And her body noticed all too clearly the hard planes of his chest and upper torso. Her breath fanned the droplet of water at the base of his throat.

'Be quiet unless you want to bring everyone here.'

The water lapped around his knees. The hem of Annis's shift touched the water. What exactly was he planning?

'Put me down this instant!'

'As my lady commands.'

His arms released her. Down, down she fell into the water. Her feet touched the bottom and she rose up, spluttering, pushing her hair away from her eyes.

'You did that on purpose!'

'You said you were hot, bothered. I thought to refresh you.' Haakon wore an unrepentant look.

'I am not a good swimmer.'

'I would have saved you.' His eyes became serious. 'The water is not deep. It only comes to your hips. You did say that you sought relief from the heat.'

'Being cool is one thing, being wet is another.' Annis pushed out with her hands, connecting with his body, pushing him backwards. 'You look a bit hot. I think you should try it.'

He fell backwards, with an even louder splash. Within a heartbeat he rose. Water streamed off him, moulding his shirt to his every sculpted muscle, leaving little imagination, reminding her of her earlier view. His eyes darkened and Annis realised with a start that her dress had become transparent.

'You shall pay for that,' he growled and sent a splash of water, covering her.

She had to admit that it was refreshing. A bubble of laughter filled her. She splashed him back. 'And I did not ask for that.'

'So you gave it back.'

'I am drenched.' Annis held up her arms and the water streamed off her. 'I look like a drowned rat.'

'You look like...' He took a step closer.

'Like what?' Her voice seemed different to her ears. She found it impossible to move. His eyes changed, reflected the grey blueness of the lake, so deep that she fancied she could easily drown in them.

He reached forward and pulled her into his arms. She tasted the cold water, followed by the heat of his tongue tracing the outline of her mouth. Gentle, persuasive. A different type of kiss to the one they had shared at the feast. At the feast he had sought to dominate her, to demonstrate his claim on her, and now he asked. He captured both sides of her face, held her still as their lips clung.

The kiss became a long, slow exploration. Deep. Intense. Retreating, advancing and then retreating. Leaving her wanting more. She moaned slightly in the back of her throat. Her hands reached for his head, his shoulders, held him still, while her body arched towards him and her nipples contracted to hardened points.

His hands slid down, encircled her bottom, pulled her closer, so that their bodies collided. She could feel the hardness of his arousal through garments that provided only the thinnest of cover. She shivered slightly.

Haakon lifted his head. He pushed a wet tendril of hair back from her face. His chest expanded, drawing his tunic tight against his muscles, and his breath was ragged as if he had swum across the lake. 'We should go to somewhere warmer.'

'Not the hall. Not your chamber.' Annis ran her tongue over her lips. She couldn't go back there to that heaving mass of people. What she and Haakon had shared was private. But he was right, they could not stand here for ever, kissing in the middle of the lake.

He shook his head. 'I know of somewhere else, where we might be able to dry your wet things.'

Annis wanted to ask whose fault was it that she was dripping wet, but she found the quick words of refusal stuck in her throat. Her body demanded the feel of his hands against her. She mutely nodded.

He scooped her up again, and strode through the water. This time Annis lay still, savouring the strength of his arms, carrying her.

He opened the door of the small hut as he allowed her to slide down the length of his body. 'I came here, heated the rocks in the fire and bath. It is for my own private use. No one will disturb us.'

The warm air rushed out at her. Annis bent her head. The room smelt of wood smoke and steam. She put a hand on the wooden frame and felt the stored heat. Inside, low benches hugged the walls, and a pile of stones sat in the exact centre.

Her mouth grew dry as the enormity of what she was about to do washed over her. Sweat baths were pagan. Good Christians shunned them. Neither did they passionately kiss men. Annis swallowed hard, feeling as if a bucket of ice water had been thrown over her. She had done so many things lately that a good woman was not supposed to do. A good woman would now be dead. She was wicked. Wicked.

She drew back, her hand clutching the neck of the linen shift where it had gaped open. She wanted to find a reasonable excuse for her behaviour, but none would come.

Haakon sensed her withdrawal. Where a heartbeat ago she had given measure for measure with his kisses, now she hesitated, turned her face and her eyes were cloudy, troubled.

Exactly what was her concern?

He was not going to let her depart like that. His body demanded her, ached for her. He had spent the better part of the night thinking about her after their game of *tafl*. But he wanted a willing partner.

'Stay with me.' He kept his voice low and softly touched her shoulder.

'I should go…. There is work to done…. Thrand's burns…' She started to edge past him, but he blocked her way, moving to stand between her and the door.

'Do you intend to tease?'

'I…I have no idea.' She looked down at her hands. Innocent, vulnerable and thoroughly desirable.

He was going to end his torment now. He would not force her, but he would show her how good it could be. He had seen her response in the lake. He would have taken her there, but he had no desire to become gossip for bored kitchen maids. His lovemaking was private, not a spectacle for any passing warrior.

Desire smouldered in her eyes underneath the hesitation. He had to stop her from thinking.

He bent his head and ran his lips down the white column of her throat. She gave a sigh, no more than a breath.

'You will like this, Annis.'

'Do I have a choice?' Her eyes were dark pools and her lips full.

'No.' He pulled her more firmly in his arms and recaptured her mouth.

His tongue touched the little parting of her lips and she opened, allowed him entrance. He feasted on the dark inner reaches of her mouth. Hot, sweet, holding intense promise.

He took his time, exploring, until once again her body began to melt against his. Her breasts brushed his chest and, with a surrendering sigh, she fastened his arms around his neck.

Success.

He ran his hand over her shoulder, moulding the wet cloth to her body. 'Time to get you dry. I don't want you to catch a chill.'

'You were right.' Her voice held a husky note. 'This is different. It was not like this before…with my husband.'

He reached down with one hand and pulled the linen shift over her head. With the other, he held her waist firmly. He brought her soft curves against his body.

'We go slow, Annis. You set the pace. Feel what you are doing to my body.'

She did not stiffen or draw away as Haakon ran his hands down her smooth skin, cupping her bottom, pulling her closer.

'You're wet as well,' she whispered.

'All in good time.'

He bent his head; his tongue made traces of fire down her body.

'What are you doing?' she gasped out as his mouth moved lower, covering her body with open-mouthed kisses.

'Drying you. Your skin tastes of honey and wildflowers,' he murmured as his tongue reached out and licked the hardened nib of her breast.

He circled, suckled and then circled again. All the while the heat grew within her, intoxicating her with a languor more potent than the strongest mead. Annis trembled. She ached in places she had never dreamt of. Her body demanded more. Her hands reached out and buried themselves in his hair as he continued sinking, his hands sliding down her back. His tongue touched her navel. She gave a small moan as he leant forward and sucked.

Annis's legs gave way as desire curled around her with an unforgiving intensity. Her hands clung to his damp shirt, but she felt herself being lifted and placed against the smooth ground. The heat from the bath rose up to encircle her, caressing her skin.

Above, Haakon loomed. He slowly peeled off his shirt, revealing the gleaming muscles of his chest. Then he pulled off his trousers and placed them on the hot rocks where they gently steamed. Up close he was more magnificent than he had been when she had glimpsed him by the lake. The small door gave a little light and Annis watched the interplay of shadows on his muscular chest and arms.

All she could think was that she had been safe in those arms. He had saved her—twice—and now he offered to take her somewhere she had never been before. A place her body needed to be. She wanted to be here with him. She wanted him, and she'd think about everything else later.

She reached up and touched his warm flesh. One or two droplets of water remained on his skin. She gathered them with her forefinger and then brought the drops to her mouth. Sweet, clean and yet containing something that was indefinably him.

What was happening with Haakon was different from anything she had experienced before. Before her husband had taken his pleasure, grunted, then fallen asleep, leaving her dissatisfied. There had to be more to lovemaking than that or else why would the maidservants gossip about it behind their hands, laughing and comparing, when all she did was endure? Now she knew all her previous ideas had been wrong. It was not she who was at fault. It had been her late husband.

Her hands curled upwards and brought his face back down to hers. She felt the full length of his body meet her. Softness giving way to the hardened masculine flesh. She knew that she had to feel all of him, to experience everything.

She ran her hands down his back, a mixture of smooth flesh and scars from earlier battles.

'Haakon—'

He put his finger to her lips. 'Shh. Let me show you what it can be like between a man and a woman.'

And then once again his mouth made fiery trails over her until he reached her soft curls. She needed to know what came next. He lowered his mouth and explored her hidden recesses. Cool against the burning need of her. Her hips rose, inviting him, and he drove deeper.

And she forgot everything except the feeling of his tongue against her burning flesh.

She needed more than that. A great burning developed inside her. She wanted him joined with her. Her hands tugged at his shoulders, pulling him upwards.

'Slowly, slowly,' he murmured pressing open-mouthed kisses on her fevered skin.

Her thighs parted as he entered her. Entered and then retreated, leaving her longing. She pushed her hips upwards, her flesh expanded, welcoming the full length of him.

Then with a sudden assurance she began to move, slowly at first, then faster. He matched her rhythm as her hands grasped his shoulders. She wanted him, deeper and deeper still, until a great shuddering overtook her, and a cry was torn from her innermost being.

Haakon raised himself up on one elbow and looked down at the woman. Her face was a pale oval against the dark brown of her hair that flowed out like a carpet beneath them.

He had thought once would be enough for him. But he knew now that a hundred—no, a thousand different times would make him still want her.

He could feel himself growing hard within her again, but he could also hear the sounds of activity. Today would bring more people from the estate's outlying farms. People who would expect to be fed, to be greeted and their disputes resolved.

Today was not a day for lingering with Annis—as much as he might like to. He had responsibilities. This was his land, his people, the reason he braved the sea. He refused to abandon them.

There would be time afterwards.

He pressed a kiss against her forehead and eased himself out of her, his flesh protesting at the sudden move. He rolled away, and reached for his discarded trousers.

'We need to go.'

Her eyes blinked open, focused in the dim light. She looked confused, then appeared to remember where she was. She sat up, drawing her knees to her chest. 'Go? Go where?'

'It is late morning.' Haakon pulled on his damp clothes,

knowing that if he looked back at her, he would give in to his desire. He could not do what was best for him, but had to consider the rest of the estate. They depended on him. 'There are things to be done.'

Annis forced herself to stand and to pull on the creased linen shift. It was dry in places and wet in others and hung about her like a sack. The enormity of her actions washed over her. She had given everything and he wished to discard her. Selwyn was like that as well. Except this time she had experienced pleasure. She would now have to walk from this secluded hut to the main house in her damp clothes.

Haakon had his back to her as he fastened his sword belt around his waist.

Her brow wrinkled. No one had seen them together. She might be able to go on as before—to glide over the water like the ducks.

'What is going to happen to me?' she asked, giving voice to her fears.

Haakon paused in the doorframe. 'I am not sure what you mean. Will you come with me to the hall?' His voice broke into her circling thoughts.

'I can make my own way.' Annis kept her chin high. 'I would not want it said that you were favouring a captive.'

Haakon's eyes became hard points of sapphire. His mouth tightened to a thin white line, but Annis stood watching him. She had no wish to become the target of Guthrun's or Tove's spite. What had happened here must be locked away, deep within her. And she needed to do all within her power to prevent it occurring again.

'You will return shortly or I shall send men to fetch you.'

Haakon left without a backward glance. Annis took a few moments to arrange her hair into a loose plait and to straighten her shift. Then she left the small structure, closing the door with a gentle click.

What had happened here changed nothing, she repeated over and over, willing her body to believe it. But her heart kept saying—Haakon has changed everything.

Chapter Nine

'It has gone!' Guthrun said, her voice rising to a screech
and sending the lounging cats racing for cover. 'Vanished
without a trace.'

Annis's hand froze on the door handle. She had found
another older shift, changed and returned to the kitchen. Tove
and Ingrid looked at her speculatively and she wondered if
her encounter with Haakon showed in her face.

'What is going on?' Annis mouthed at Ingrid as Guthrun
stamped up and down the room.

'Looking for a missing loaf,' Ingrid whispered. 'Her
special wheat bread.'

Bread. The loaf of bread she had given Aelfric earlier—
she had assumed it was barley. She hadn't thought, just
reached and grabbed. She swallowed hard. No, it couldn't
have been. She knew the difference. The loaf she had given
Aelfric was barley.

Tove and Ingrid looked at each other and put down their
spinning with apprehensive expressions.

'We know nothing about the loaf of bread,' they chorused
along with the other serving girls.

'And you?' Guthrun walked up to Annis and snapped her

fingers under her nose. 'What do you know about this bread? Maybe you have turned it into an ointment or another medicine.'

'I have no idea where it is.' Annis kept her head and met Guthrun's gaze full on. 'Bread—wheat or barley—is not a usual ingredient in my medicines. Is it in yours?'

Guthrun's cheeks reddened and took on a more pinched expression as if she had swallowed a sour plum. 'I don't make medicine. I leave that for the soothsayers and the healers.'

'The more is the pity,' Annis murmured, but forced herself to smile sweetly.

Guthrun stomped over the kitchen, throwing open chests. At last she discovered the missing loaf, under a white linen napkin.

'Hmm, I want a thorough search of the hall, in case anything else has gone missing.' Guthrun pressed her fingertips together, and her black eyes sparkled. 'We may have a sneak thief.'

'With so many warriors about?' Ingrid asked under her breath as she broke the thread of her spinning. 'Who would dare? Guthrun wants to cause trouble. Watch your back, Annis. Our mistress looks for an excuse to punish someone when she is in one of her moods and even Haakon will not be able to protect you.'

'Why? I have not done anything wrong.' Annis wrapped her arms about her waist. Guthrun could not suspect about Haakon and her. It was too new, too soon.

'She fears you and your power to heal.'

'What was that?' Guthrun demanded, her eyes narrowing as she slapped her hand against her hip.

'Nothing. We are happy to search.' Annis stood up and wiped her hands against her apron-dress. 'Tell us, what are we looking for?'

Guthrun harrumphed and marched over to the large chest that dominated one side of the kitchen. She withdrew a key and threw back the top. The contents were thrown about, not neatly placed. She withdrew Annis's gown, Haakon's cloak, but not the cross. Annis swallowed hard and restrained herself from running and tugging the gown away from the woman.

'They are gone!' Guthrun shrieked as she reached the bottom of the chest.

'What's gone?' Annis asked, peering at the chest along with Ingrid and Tove. Ingrid's face crumpled.

'We are in for it now. She wants to use the birch to beat us,' Tove muttered. 'Who could have been so stupid to leave the chest in that disarray?'

A sob escaped from Ingrid. She stuffed her hand into her mouth in response to Tove's filthy look. A prickle of fear ran down Annis's spine. What was it about Guthrun's punishment that had Ingrid so afraid?

'My second-best oval brooches, my amber beads that Thrand gave me at the last harvest and…the silver cross.' Guthrun started to pull at her hair. 'Who could have taken them?'

'You must calm yourself, Guthrun. It will not do you any good,' Tove said in a soothing voice. 'I am sure there is a simple explanation for this. Perhaps they are in a different chest.'

'No, I always keep them here.' Guthrun's voice rose to a piercing shriek. 'You know that, Ingrid, Tove. And they are missing. Somebody took them.'

Annis grew cold. She wanted to cry. The cross had been her last link to home. She had held out some hope that it might be returned if ever the ransom arrived. The fact that it was in that trunk had given her hope. Some day, she would get it back, and would once again be more than a captive. But now it was gone—gone into someone's greedy purse to be melted down.

'Is there a problem here? The noise of wailing can be heard out in the barns.' Haakon strode into the kitchen and stopped as he saw the piles of linen and clothing on the floor. 'What exactly is going on?'

'My best amber and a few other things have disappeared from the linen chest.' Guthrun dabbed her eyes. 'I have no idea what the world is coming to—even my own personal chest is not safe any more.'

Haakon went over to the chest and methodically went through the contents. He sat back on his heels, shaking his head. 'You are correct. There is nothing valuable in this chest. Who has had access?'

'I have always kept it locked,' Guthrun said. 'I know what some in the *felag* are like—wouldn't hesitate to take from their mothers if they thought they could get away with it.'

'The lock has not been broken.' Haakon put his hands on his hips, his eyes glittering darkly. 'Who did you lend the key to, Stepmother?'

'All the kitchen staff know where I keep my keys. Ingrid used them recently to get linen for Thrand,' Guthrun said decidedly as Ingrid covered her mouth in horror. 'Annis required it for her healing and I was occupied with other things. Shall we have a look at their possessions?'

'If you wish, but I doubt you will find anything.' Haakon rolled his eyes upwards. 'Is it possible you stored the beads in another chest? Like you did when you accused me of taking the drinking horns?'

'That was different.' Guthrun clapped her hands against her cheeks. 'I demand a search! I am within my rights, Haakon, as mistress of this hall.'

'As you wish, Guthrun, but I doubt a thief would hide something in here where it would be easily found.'

The bedding was all turned out, one by one. Annis was secretly relieved that, each time, none of the maidservants had anything. She gave Ingrid's icy hand a squeeze when Guthrun shook her fur out. Ingrid gave her a tiny nod.

Finally, Guthrun came to Annis's bedcovers. Guthrun gave the fur a practised twitch and the silver cross slid to the earth floor with a tiny tinkle. It lay there, gleaming silver against the packed earth. Annis stared at it in disbelief as Guthrun reached for it, holding it between her claw-like fingers as a wide smile crossed her lips.

'You see, Haakon, I told you that she was untrustworthy.' Guthrun's eyes narrowed as she shook her fist at Annis. 'Where is the rest, captive? Where have you hidden my things?'

'How…how did it get there?'

Annis held out her hands palms upwards, appealing to Haakon where he stood, his face all hard planes and his eyes an icy shade of blue. His shoulders had become set, forbidding. Annis allowed her hands to drop to her side, forcibly keeping them apart rather than twisting her apron. Already the other women gathered behind Guthrun, whispering behind their hands, and staring at her with accusing eyes. Haakon was her last hope.

He had to understand that she wasn't a thief. She had not stolen the items. How could she? She had no idea where the key to the linen chest was. She was innocent and he was her last hope.

Haakon's hand closed over the cross, tucked into his belt.

'It was not there when I straightened my fur yesterday morning.' Annis tried again, hoping for an answering spark of understanding in his eyes, trying to keep the desperation out of her voice. 'I spent the night in the kitchen, watching over Thrand, sitting by the baking oven, just in case he needed more ointment.'

The silence was deafening. He had to believe her. Surely the time they had spent together in the sweat-hut would mean something to him.

Annis pressed her fingers to her eyes, willed him to speak, to defend her. He did nothing but stand there, with drawn-together eyebrows and his arms crossed, the formidable warrior, not the gentle lover from the hut.

'When did you last see your brooches, Guthrun?' Haakon asked in a calm voice. 'There is much to be done today, and I would like to solve this little mystery speedily. Neither do I wish for anyone to be punished unnecessarily, simply because you can't remember.'

'Annis is lying. See how her cheeks flame.' Guthrun snapped, pointing an accusing finger. 'She has hidden them somewhere else. Who could be in league with her? One of the monks?'

'I heard Annis speaking Latin this morning,' Thrand called out from where he lay. He raised himself up on his elbow, the white of the linen hiding the redness of his face. 'I thought I was dreaming, but then I realised what it was—a man and a woman talking, arguing in Latin. Annis is the only woman who knows Latin here.'

'Did you make out what they were saying, my son?' Guthrun asked in an eager voice. 'What they were plotting?'

Annis's mouth went dry. This was like a nightmare. She tried to remember what she had said to Aelfric. She had been unguarded, but she had tried to keep him from running away. She felt as if the whole world was threatening to tumble on top of her. She struggled to draw a breath and not to panic. What was the worst that could happen? She was already a captive and Haakon wanted the ransom.

'Alas, no.' Thrand held out his hand and Guthrun squeezed it to her chest. 'I stayed here with *you* while my brother went to Charlemagne's court. I only speak Norse as you know, Mother. I did see her put something into his hands.'

Annis let out a breath. She had to speak, undo the damage. 'The monk Aelfric came in here, that is true. I gave him a bit of my bread, the bread I had for my breakfast, as he looked hungry. Then he left. He wanted to know if I needed more herbs. He is more…more comfortable speaking Latin.'

Her voice trailed away. It was a poor explanation, she

knew, but she refused to betray Aelfric. The punishment for trying to escape would be as harsh here as in Northumbria, possibly worse. She had no wish to see any of the monks punished on her word. And she had no idea where he went after he left the kitchen.

She waited, but Haakon merely lifted an eyebrow and his face appeared sterner than ever. He turned his back on her without acknowledging her words.

'Shall we summon the monks?' Haakon asked in a bored tone. 'And question them? I fear you will give me no peace, Guthrun, until I solve this little mystery.'

'By all means, Haakon. You are the Jaarl here.' Guthrun oozed triumph. 'All I want is to have the proper order restored.'

Haakon barked an order and all the monks were brought in, shuffling with their heads bowed as if in prayer. Annis counted once and then again. All the air vanished from her lungs. The room swayed.

Aelfric was missing.

Gone.

He had carried out his escape plan. How long since he departed, she could only guess. But he had escaped and it would be discovered. Those who remained were sure to be punished, particularly with Guthrun in her present mood. She went cold and then hot as she remembered Haakon's words from the first day that she had arrived in Viken.

What would happen to Aelfric when he was caught? And what would happen to her? Would Haakon understand that she had nothing to do with it? He had to. She had been with him. Her eyes darted from Haakon to the monks and back again.

'Which is the monk Aelfric?'

The monks shuffled their feet, mumbled in Latin. All turned their eyes, appealing to Annis.

'Aelfric is not here, my lord,' Annis said quietly. 'All the other monks are, but Aelfric is missing.'

Haakon put his hand to his sword belt and seemed to grow, to become more formidable. The hunt for the missing items had ceased to be a joke. 'Not here? Where is he?'

'I have no idea.' Annis's eyes flicked from his face to where the monks stood, never staying still. The note of panic rose in her voice. 'The last time I saw him—'

'Yes, yes, I know.' Haakon lifted his hand to stop the flow of words. 'You may stop the protestations of innocence, Annis. I do not believe that you had nothing to do with this. You were speaking to the man this morning. In Latin. Why did you need to speak Latin?'

Annis became intent on a pebble. She whispered something that did not carry.

'Annis?' Haakon said through gritted teeth. He had no time for games. She knew far more than she was willing to say. He could see it in the way she stood. She had used him. She had gone down to the lake for one purpose only—to seduce him. She had seduced him so that this monk could escape. And, what was worse, he had allowed himself to be used. No more.

'I told you why!' She clenched her fists.

'Has one of your captives gone astray?' Guthrun asked with poisoned sweetness. 'Are you sure you have looked in all the chests?'

'The monk will reappear in one form or another,' Haakon said. He turned to the men guarding the prisoners. 'Is there any reason he might be missing?'

'No, my lord.' One of the guards shook his head. 'They were all here earlier. Me and the lads started having a wrestling match, and he was gone, like.'

'Just like that.'

'Yes, sir.'

'And whose idea was it, this *wrestling* match?'

'I don't rightly remember.'

Haakon gritted his teeth, struggled to keep a leash on his temper. And all the while, Annis looked at him with big eyes, eyes that demanded he trust her. She had betrayed him! Used him! What an accomplished liar she was!

'I want him found! Now!'

Haakon raised his arm and signalled for the alarm to be rung. A loud horn resounded throughout the hall and farm. A call to arms. A cacophony of barking and shouts filled the air. Men ran in every direction, calling the dogs. Horses were brought, mounted, as Haakon issued orders, directing his men.

A cold, furious rage descended on him. He had warned the captives. He treated them properly and they chose to take advantage of it. The monk had not acted on his own. He could not have. Someone had helped him.

He would see that *someone* punished.

Annis pressed her hands together as she watched the search being organised. It seemed the space of only a few breaths and the searchers were gone, and all that remained were the monks, Haakon, Guthrun and the women. The shouts and barking grew ever more distant.

Had he in truth escaped? Was he even now marching along the road towards freedom? Head held high? But for how much longer? Would he be brought back, arms tied, dragged behind a galloping horse? Or worse. Annis pressed her hands against her cheeks at the thought. She knew how barbaric the Viken could be. Lindisfarne haunted her dreams.

She might have counselled Aelfric against leaving, but she certainly did not want him found. And she could not betray him. He must have been the one to steal the brooches, and the amber, but how did he get access to the trunk?

She held out her hands to appeal to Haakon. His face had

hardened, all angles and planes with nothing soft. A cold shiver went through her.

She glanced right, left. Everyone had moved away from her. The baying of the dogs grew fainter with every passing heartbeat.

Haakon's piercing gaze never left her face. His fingers drummed on his thigh. His cloak fluttered in the breeze, making a flapping sound. The leader. In command. Dangerous.

'You must punish her.' Guthrun's voice rose to a shriek. 'She has defied me! Defied you! She helped a fellow captive to escape and all you do is stand there and gaze into her eyes.'

'Punish me?' Bile rose in Annis's throat and her arms started to shake. She held back the words, accusing him of using her for his pleasure. 'I have not done anything. I had nothing to do with the theft, and I did not help Aelfric escape. I am innocent.'

Haakon felt fury building within him as Annis's eyes shimmered with unshed tears. Mock tears that she mistakenly thought would tug at his heartstrings. He pressed his lips into a white, tight line. He had seen such weapons deployed against his father many times and had resolved to remain unmoved by such things.

His gut turned over. Betrayal. He had trusted Annis and she had betrayed his trust by helping this monk to escape.

He had believed that there was a friendship building between them. And now she protested her innocence. By her own admission she had spoken to the monk this morning. They had spoken in Latin, rather than in Northumbrian. He was convinced that it was because they had not wished to be overheard plotting. Then she had gone to the lake and seduced him. She had taken him for a fool, played on his desire for her, and now she expected to walk away unpunished.

Annis looked up at him with her big eyes and trembling

red lips. Did she not understand how well she had been treated? Obviously not. Unfortunately, Guthrun was correct. He would have to punish her or risk losing control of his entire estate and his men. He had no choice.

'When you first came here, I treated you as a hostage, rather than as a captive. I expected certain behaviour in return.'

'But I have. I have done everything you asked.' She paused. Her body started to shake uncontrollably as fear coursed through her. 'Believe me…please.'

'I believe the evidence of my own eyes.' Haakon put his hand on his sword belt, restrained his fury.

The words caused Annis to lift her head, square her shoulders and stand upright. Her green eyes blazed.

'Tell me what I have done! I never went to the chest. Ask Ingrid. She knows.' Annis pointed towards the women. 'I had to ask for more linen last night. I did not know where it was kept.'

Haakon glanced over at Ingrid, who stood there white faced but unmoving. She gave a small shake of her head and then appeared to sway. Tove and two of the other women grabbed her under her arms and held her upright.

'Ingrid has served in my household for over two years and never has she taken one thing. She has gone out of her way to comfort and help those new to the household. You should be ashamed of accusing her. Do you have proof?'

'I have no proof, but I know I am innocent.' Where he had heard desperation before, her voice held a measure of calm. 'As God is my witness, I am innocent.'

'And do you deny you helped the monk Aelfric to escape?'

'I gave him a bit of bread. That was all. I did not aid him in any other way.' Annis brought her hand up to cover her mouth as if she was frightened of allowing the truth out.

'Is this true?' Haakon turned to the oldest monk.

The oldest monk bowed his head but made no reply.

'Tell me. Who helped him to escape? I do not believe he acted on his own.'

The brothers looked at each other and then at Annis. Several shifted in their boots. One raised his hands towards the heavens in prayer.

'Quickly now, or it will go worse for you.'

'We did not aid our brother, believing him to be mistaken.' The eldest monk bowed his head and began to speak in slow Northumbrian. 'We understand he had help from the kitchen. I have no idea who the woman was. I did not wish to know. He broke the rules of our order, the rule of St Benedict.'

'That woman was not me!'

The light breeze whipped Annis's hair from her face. She sounded so noble and sure when she said the words, but Haakon knew them for a lie. He was not blind. He could see what had happened. Somehow Annis had got into the chest, given the goods to Aelfric, but had been unable to resist keeping the little cross for herself.

The only mystery was she had not attempted to escape at the same time. Or perhaps she had planned to and Aelfric betrayed her and slipped away while the guards fought amongst themselves and she sported with him, preferring to go on his own. And Annis had probably taken the gamble that his desire for her would provide protection from any storm. She had guessed wrong.

Haakon refused to let emotion sway him. He was the Jaarl. He had to decide what was right and proper for his people. It was his first duty.

'Very well, since you persist in telling tales that only a child would believe, you shall be marked as a captive so that all the world will know at a glance what you are.'

He signalled to two of his men, who pinned her arms to her sides. She fought against them, her calm deserting her.

'What do you mean?' Annis's voice held a note of panic.

Haakon gritted his teeth. Did she think he'd be lenient because they had lain in each other's arms?

'Cut her hair. Place a collar about her neck. Then put her in the pigsty where she can contemplate what she has done.' Haakon stared at her, hating her. She had lied to him, whispered soft words and given advice. Asked what the lands to the south were like.

He had liked her, lusted after her body, wanted to spend time with her, and all the while she wanted to betray him. He should have remembered the lessons of his youth—women were not to be trusted.

'She can stay there and see if she enjoys that sort of Viken hospitality more.'

He thought she might break down in tears and make a play for his pity, but she stood with her head held high.

'And the others?'

'Put collars around them. If they try to escape, people will recognise them for what they are—my property.' He nodded towards his stepmother. 'The punishment may begin.'

Guthrun advanced towards Annis with a purposeful step and her scissors gleaming in the afternoon sunlight. Annis's stoic calm deserted her as the first lock of hair was cut.

'Listen to me! I am innocent! I have not done anything wrong! Please believe me! You must believe me!'

She struggled to move her head and break free, but to no avail. The pieces fell in great chunks to the ground until she had a carpet at her feet. Haakon's heart clenched as he remembered how he had run his fingers through it. He pushed away the thought and forced his face to stay stern. As the last piece of hair fell and the collar was clamped around her neck, she fell silent and stared defiantly at him, her eyes accusing him.

Haakon turned his back and strode away, but the anguished look haunted him.

Chapter Ten

Annis lay on the straw, face upwards. A little light filtered through the cracks, but that was all. She had heard the dogs and the men returning a short while ago, but she assumed they had not found Aelfric as no one had come to release her.

How had it come to this? An itchy collar about her neck and her hands chafing from the rope that bound them behind her. Surely she could not sink any lower and survive. She with her proud heritage, a captive in a filthy sty! Being married to Eadgar could not have been worse than this.

She gave a bitter laugh. She had trusted a Viken. She had lain with him, voluntarily. She had believed Haakon was somehow different from the others. He spoke Latin, and she had seen his kindness, his humanity.

A faint sob escaped her lips.

It did not matter now that the ransom would not come. She had been content to wait, hoping against hope that she could convince Haakon to allow her to go free when the time came.

She had saved his life. And this was how he treated her!

Now she knew freedom was a distant memory, a condition confined to her dreams. She had been marked as thrall, and would end her days as one, unless she took matters into her own hands and escaped.

Escape. The very idea made her heart quicken. Aelfric had been right, as much as she hated to admit it. It was the only way.

But how? And, once free, how would she make her way back to Northumbria?

She kicked a bit of straw with her foot.

They would be watching her now, looking for any little infraction—real or imaginary.

Despite what they had shared, Haakon had chosen to ignore her. It made it worse. The stony expression on Haakon's face as Guthrun cut her hair. His hands shoving her into this pigsty, and most of all his look, as though she had been the one to betray him! She felt used and worthless.

Annis moved her arms, rolling in the straw, trying to get into a more comfortable position, then recoiled as her right hand hit a metal spike. She ran a finger down it. It was only slightly sharp, but was the only piece of good fortune she had had lately. She set to work, rubbing the rope that bound her wrist up and down against the metal spike.

It seemed to take for ever and the heat in the pigsty was awful. Small flies, attracted by the sweat, came and buzzed about her, getting into her nose and mouth. Annis wished she could wipe the sweat from her eyes or scratch her nose, but all she could do was, rather ineffectually, rub her face against her shoulder. And still the rope wouldn't budge.

Was this sent to torment her?

She redoubled her efforts and then suddenly and without warning the rope gave way and Annis was free.

Immediately she brought her wrists around, shaking them, trying to get life back into her fingers.

She touched the collar that now fastened around her neck. Truly a slave. She could live with the short hair; it was cooler against her neck. But the collar? Never! She was freeborn, a lady. And she had done nothing to deserve such treatment.

This was war. And she, a prisoner.

She would follow the directions Aelfric had told her and hopefully he would prove to be right in his estimations.

She scrambled all over the pigsty, but Haakon had locked it securely. Annis muttered a few choice phrases under her breath. The Viken was nothing if not efficient.

Her neck and her arms ached, but what hurt the most was the knowledge that Haakon had given her no time to explain or to listen to her explanations. Surely he had to see that it would make no sense for her to hide her own cross in her bed. He had abused her trust.

'Annis,' she heard Ingrid softly calling. 'Are you awake?'

Annis hurried back to where she had been sitting and arranged her arms behind her. What did Ingrid want? She thought the woman was her friend, but she had not lifted a finger to save her. She *knew* that Annis had never been near that chest.

'I am here at the back, Ingrid. What do you want?'

'I have brought you some food. I hated to think of you going hungry. Sorry it took so long, but I had to wait, you see, until the others were eating.' Ingrid appeared in the doorway, carrying some bread and cheese. She put it down cautiously at the entrance. 'I thought you might need some food. You did say that you had given your breakfast to…Aelfric.'

There was something in the way she said the monk's name with a slight tremor. Annis thought back to that morning after the feast. She had not thought to question why Aelfric was there. Had he been planning and scheming even then? Had he used Ingrid?

An idea formed. Ingrid might prove very useful. If only she could get her to come closer… She had loathed her father's lessons in protecting herself, hating to learn how to shoulder charge or tackle. But now she had need of them. She had to remember the rusty skills.

'It is too far away. I will have trouble eating it with my hands tied.' Annis made her voice sound feeble, tired and without hope.

Ingrid stepped into the pigsty and shoved the plate forward. Close, but not close enough. Her expression was just visible in the dim light.

'I am sorry I can't untie them, Annis. I know you must be in pain.' Ingrid shook her head, making a clicking noise in the back of her throat. 'Haakon would be furious. I don't think I have ever seen him so angry. He is shouting at everybody. The cats hid behind the butter churn, knocking it over.'

'Serves him right,' Annis muttered.

'He did it to protect the estate. Haakon is in charge. Those who do wrong must be punished.' Ingrid widened her eyes and pursed her mouth. 'Surely it is the same where you come from.'

'I am innocent. I have done nothing. You *know* I never went to that chest.' Annis barely restrained herself from banging her fists together in annoyance. She had to be cautious. She had to find out what Ingrid knew. It was more than friendship that brought Ingrid to the pigsty. Aelfric had used someone else in his escape. He must have done.

Ingrid?

Annis thought back to the time she had seen him in the courtyard. Why had he been there? And Ingrid had come into the kitchen shortly after Aelfric departed. It had been her suggestion for Annis to go down to the lake. Or had Ingrid been following Aelfric's suggestion?

Ingrid gave her a worried look. 'You do understand. I have taken a massive risk, bringing you the food here.'

'I am not asking you to untie my hands, just bring my food nearer. I don't bite.' Annis gave a little laugh, making her voice sound light, and willed Ingrid to come closer.

Ingrid advanced one step at a time.

Annis waited, her muscles tense, her breathing still. Closer, closer. Annis caught her tongue between her teeth, forced her body to wait.

Ingrid put the food down, almost under Annis's nose and then started to back away.

A step, two. Ingrid nodded slightly. Annis bit her lip. Waiting, waiting. Now!

Annis sprung, tackling Ingrid and bringing her down on to the soft straw.

Ingrid squirmed, lashing out with her hands, striking Annis's face with her nails. Annis captured one hand, then the other, but Ingrid bucked her body, forcing Annis to the floor.

The straw got into Annis's nostrils and eyes, but she brought her knees up and connected with Ingrid's stomach. Again they flipped, with Annis on the top this time. She grabbed Ingrid's upper arms, overpowering her, pinning Ingrid to the ground with her knees.

Ingrid gave a cry of surprise, but Annis put her hand over Ingrid's mouth and nose. Annis controlled her breathing, wanted to wipe the straw and dirt from her face but did not dare.

'I want you to answer my questions by nodding or shaking your head. Do you understand?'

No response from Ingrid. Annis shook Ingrid's shoulder and was rewarded with a quick nod.

'I mean you no harm, but I intend to leave this place with the truth.' Annis put her face close to Ingrid's. 'You allowed Aelfric into the linen chest, didn't you? You were the one from the kitchens who helped him.'

Ingrid blinked up at her. A single tear ran down her cheek.

Annis damped down any feelings of pity. This woman was responsible for her punishment. She had stood by and allowed Haakon to believe she had lied.

Annis angrily gave Ingrid's shoulder another shake. 'Answer me!'

Ingrid nodded slowly and then muttered against Annis's hand. A mumbled justification, no doubt blaming the whole thing on Aelfric's charms. Annis's mouth twisted. She had trusted this woman.

'That should teach you to believe strange men.' Annis gave a short, bitter laugh. 'I don't suppose you knew that he intended to steal Guthrun's necklace. He probably gave you a plausible story. He possibly even gave you an excellent reason why I needed to go down to the lake.'

The mumbling stopped and Ingrid nodded vigorously.

'Is there anyone guarding me?'

Ingrid hesitated, her brow puckered as she appeared to think. Then she slowly shook her head.

Annis regarded her captive.

Did she believe her?

She glanced over her shoulder to where the sunlight shone golden through the door. Impossible to say what time it was, but she fancied she could hear the clanking of the plates. Supper time, and so less chance of anyone being about.

She had started so she had to go on, and keep going until she was free or she died. Ingrid could be sending her out into a trap, but it was too late. She had to trust her instincts and her instincts told her that Haakon thought her secure.

He would not waste one of his warriors guarding a captive who had no means of escape.

Ingrid made some more grunting noises.

'I hate to do this, Ingrid, but here you and I part company.'

Annis worked quickly. She pulled off Ingrid's kerchief and stuffed it into the woman's mouth. Used Ingrid's apron-dress to tie her hands behind her back. Finally she removed the metal spike from the straw and dropped it near the entrance with a loud clatter.

Time stopped. Annis peered out of the pigsty. Ingrid had told the truth.

No warriors. And, more importantly, no dogs.

Annis closed the pigsty's door with the barest hint of a click and darted across the open space to the shelter of the barn.

The horses gave a slight whinny, but Annis rejected the idea of capturing one immediately. The noise was sure to alert Haakon or one of his warriors.

She would have to go on foot, and hope.

Soft laughter floated towards her—Tove's and a deeper, unknown voice. She froze, saw a couple engaged in an embrace at the end of the barn and backed away slowly, her heat pounding so loudly she thought they must hear.

When she reached the sweat-bath by the lake, she glanced back over her shoulder.

Nothing. She had made it.

The walls of the hut were cold and she did not linger.

She skirted around the lake and entered the pine wood, being careful to walk up the small stream so that the dogs would have difficulty tracking her scent. Then she started south, changing direction, doubling back several times.

The trees thinned and she discovered a dirt track, running almost directly south. Her heart beat faster.

There was every possibility that Aelfric had told the truth—the way to Thorkell's court might be easy. She kept to the trees at one edge of the road, ready to run and hide if anyone should appear.

She rounded a bend and saw the road stretching out in front of her with nothing but pine trees behind her. She had done it. She had escaped and her whole life lay before her.

'You are not paying attention, Haakon. Your king is in jeopardy and you have not made your move.'

Haakon lifted his gaze to his brother. Thrand lay back against the multitude of furs and pillows. Fress and Kisa purred softly at the foot of the bed. The linen bandages half-covered his face, but his eyes were as sharp as ever. Haakon had assumed the game of *tafl* would distract his thoughts from Annis but it had only reinforced his disquiet.

How could someone who played *tafl* so well, who seemed so intelligent, leave the cross entangled in her own bedding?

'It makes no sense.' Haakon moved his knob and effectively blocked Thrand.

'What makes no sense? Your move?' Thrand took Haakon's piece.

'She is an intelligent woman. Why leave the cross where it would be easily found?'

'If I understood the ways of women, I would be a very wealthy man indeed. Take Ingrid, for example—all hot for me before we left. Now that we have returned—successful—she has been cold. All because I made eyes at Tove. Then she was weeping over me when she changed my bandages earlier… overcome by my injuries, no doubt. And I thought she was going to come back to plump my pillows, but she has disappeared again. Gone. Vanished without a trace.'

'Weeping?' Haakon lifted an eyebrow. 'But the burns are fading fast. Annis is a talented healer. Her ointment has worked wonders. I doubt there will be much scarring. Ingrid's actions do not make sense. She was not weeping over you, my brother.'

'As I said, there is no accounting for women.' Thrand put his hands behind his head. 'Can I help it if I am devastatingly handsome?'

'But you said she vanished.'

A cold prickling went down Haakon's back. Had he made a mistake? Had he blamed the wrong woman? Had he been searching for a reason to mistrust Annis?

She had been in his mind, haunting his dreams. He knew he wanted her, more than ever after their encounter in the lake, but the depth of his feelings frightened him. It made him vulnerable. It made him think he was becoming like his father. He remembered his father's grief at his mother's death in childbirth and then how his proud father had become Guthrun's thrall. Haakon had promised himself that he would never behave that way.

Then this happened, and it had appeared clear who was to blame. She had lured him to the lake, made love to him only for the sake of the misbegotten monk. He refused to be a laughing stock. Haakon's neck muscles became rigid, his head pounded. He refused to become his father.

'When did Ingrid vanish?'

'Ingrid will be back soon.' Thrand made another move. 'It is just that I expected her before now. My mother has probably given her a job to do.'

Haakon grunted and turned his attention back to the *tafl* board. There was some key that would make this whole episode clear, but he couldn't find it. He tapped his fist against his mouth.

Why had Annis behaved that way?

'You know,' Thrand said, moving his next piece, 'it does make me wonder. Why didn't he take her with him? I mean, Annis is able bodied and all, but she stayed behind. Why?'

'The monks stayed as well.' Haakon tried to forget the accusing sea-green stare.

'But Annis was talking to him. I heard raised voices. And if she objected to his escaping, why didn't she want anyone to know? Why didn't she tell you?'

'Thrand, would you warn anyone if a fellow captive was about to escape?'

Thrand was silent as he toyed with the king piece that he had just won. 'You are right. I don't know Latin. I only know they were arguing. He shouted at her. She shouted back. Then he left. She stormed out shortly afterwards, telling Ingrid to change the bandages.'

'Why tell it differently before?'

'You know what my mother is like. She wanted to punish Annis. She was looking for an excuse.'

Haakon shifted on his stool and resisted the temptation to throttle Thrand.

'And the linen chest? And the cross in Annis's bedding?'

Thrand collapsed against his pillows. He pressed his fingers together and gazed up at the ceiling. 'I have been thinking about that as well. I had to wait while Annis found Ingrid and the key. My face hurt like it was on fire. Annis never went near the chest.'

A stab of remorse coursed through Haakon. Had he believed the worst of Annis because he too was searching for an excuse? Because he was afraid to trust? Haakon shook his head, trying to rid it of the doubts. Thrand was correct. He needed answers and he needed them fast.

The air in the kitchen was hot, overpowering, preventing him from thinking clearly. He stood up, started to head for the door.

'Where do you think you are going? We have not finished the game. Don't you want to hear more of my theory?'

'I am going for a walk around the farmyard to make sure that everything is safe and secure.'

'Haakon?' Thrand called from his bed as Haakon was about to walk out the door. 'When you speak to Annis, give her my regards. Her ointment comes from the gods.'

Haakon slammed the door with a satisfying crash.

Annis's feet ached. Her boots were soaked through and now pinched her toes. How long she had been running and half-stumbling down this road, she had no idea. She had given up counting trees and bends in the road or even places where the road became muddy and rutted as it crossed a stream.

Once she had to skirt around a farmhouse where a lone dog barked and a baby wailed.

The sun barely moved at this time of year and late at night had the same light and shadows as mid-afternoon.

A wolf's howl filled the air, chilling her to the bone.

She quickened her footsteps, nearly a running pace, but still walking. She glanced over her right shoulder and then her left. Nothing, just the vast emptiness of the woods.

Where sunlight had played, she saw the shadows move, hold still and then begin to move again. Something was out there. Something was tracking her.

Another howl, and the cracking of twigs. The noise came far closer. Annis froze and tried to remember what she had to do, but her mind was blank.

Above all she had to survive.

Haakon frowned. The courtyard felt different. Something had changed. Almost as if something was missing. He dismissed the thought, continued on his tour and then doubled back to the pigsty.

The catch was not closed properly. Someone had forgotten to loop the rope up. If Annis pushed hard, she'd be out. Haakon frowned. Who had done this? And when? He had twice checked the fastening when he placed her there.

Floki whined and pawed at the door.

'Annis? Are you in there, Annis?'

He stooped and peered into the gloom. A figure thrashed about on the floor, making muffled noises, kicking out with its legs. But it was the wrong shape. The hair was long, blond. Floki gave a soft growl in the back of his throat and then proceeded to lick the woman's face as she struggled to get away from him.

Annis had vanished.

Haakon reached the prone woman, elbowing Floki out of

the way. Ingrid! Haakon pressed his lips together and resisted the urge to shake her.

What in the name of Odin was *she* doing here? A willing partner or another victim of Annis's treachery?

He pulled the kerchief from Ingrid's mouth.

Ingrid made spluttering and gagging sounds. She looked up at him with piteous eyes. A tear trickled down her cheek. Haakon raised his eyes towards the roof. Every single time, women cried. Give him a woman who fought back, rather than this limp rag doll who did not even have the sense to spit out the kerchief.

'I want an explanation for this,' Haakon said, placing his hand on his hip. Had this woman voluntarily agreed to take Annis's place? Or had somehow Annis tricked her?

'That witch tied me up! I came here to give her food and she pounced on me. She tricked me.' Tears streaked Ingrid's face as she rested her head against her knees. 'That's gratitude for you. I befriended her, you know, felt sorry for her, and she did this to me.'

'Truly?' Haakon gave Floki a pat on the head before he started to work on the simple knot that bound Ingrid's hands together. He had a grudging admiration for Annis and she certainly displayed ingenuity. 'Her hands were tied when she was put in the pigsty. I have always thought it difficult to tie someone else when one is bound, but perhaps I was mistaken.'

'Her hands were free. Maybe someone did not tie the knots properly.'

Haakon kept a tight rein on his temper and only raised a single eyebrow. 'And who gave you permission to bring Annis food? Or was it something you decided for yourself, Ingrid?'

'Please release me.'

'Tell me what happened in your own words.' Haakon moved to undo the simple knot. If Ingrid had possessed an ounce of courage, the knot would have fallen away.

'I don't know what happened. Truly I don't! I felt sorry for her. I told you we were friends and she did save Thrand, after all.'

'And after that? Did she ask you to help her?' Haakon asked silkily, in a deceptively quiet voice. He struggled to retain the last vestiges of control and not shake the answers from the woman.

Ingrid rubbed her wrists and stuck her bottom lip out. 'I only know my head aches like Thor's hammer hit it.'

Haakon closed his eyes. Counted slowly. Controlled the surge of anger that passed through him. He had no wish to frighten the woman.

Somehow, Annis had found a weapon and had not hesitated to use it, but something in Ingrid's story did not sound right either. Ingrid had been weeping before. And she had no history of disobeying his orders. Why did she feel the urgent need to see Annis? Annis had only been confined for a few hours. The first of Aelfric's search party had recently returned.

'Can I go now?' Ingrid asked in a slightly petulant tone as she rubbed her wrists. 'The cats will be missing me and I promised Thrand—'

'You know more about this than you pretend, don't you?' He caught her arm and forced the reluctant woman to look at him. He had always thought Ingrid was kind hearted, but she would have never taken Annis's place voluntarily. She knew the penalty for helping prisoners to escape.

Ingrid hid her face, but Haakon took her chin between his fingers and forced her to look him in the eye. She jerked her head away. Haakon recaptured Ingrid's face and then let her go. She stumbled away from him. 'Tell me what you know!'

'I have no idea what you are talking about. I brought Annis supper because she has been helpful. That is all.' Ingrid wiped her face against her sleeve. 'And this is how she repays me. You know, I even got her fresh linen when she asked for it as she had no idea where it was. Otherwise, she might not have succeeded with Thrand's face. But did she thank me? No.'

Ingrid gasped and put her hand to her mouth. Then very slowly she lowered her hand.

Haakon clenched his fists and contented himself with slamming one of them into a post with a satisfying thump. Ingrid jumped.

'You have to understand I did not mean Annis any harm….' She sank into a ball and wept. Great gulping sobs.

Haakon regarded the woman. He wanted to feel pity for her. But he could see all too clearly what had happened. He had been a fool, and far too anxious to believe Guthrun. And Annis had vanished.

'You were the one who had the key to the linen chest. Annis never went near it. She was surprised to see the cross, but you weren't,' he said, remembering Annis's shocked expression.

'How did…?' Ingrid paused and swallowed hard. Her tone became more respectful. 'Yes, I did, but I didn't take anything.'

'Who was with you? Tell me quickly or it will go ill with you.'

'Aelfric,' came the muffled answer. Tears started to stream down her face. Then she dissolved into great noisy sobs, sobs designed to tug at the heart and make a man feel helpless. Haakon gritted his teeth. 'He put the cross in her covers as a reminder, he said. He promised to send for me once he'd escaped. He said that he would take me back to his house and I would live like a grand lady with plenty of servants to wait on me. He is the son of a great noble. If I stay here, all I will be is the concubine of a lowly warrior.'

'Aelfric is a monk.' Haakon stared at the woman. 'A tonsured monk! He follows the rule of Rome!'

'I don't understand.'

'Monks don't marry, Ingrid. They have sworn their lives

to their Christ. It is why they shave their heads to show they are at one with their God's suffering. He lied to you.' Haakon felt a twinge of pity for the girl. She was an innocent in many ways, but an innocent who had caused a great deal of trouble, possibly more than she could ever guess.

Annis had escaped, but could she survive?

'He lied to me?' Ingrid scrubbed her eyes with the back of her hand. 'He couldn't have done. He was so kind and gentle. He was nice to the cats, picking them up, even though Fress gave him the sneezes. And he kissed me on the forehead, not pawing at me as some of the Viken warriors have done. He can't have lied.'

'He did, you know he did and you let an innocent person pay for your mistake,' Haakon ground out between his teeth. 'You stood by and let Annis get punished for something you had done. Now, do you have any idea where either might have gone? Any clue?'

'How can I? I was tied up and knocked out when that witch left.' Ingrid shrugged as her face became mutinous. She pushed past him and out into the yard, where she breathed deeply. 'You have no idea how much a pigsty smells.'

Haakon resisted the temptation to shake her. But he had no time for such things. He had to find Annis.

Ingrid was of no further use to him.

He hooked his thumbs into his sword belt in an effort to control his temper. Her lies and selfish disregard for everyone but herself had led to this and he suspected she was lying to him even now, trying to protect her lover, Aelfric.

'When I get back, I want you and all your belongings gone from my estate.'

The colour drained from her face. She swayed where she stood. Haakon felt a grim sense of satisfaction. Whatever she had expected, it was not that. No doubt she thought it would all be overlooked as her father was an important freedman, the owner of a large farm. It had been an honour to have her fostered here—Guthrun had pointed it out several times. He had even once considered her for Thrand. All that had changed.

'But…but what about my parents? I can't go home in disgrace!' Ingrid wailed. 'They have plans. I am supposed to find a husband and learn to be a good housekeeper. You can't send me back.'

'You should have thought about them before you believed the blandishments of a captive monk.'

'Thorkell's court—to the south.' Ingrid spoke to the ground. 'Aelfric thought Thorkell might be able to help him. He said that the king knew nothing about the raid and that a great evil would befall any who had taken part in it.'

'Aelfric obviously does not know our esteemed king. He has no great liking for monks.'

Haakon turned his back on the woman, and headed towards the barns. He wanted to rush, but forced himself to plan, to think. How far had she gone? She had fled from the danger here, and had placed herself in even more danger.

He had to find her.

Floki ran along beside him. He quickly saddled the nearest stallion. He started to ride out and then stopped, went back to the hall and retrieved Annis's gown from the chest. He held the gown under Floki's nose.

'Find her,' he said.

Floki started sniffing, gave a bark and then was off, headed down the road to the south. Haakon tried to concentrate on the road ahead and not the bears and wolves that he knew lurked in the woods. He would find her, and bring her back alive. He would right the wrong he had done her.

She had to be alive.

Chapter Eleven

Annis abandoned the increasingly faint track for a copse of birch and larch trees, looking for somewhere to shelter for the night. Her legs ached from running and red welts shone on her wrists and hands where the rope had chaffed. She wanted to find somewhere to lay her head and sleep. And she prayed it would be a dreamless sleep, with no black-haired Vikens with broad shoulders and a tender smile who bestowed kisses and then betrayed her.

The howl of the wolves lingered in her brain. How close were they? If the wolves were about, she wanted to be up high as she had no means of making a fire—no flint, no steel, not even something to catch a spark.

Annis pressed her hands into her eyes. She had to keep calm. Panic led to death. She had learnt that lesson at Lindisfarne.

She had been foolish in escaping, without a knife, without any means of surviving. She did not even know how long her journey would be. Her stomach growled slightly from hunger; despite the warmth from the sun, Annis shivered. How cold would tonight be?

But had she really had a choice?

Staying there would have meant another type of death. At

least she had her pride. She was not a thrall. If Haakon was willing to punish her severely for something she had not done, she hated to think what his temper would be like when the ransom failed to arrive. He was wrong. There was nothing worse than being his captive.

The trembling in her limbs started anew and she forced her feet to move a few more steps, away from him and his so-called protection.

She fingered her shorn head. Little wisps curled up and her head was much lighter, but she had been proud of her hair. Her uncle had been displeased when she laughingly suggested the necessity of cutting her hair would prevent her from ever joining a convent. He had called her vain. What would he say if he saw her now? A just punishment for a woman who could not please her husband? Her uncle had blamed her for Selwyn's mistresses, and for that fact she had not been able to persuade him to give a bigger donation to the church.

Her hair would grow long again. It was a small price to pay for having her illusions shattered. Haakon had proved that he was made from the same cloth as Selwyn. Unyielding and unwilling to listen.

A bramble scraped her shin before entangling itself in her shift, capturing her, forcing her knee down on to a rosette of foxglove leaves. Annis bent and pulled it off with impatient fingers. Even the plants were trying to hold her prisoner.

She froze.

In the growing darkness, a pair of yellow eyes, white dripping teeth and a dark muzzle stared out at Annis from the undergrowth. She backed away slowly, her mouth dry. All around her she heard the padding of soft paws. She blinked and they disappeared.

Her imagination playing tricks?

She wiped her hands against her shift, stood up straight. It had to be. Wolves were wary of man. They hid and slunk away at the sound of footsteps and voices. Annis forced a tune from her mouth. It sounded small and lonely in the great wilderness that surrounded her. When that song was finished, she began another—a louder drinking song that her husband and his cronies had sung late in the night. She stamped her feet and marched. A shiver ran down her spine as if eyes watched her from the shadows.

The song died on her lips. All was silent, but the leaves of a bush swayed. She needed to find shelter for the night, quickly.

Something scraped her shoulder. She looked up. There was a larch and one low branch that looked like it might bear her weight. She had to try or run to the next tree.

She saw a shadow move and knew she had to climb. Now.

Annis turned and tried to find a foothold on the smooth bark. One and then another. She slipped back as the first wolf broke cover, snarling and wild eyed.

Her hands reached up again, fingernails digging into the bark, pulling. But nothing, only a slight hop off the ground. Annis gritted her teeth, summoned all of her remaining strength and pulled upwards.

This time she moved upwards and then along, dangling from the branch while the wolf snapped at her feet. Her hand clung, hurting, hanging on. She swung her feet and locked them around the branch and then looked down. The world turned upside down. Annis wished she hadn't looked.

The wolf made a leap, but fell back, his claws scraping the bark and his long, low howl of frustration chilling her to the bone.

The wolf had to leave. To go. It had to see that it could not get her. Annis nodded towards the undergrowth.

'Go on. Get out of here. You are not wanted. I shall sing again.'

The wolf started to move away. Annis released a breath and felt her palms grow slippery with sweat.

The wolf sat down and tilted its head, regarding her with its yellow stare, and then began to pace around the bottom of the tree.

Annis tightened her grip on the branch. The impossibility of hanging there for ever like some demented bat crashed in on her as her limbs began to ache and her head spin. She had to move.

One by one, she forced her legs to unhook and used her arms to propel her upwards, until very ungracefully her middle was over the branch. Slowly she turned over, found she could sit and surveyed the scene below her feet.

Two more wolves had joined the first one and they padded around the base of the tree. Every so often one would give a yellow-eyed glance upwards. Above her, a horde of ravens circled, cawing loudly.

Annis hugged the trunk of the tree tighter and began to wonder when they would tire of the game and disappear. They had to go.

One wolf threw back his head and gave a long howl of frustration.

The wolf's howl echoing through the woods caused Haakon to stiffen on his horse. All his thoughts became concentrated on what lay ahead. The sound was enough to send a chill through the body of the most hardened warrior—a wolf pack on the move and hungry.

Floki pricked up his ears, sniffed the air and gave a low growl.

'Yes, I know. The wolf packs will be out hunting. They have young cubs to feed. It is the time of year.'

Haakon forced his lungs to fill with air. One more worry to add to his mind.

How had Annis escaped from the farm unnoticed? His men were supposed to be on guard. No doubt they had underestimated her resourcefulness and determination.

He made a disgusted noise in the back of his throat.

They all had. He, most of all. He had put his pride before his common sense.

And did she realise the danger she was in? Did she have anything with her or had she simply escaped?

Floki appeared to pick up her scent a little way south of the lake. His ears pricked up and his paws began to move faster as he worked from one side of the road to the other. Floki sniffed the air, gave a decisive bark and headed south.

Luckily she had found the track that led to some of his outlying farms, rather than stumbling blindly through the woods.

There was always the possibility that the wolves and bears would avoid the road because they did not like to encounter man, but he knew there were dark stretches where the birch and pine touched over the road. But now a wolf pack was on the move and would find a lone human.

Another wolf sounded. Floki picked up speed, his plume tail streaming as he ran. Haakon urged his horse forward. The horse responded, going from a trot to a gallop and finally to *skied*, its flying pace with all four hooves raised off the ground as the horse easily kept up with Floki.

What had the dog sensed?

Annis?

Annis shifted her weight, easing her body to the right. She had been in the one position so long that her legs were starting to feel numb. And still the wolves circled the tree, and every now and then the silver-tipped wolf threw back its head and howled, a long, lingering howl that sent shivers down her spine and chilled her blood.

As much as she hated to admit it, Haakon was right. Out here beyond the limits of the hall, it was a different, dangerous world. She had been naïve to think otherwise. Just as he had told the truth about keeping away from the priory, he had told the truth about Viken. This land was far from safe. She should have listened. And what was worse, she wanted to see him again. To apologize.

She laid her face against the rough bark of the tree.

Above all, even after everything she had gone through, she wanted to feel his strong arms around her, hear his voice reassuring her. But that was impossible. He was not the man she had thought him.

Once her escape was discovered, his men with dogs and horses would hunt her, while Haakon stayed within the safety of the hall. He had finished with her. The thought was not a comforting one and she tried to push him out of her mind.

Her mouth became drier than ever and she tried to ignore the rumbling in her stomach. She had to concentrate on survival—food would come later. She would find a stream, and hopefully berries to eat. There had to be something. She put one hand to her head and tried to peer through the woods for a glimmer of blue.

Nothing.

She turned her body to look the other way, towards the dark mountain.

A distinct crack and the branch that seemed solid beneath her before appeared to slip. It had to be her imagination. She glanced down and saw fresh broken wood.

She closed her eyes and whispered a prayer.

'Don't let it fall, please, God. Not that!'

At the sound of the creak, the wolves froze, motionless statues. She saw the long pink tongue of one lick its chin. Annis pressed her body tighter into the tree, and heard the branch give out another moan, protesting at the unaccustomed weight.

Her place of safety had been illusion, a trap. Once again she had to escape. Despite the warmth that hung in the air, her teeth began to chatter and her body was racked with uncontrollable shivers.

She glanced upwards into the canopy.

Where else could she go? This branch was not going to take her weight much longer. The other branches were too far above her for her to grab. And the one below looked insubstantial. She had to do something. She had to prepare.

She tensed her muscles, ready to jump. It was the only way. She had to control where and when she fell. She pushed away from the tree, aiming for a spot a little way from the wolves.

As she left the tree, the branch fell with a heavy crash. Annis landed to the right of it, rolled and then righted herself.

The noise had caused the wolves to scatter, vanishing into the undergrowth.

Annis broke a substantial piece of the branch off. It was a weapon of sorts, a club, if the wolves returned. She looked for another tree to climb. Then froze as she caught a glimpse of luminous yellow, moving stealthily.

The wolves were back, and in greater numbers, scenting easy prey.

Silent. Deadly.

The grey-and-black shapes crept closer towards her. She looked left, right. Where would the attack come from? She retreated until a tree was at her back. The bark scraped at her, but it was firm and solid.

'Help me! Anyone, please help!'

She raised her club, prepared to fight. This was it, her last stand. She had escaped the Viken, only to perish from wolves. She raised her club, ready to strike the first wolf down.

A streak of white and grey came from the right, leapt on the lead wolf with a fierce growl and rolled over and over in the dust and leaves beneath the tree.

A wolf? A dog? Did it matter? Someone had heard her prayer.

The dog grabbed the wolf by its neck, shook it and threw it into the air. It fell to the ground. Then the dog stood, back to her, facing the wolves, teeth bared, daring the wolves to attack again. Annis heard the whimper, saw the white eye-patch and the plumed tail.

Haakon's dog! Floki!

If he was here, was Haakon?

Her heart leapt. She had a chance. If she could hold on long enough, she would be saved.

'Haakon! Help me, please!'

The only answering sound was the snarl of a wolf. Annis shivered. Was she truly alone?

The scent of blood maddened the wolves and they advanced again, this time growling and snapping at Floki. Floki braced his paws and snarled back, challenging, defending.

One wolf charged forward.

Annis aimed a blow at the wolf's head, brought it down with all her might, felt it hit true. The wolf paused. She hit again, brought the wood down so hard that she heard it crack and watched the wolf stumble. Floki snarled and bit its neck. The wolf jerked and lay still. Dead.

The other wolves regarded the two dead of their number, appearing to reconsider.

Annis reached out a trembling hand and patted the dog's ears. Had Floki come alone?

'Haakon! I am here, Haakon!' she cried again. He had to come. She wanted him to be there. She needed him.

'Catch on to my hand! Annis, do it now!'

Haakon! On a horse with thundering hooves. Bending towards her with an outstretched arm.

Annis didn't stop to wonder why or how. She reached out and felt his strong fingers curl around her wrist, lifting her upwards.

Back to safety. Back to captivity.

Annis couldn't think. All she knew was that this man had saved her from certain death. She wanted to bury her face in Haakon's chest, and revel in his masculine scent. He was solidly real and her ordeal had ended.

Haakon whistled to his dog.

A wolf bared its teeth, leapt and its outstretched claws raked the horse's side.

The horse reared upwards, overbalanced, throwing Haakon and Annis to the ground. It bolted, and its thundering hooves could be heard in the distance.

Haakon took the brunt of the fall as Annis rolled on top of him. She pushed against the earth, forced herself to stand. Haakon had not moved. He lay splayed, face down on the ground. He had to move.

'Get up, Haakon. Get up!' She tugged at his leather tunic.

He gave a groan and began to rise, using his sword for support, but collapsed back to the earth.

The wolves crept forward, advancing once again.

Annis glanced to her right, to her left. She needed a weapon. Her broken branch was several feet away from her.

Floki broke off his run, leapt towards their defence, his hackles raised, growling. Blood poured from his hind leg, streaking the brown earth.

A wolf started towards them. Floki gave another warning growl and leapt. They tumbled over and over until this time Floki lay still.

Annis resisted the urge to bury her face in her hands. Her hand stretched for the branch again, but Haakon was already on his feet, brandishing his sword.

'Stay back, Annis! Stay still. If you run, they will be after you.'

He went forward, swiping the air with his sword, his eyes darting first to the right and then to the left.

'What are you going to do?'

'Fight. It is what I am good at.'

His sword gleamed in the fading sunlight as he waded into the wolves, stabbing and slicing, attempting to reach his dog.

The first wolf fell and then another.

The others of the pack ran. But Haakon kept on stabbing and slashing, defending her and the fallen Floki until all the wolves were gone. Then he lowered his sword, his face bloodied and wearied.

The silence that followed came without warning. Annis at first thought she must be mistaken. No howls, no rustling in the undergrowth, just the breeze whispering through the leaves of the trees.

She stumbled over to Haakon, who reached out an arm and gathered her close. A moan escaped her throat.

'Shh, it's all right,' Haakon murmured into her hair. 'They have gone. You are safe now. You are here with me.'

'You came after me.' Annis's hands touched his chest, his arms. She had to sure he was real, breathing, alive.

'Did you really think I'd let you go that easily?'

'I had no idea.'

She lifted her face to meet his lips, but he clasped her to him. She buried her face in his leather tunic as his hand stroked her shorn hair. There was no need for words. His heartbeat resounded in her ears and that was enough.

Once the shaking in her limbs stopped, she pushed back. His arms fell away and she took three steps backwards.

Five wolves lay dead and Floki whimpered on the ground. Annis knelt in the mossy earth by his side. The dog gave a small whimper. She could see bite marks on his side. The dog had tried to save her and had nearly lost his life in the process. She should be the one bleeding on the ground, but instead it was the dog.

He couldn't die, not after all he had done.

'I think he might live with the right attention.' She started to tear strips from the bottom of her linen shift. 'If I bind his leg and then we keep him quiet for a few days, he might regain his strength.'

'This glade is far too open. It is impossible to defend.'

Haakon's voice was hard. 'We are in danger here. We must go. Come away now.'

Annis glanced up at him and saw the stern planes of his face. He was looking at her as if this was all her fault. She had not asked for him to come after her. Or for Floki to charge forward. The dog had saved her life. And now she had a duty to this dog.

'You can't let this dog die. He saved my life. He tried to save yours. He needs our help...please.'

Haakon made an exasperated noise as he wiped his sword, staining the green moss red. 'The wolves will regroup and be back. They can smell the blood. Floki cannot walk on that leg. He will not last long.'

'Maybe it would be better if I stayed then, faced them down if they return.' Annis started to probe the wound, and the dog gave a small yelp.

'Are you being a fool?' His hands gripped her arm in a vice. 'I did not come out here to find you just to let you die. Are you going to let this dog's sacrifice be in vain? Stay here and all that he suffered on your account will go to waste.'

Annis pressed her hands into her thighs. She had to control her temper. Shouting back would do no good. She counted slowly, breathed a deep cleansing breath and regained control of her temper. 'Help me to save this dog. Take him with us. He is a good dog.'

'Don't you think I know that?' Haakon's voice was quieter. He knelt by the dog and gave him a stroke. 'I raised him from a puppy, Annis. But it is a bad wound.'

'I can save him. Give me a chance. Let me bind his wounds.'

Haakon sighed and slung the dog over his shoulder, and started to march off, not towards the road, but deeper into the woods. Annis ran after him, struggling to keep up with his long footsteps as he appeared to be heading deeper and deeper into the wolves' territory.

'Where are you going? The road is the other way.' Annis gestured with her hand. Had the fight confused Haakon? 'Are you planning to carry him all the way back to the hall?'

She wasn't ready to go back there yet. She refused to go back to the darkness of her prison.

'I know where we are.' Haakon's pace did not slacken. 'There is an old woodcutter's hut up here.'

'What good will that do us?' Annis glanced over her shoulder, half-convinced that the bushes were moving and eyes were following her. She put a hand on Haakon's elbow.

'We can shelter there. You can attend Floki. Maybe you are correct and he will not go to Valhalla.' His voice broke slightly. 'For surely if ever a dog deserves to go there, it is Floki for his bravery.'

'How do you know that there is a hut?'

Haakon swung around. His blue gaze pierced her. 'This is my land, and I know every inch of it, every rock, every tree.'

Annis stopped. Despite all her running and scrambling, she had not managed to even leave the estate. How pitiful her escape attempt must seem. She put her hand to the collar she wore. 'Not every rock, surely.'

Haakon smiled, and adjusted the dog's weight on his shoulder. 'I like to think so, but I know the hut because it is where I used to run to as a small boy when I was trying to avoid being sent away. The woodcutter was a friend, a former sailing companion of my father's. He taught me about the woods and how to read them, to understand their moods.'

'And did it work?'

'My father found me.' Haakon was silent and his eyes took on a faraway look. He gave a half-smile. 'Gorm refused to hide me. He turned me over and I learnt to accept my punishment like a man. I left this land without a backward glance, and in my heart I swore I would return and I would make this land mine. It was ten long years before I returned, but I did return.'

'How old were you when you left?'

'Seven.'

Annis bit her lip. What lessons had Haakon learnt? Did he understand her desire to go home? He had to.

'And was it the same when you came back?'

'The same as I remembered?' Haakon gave a quick shake of his head. 'No, things had changed. My father was ill. He had neglected the land. Much had to be done. Much work still has to be done. My people deserve it.'

'But—' Annis wanted to find out more '—it is prosperous now. I have seen the grain stores, and the animals.'

'Come on, keep up. We have a way to go before we are safe and behind a bolted door. Remind me to tell you the tale some winter night.' Haakon strode ahead, a look of determination on his face.

Annis started to follow but her legs refused to obey. She sank down. 'Please wait. I need to rest.'

'You can rest at the hut.' His voice was uncompromising. 'We must go on.'

'But everything hurts.' She hated the way her voice cracked and the tears that sprung to her eyes.

He stopped. 'Did you get bitten?'

She shook her head. 'Miraculously, none of the wolves touched me. The skirt of my shift tore slightly when I jumped from the tree, but I need to catch my breath. I must rest.'

She put her hand against a birch tree, feeling the coolness of the bark beneath her palm.

'Then you can walk. When you get to the hut, you can rest, but we are in danger here in the open. Haven't you caused enough trouble already?'

She wanted to open her mouth and pour out the story about Ingrid and Aelfric, but what good would that do? He would probably only blame her. She wanted to put the whole episode behind her. She had tried to escape and had failed.

'Who else do you have looking for me?'

'I am the only one.' He shifted Floki to his other shoulder. 'Now walk, because I cannot carry you both. It is over the next rise, I promise.'

'I never asked you to.' Annis forced her feet to move. She would make it to the hut on her own. Then she would decide what she would do.

Chapter Twelve

❧

As Haakon had promised, a wooden hut came into view. The struggle had ended. She half-ran, half-stumbled towards the building. Her fingers fumbled with the catch.

'It's bolted shut.' She wanted to drop to her knees and weep. Four strong walls and a door, but locked, barred against intruders. Safety so near and yet it was beyond her grasp. But after all she had been through, tears seemed very far away.

'Allow me. There is a slight trick to it.' Haakon opened the door to the hut with ease.

Although small and compact, it was snug and dry. A pile of dry leaves graced the central fire, and a snow-white owl peered out from a corner. It hooted twice, before flapping its wings and disappearing through the smoke hole.

Annis collapsed on the floor as her limbs started to shake. The enormity of what she had been through washed over her. Every time she closed her eyes, she saw the snarling fangs of the wolf pack. She wrapped her arms about her knees, resting her head.

Haakon placed Floki down and shut the door, bolting it from within. A solid, reassuring sound. 'We will stay here. The door is thick birch. It will keep out the wolves and other predators. You have nothing to fear here.'

'I am so cold, so very cold, now.' Her teeth began to chatter.

'Luckily, I keep my fire-steel, flint and touchwood hanging from my belt.' Haakon pulled the items from his belt. 'The hut will soon be warm. I have a bit of bread and cheese as well that we can share.'

Food. Annis's mouth watered. Never had dry bread and cheese sounded so good. She waved a hand. 'After I examine Floki.'

'You are in no fit state. Floki's bleeding has stopped. Eat. Get warm. The shock will wear off in time.'

'I will still need to examine him.'

'Later. You need to recover first. You will examine Floki when I say so and not before.'

Annis's protest died on her lips. Haakon was correct. Her hands trembled too much. She would do more harm than good in this state.

'Thank you.' She reached out a hand. 'Thank you for everything.'

He shrugged out of his leather tunic. 'Do you believe me now? These woods are far from safe. Your best chance of survival is with me.'

'Are you going to tie me up again?' Annis tilted her head. She wanted to ask him why he had come searching for her. Was it because he had been frightened for her safety or because he could not stand the thought of losing a valuable captive? Her lips twisted upwards. It did not really matter. Without his help, she would now be dead, and her body torn to shreds, a possibility that did not bear thinking about.

'If I tie you up, you will not be able to heal Floki.' Haakon ran his hand through his hair. 'And where would you run, Annis? Do you want to die amongst the wolves? It is not a pretty death. We were lucky back there. Neither of us was severely injured.'

Annis put a hand to her head and tried to think. Everything

was spinning out of control again. She knew she should hate being recaptured, but it came as a relief. She did not have the tools to survive in this wilderness. But there again, what sort of life was it to be treated in the way she had been treated? And all she wanted to do was to rest her head against his chest.

'I thought I was going to end my days, particularly when the horse threw us.'

'We won. We're alive and that's all that counts.' Haakon briefly gave her shoulder a squeeze before going to gather some sticks from the corner of the room.

'Thanks to Floki.' She leant over and gave the dog a stroke. Floki licked her hand. 'How did you know I was gone?'

'I discovered Ingrid in the pigsty. She was not best pleased at being tied up.'

'She came to give me food. Perhaps I was unkind to her.' Annis bit her lip. Should she tell him about what she had learnt? Who the true culprit was? Or was it really important after what she had been through? 'It seemed the only way at the time. I had to leave.'

'How did you manage it?'

'My father made me learn how to bring down a man. He believed in being prepared for everything.'

'Nothing you use regularly.'

'Never had to before.' She gave a quick smile. 'I hope never to have to again.'

'It is good to know that your father cared about your safety.'

'My life was not the same after he died and my mother re-married.' Annis ran her hands through her hair. 'He cared about me. I was his only child to live past infancy.'

'I have sent Ingrid away.' Haakon's words resounded off the walls of the hut.

Haakon started to build the fire, methodically placing the sticks. His back was turned away from her. Annis pressed her hands together. Had he sent Ingrid away because he thought she had helped Annis?

'Sent her away? Why?' The words escaped before she had a chance to think.

'She was the woman Aelfric seduced. She gave him the key to the chest.' Haakon turned towards Annis then, white lipped and with anguished eyes. 'You protested your innocence and I failed to believe it. It has preyed on my mind. I ask for your forgiveness.'

Annis's throat tightened. She could do nothing more than nod. No sense of triumph, just an aching weariness. 'Continue.'

Haakon recounted all Ingrid had told him. Annis found it hard to feel pity for the woman. She had brought this all on herself, she and that false monk.

'I suppose he put the cross on my bedding to remind me of my duty,' Annis said with a bitter twist to her mouth. 'He told me that I am a wicked woman.'

'Wicked?' Haakon raised his eyebrow. 'I would have called you many things before I called you wicked, Annis. Why would this man call you that?'

'I have done things that I am not supposed to. I should be dead. He told me that.' Annis crossed her arms over her chest. 'And all the time, he was seducing Ingrid and whispering falsehoods. He put everyone in danger.'

'What did you and he argue about this morning?'

Annis put her hand to her head. Only this morning? A lifetime ago, surely. Despite everything, Haakon had come after her and saved her life. She owed him the truth. 'He wanted to escape, offered to let me join him, but I refused. I told him to think of the others. Obviously he didn't. Ingrid thought I looked heated and suggested I take a walk to the lake. I didn't know you were there, or that Aelfric would escape while…while we were together.'

'He was concerned solely about himself, Annis.'

'My uncle had tremendous respect for him. Aelfric was expected to achieve great things. My uncle planned to send him to Rome. He appeared so pious. He made me feel dirty.' Annis pressed her knuckles into the bridge of her nose. She wanted to explain it, to make Haakon understand why she had run away. Her voice cracked slightly. 'He made me feel as if I should have died.'

'What he told you was a lie as well,' Haakon said. His eyes softened, but he kept his hands at his sides. If he had made one gesture, she would have been in his arms, but as it was, all she could do was kneel by Floki. 'You have done nothing to be ashamed of. You survived.'

'But…but…' Annis tried to think of a logical argument, one which would explain why Aelfric was right, but she wanted to believe Haakon. Surviving was not evil.

'It would be a great loss to the world if you were dead. You have a great power to heal. You saved Thrand from permanent disfigurement.' Haakon knelt by Floki's side and gave him a stroke. 'Who would save Floki, if you were dead? Better to concentrate on the living, than to berate yourself for not having died.'

Annis turned her attention to the dog. The gash on his hind leg was deep; as she touched it, the clotting fell away and it began to bleed profusely again. Annis shivered slightly as she thought of how Floki had shaken the wolf by its throat.

All she had to do was to stop the bleeding and bind the wound. All! She knew how much she owed this animal. She had to save him.

But how? She tore another strip of cloth from the bottom of her shift, and applied pressure, but still the wound oozed.

Annis glanced about her. She needed something to stop the bleeding, but the tiny room was bare except for the leaves. Haakon had bent down and had his fire-steel in one hand and the charred touchwood in the other.

'Can I have a piece of your touchwood before you put it away? I need it for Floki.'

'You may, but what good can the touchwood do?' Haakon broke a bit of the soft charcoaled fungus off. She caught the piece in her palm, being careful not to touch Haakon. But the heat of his fingers brushed her, sending a spark shuddering through her. 'It is excellent for lighting fires and that is about all.'

Annis crushed the fungus between her fingers and rubbed it into the wound on Floki's hind leg. The bleeding stopped almost at once. Then she started to bind it up. Small, simple movements, anything to keep her mind off the large man who was standing so close to her. 'This should keep it from bleeding as much. I have seen it used to good effect before.'

Haakon nodded. He made the spark leap from his ornate fire-steel to the touchwood and then, after he had captured the spark, to the twigs in the fireplace. The fire-steel, different from the Northumbrian ones, was curved and decorated with serpents, and he hung it back on his belt along with the flint he had used. The fire crackled and grew as the dry wood caught readily, filling the room with light and heat.

Annis finished binding up Floki's wounds and then sat back on her heels, holding out her hands to the fire. 'It is odd. I thought this morning that the day was warm, but now my entire body is cold.'

Haakon resisted the urge to bury his face in her shorn hair and beg her forgiveness again. He knew it had been his jealousy and fear that had driven him to punish her. How could he begin to explain how it had chilled him to find her surrounded, battling for her very life? Then, afterwards, her first concern had been for his dog.

'Your ordeal is over.' He held out the bread and cheese— a peace offering of sorts.

She took them and buried her white teeth in the loaf, eating as if she had not fed in days. He thought she might eat it all, but she carefully left half for him.

'I survived thus far,' she said, handing the remainder back. 'It remains to be seen what happens to me next.'

'You will take no further harm from me, I promise.'

She turned anguished eyes to him, and he drew her up and into his arms, intent on capturing her lips. He winced slightly as his ribs began to ache in earnest. A small gasp of pain escaped his lips. She turned her head and drew back.

'You're hurt. You should have said. I would have helped.'

He glanced down and saw a few dark stains on his under-tunic. 'A bite to my arm and a few scratches, that is all. The wolves fared much worse than I. You will not need any more touchwood for me.'

'Take off your undertunic. Let me be the judge of that. I am the healer.' She nodded towards where Floki slumbered.

He obeyed and took off his undertunic, standing there. 'You see. It is nothing to worry about. I have suffered far worse in my time.'

'They are not deep, you are right. You will live. A few days' discomfort and some bruising.' Her hand hovered over the deepest wound.

He held her hand and stopped it from going farther. He wanted her. But he knew he had to take it slowly. If she touched him, he knew his desire for her would flare as brightly and fiercely as the fire now burned in the hearth.

Shock remained etched on her face. He must be patient.

He wanted no accusations that he had taken advantage of her. He wanted to unleash the passion that he knew lay deep within her. He wanted to ensure she never felt ashamed again. She had to listen to the desire in her body. But for that to happen, he had to take it slowly, to build her trust.

'There is no need to fuss. My leather tunic took the brunt of the attack.'

Annis's hand dropped to her side. 'I had no idea. It must have hurt to carry Floki as far as you did.'

'What, a little dog like Floki?' Haakon glanced at the rather large elkhound who lifted his head and thumped his tail at the sound of his name. There had been a moment in their tramp through the woods that he had thought to carry both Annis and the dog, but one look at her determined face had dissuaded him. 'I could have carried him twice as far. Shall I demonstrate?'

'No jokes.'

'It is no joking matter. I want that dog to live as much as you do. It was necessary to move as quickly as possible to a place of safety.' Haakon ran his hand through his hair. 'We will rest here until Floki is better.'

'And if I want to leave before then…' Her eyes were luminous in the firelight.

'You want to live. To go south over the mountains on your own will lead to certain death.' He reached out and touched Annis's hand. 'There is always the promise of the ransom arriving.'

He pressed his lips together. He hated to think about losing her, as he knew he must when the ransom came. She readjusted Floki's bandages, her head bent, concentrating on the job at hand.

'There is always that.'

'It will come sooner than you expect.' He put his hand on her shoulder. He did not dare tell her how much he longed for the ransom to take its time. He had come close to losing her today, and he intended to trust his instinct for the rest of the time they were together.

'Are you sure of that?' She gave a little yawn.

'It is the truth. You must sleep. Come, lean against me. I will keep you warm.'

She put her hands under her chin and muffled a yawn. Her

eyes were bruised and sunken. 'I will sleep here next to Floki, in case the bleeding starts again.'

'What are you afraid of, Annis—me or your own desire?'

There was no answer but the popping of the fire. He glanced over and saw Annis's eyes had closed and she had fallen into an exhausted sleep. Haakon put his leather tunic under her head, smoothed away her hair, and placed a kiss between her brows. There was much he wanted to say, but it would have to wait.

Annis opened her eyes. Sun streamed through the smoke hole, lighting the hut. She stretched and realised with a start that the hut was empty. She was alone except for the peacefully sleeping Floki. Annis brought her knees up to her chest and wrapped her arms about them.

Haakon had come after her—not his men, but him. It meant that he might feel some desire for her. But he had not tried to kiss her…and she wanted to feel his lips against hers again.

Haakon appeared in the doorway, closing it with a click behind him. His linen undertunic moulded to his chest, reminding Annis of the muscles that lay beneath. He moved slowly and deliberately as if his muscles ached. She watched him, wanting to hate him, but finding that instead her attention was caught by the movement of his hands and his wrists. Her body desired him.

She knew then it had not been the punishment, nor the servitude that she had tried to run away from, but her desire for him. And if that made her wicked, she would have to live it with it, because she did want to live. She only hoped he still saw her as something more than a captive.

'I have been out foraging for breakfast.' His eyes twinkled. 'You were sound asleep with gentle snores. I saw no reason to wake you.'

'I do not snore.'

'It must have been Floki then.' Haakon gave a short laugh.

At the sound of his name, Floki lifted his head and thumped his tail.

'It must have been,' Annis agreed with a laugh as she checked Floki's leg. This time the bandage had held. 'Floki appears better. The bleeding has stopped.'

'Thanks to you.'

'And the touchwood.'

'That as well.' Haakon touched a finger to the side of his nose. 'Now, will you have some strawberries? Or do I eat them all myself?'

'Strawberries?'

'Truly.' He opened his hand and Annis saw the tiny red berries glistening there. 'Later in the season there are cloudberries, and they are a feast for the gods—orange and delicious.'

'I have never tried cloudberries.'

'You will. They will be ready in a few weeks' time.'

There was a difference about Haakon today. He seemed younger, more carefree. He seemed at ease, nothing at all like the warrior she had seen in the last few days, and very much like the man she remembered from the lake. Who was he? Did she dare trust him? He had apologised, something Selwyn would never have done.

'When are we going to leave?' Annis asked. 'Surely you are not planning to remain at this hut until the cloudberries are ready.'

'Not today. Floki needs a day or two to recover. He will have to walk most of the way. It is too far to carry him.' Haakon's eyes grew serious. 'The horse has vanished. More than likely back to the hall, but I can't count on it. My men will begin to search for us soon.'

'You could return and I could stay here. With Floki.'

Haakon's eyes narrowed. 'I think not. We shall go together.'

'I will be here when you return,' Annis said quietly. 'Yesterday's brush with death was close enough for me. I will wait and hope for the ransom.'

'That is no answer.'

'I will stay. I owe you a life-debt as you once owed me.' She put a hand on her stomach. 'My stomach has forgotten the bread from yesterday, and the strawberries smell delicious.'

'It is my food that tempts you.' Haakon dropped a handful into her lap. 'I shall have to add it to my seduction technique.'

Seduction. The word sent a shiver of pleasure down her spine. Did he mean that, after all they had been through, he wanted her? A warm pit opened inside her, but she hesitated, refused to give in. To ask Haakon would be to know. What if she had read the signs wrong? She focussed all her attention on the sweet berries.

'That was good,' she said, licking her fingers.

'Juice has dribbled down your chin.' He reached over and rubbed a spot, much as a parent might do to a child.

Annis's mouth ached. She lifted her face to give him an invitation, but he made no move to lower his lips. He appeared to be searching for something in her face.

'Shall we play a game?' he asked, his voice becoming brisk. 'To pass the time?'

'What sort of game? You cannot have brought a *tafl* board along with you.' She tried a laugh, trying to keep her heart from racing.

'Gorm scratched a game board on the floor over here. And we can use pebbles for counters. Gorm and I used to play every time I visited.'

'If you would like…' She looked at the board and at once knew the game. Nine Men's Morris. The object was to get three in a row and take your opponent's pieces off the board. It would keep her from begging him to kiss her. He certainly had shown no hesitation before. Other than simple meaningless touches, he had not tried to kiss her. And she had discovered that she very much wanted him to. She wanted to feel his hands against her skin. And if he wasn't going to, she would have to try to seduce him.

'Are you afraid?'

'I faced down wolves—how could I be afraid of a simple game?' She gave a light laugh, but her insides trembled. She had to find out now if he desired her. Or was he simply interested in the ransom she would bring? She knew he had desired her once, but he had not tried to touch her since they had come to this hut. She had to take the risk. She had to discover the truth. Her breath caught in her throat. 'Shall we play for a wager?'

'I had thought simply to play, but if you insist…' He leant forward. 'What are your terms? What do you wish to wager?'

Annis ran her tongue over her lips. 'If I win, you must do me a favour.'

'It depends on the favour.'

'You will know if I win,' Annis countered.

'I warn you that I will not let you go easily.'

'Not that sort of favour.' She swallowed hard. 'Something else.'

'It sounds intriguing, but what happens if you lose?'

'Then I will obey you. I will do you a favour.'

'Done,' he said. He leant forward. 'I intend to win, Valkyrie.'

'As do I.'

He laid out the pieces and Annis made her first move. Her hand trembled slightly as she placed the counter. Haakon placed his counters and the match began, ebbing and flowing between the two.

Annis forced her mind to concentrate on the board, and not on the way Haakon was sitting or the glimpse of his throat where his tunic gaped open.

There were six pieces remaining on the board. The next

person to get three in a row would be able to remove the final piece.

Annis studied the board. It looked simple, too simple. She moved a piece. Haakon countered. She was able to move her third piece in line. 'I won, I won. I have made the final mill.'

Haakon looked at the board and counted on his fingers. 'Impossible. I haven't lost at Morris since before I left for Charlemagne's court.'

'Are you doubting the outcome?' Annis tilted her head and peeped at him from under her lashes, savouring her triumph.

'No.' He inclined his head. 'What do you want to do? I am yours to command.'

'I want you to make love to me,' she whispered quickly before she lost her nerve. She had to know.

She watched his face, waiting for any sign. Nothing but a slight flaring of his nostrils. She dropped her gaze to the board. Her hands shook as she started to put away the counters. She'd make a joke of it, pretend that she had teased him. A slight lump grew in her throat. She had thought—but she was wrong.

'Ah, Annis, we needn't have played a game for that.' Haakon ran a finger down her cheek, lifting her chin so she met his eyes that glowed with an inner fire. 'I have wanted to ever since we arrived, but my ribs are bruised.'

'I understand.' Annis kept her chin up. She felt foolish. She should have known that he would have a simple explanation. She was new at this game. She had never been any good at seduction. This was his way of politely letting her down. She forced her lips upwards to hide her chagrin. 'I see. It was a suggestion. Let me think a while and I will come up with another favour.'

'I don't think you do.' He paused and put his hands behind his head. 'If you want to make love, you will need to make love to me. It needs to come from you. I will not have it said that I forced you.'

She leant forward and gave his mouth a quick kiss, butterfly-like, then sat back on her heels, waiting. 'There, you see.'

'You will have to do better than that.' His eyes became serious. 'Annis, you said that you were ashamed before. I have no wish to make you feel that way. Show me you desire me.'

'I do.' Annis pressed her hands against her cheeks, feeling the heat rise. She had explained it wrong. 'I feel no shame when I am with you.'

'Prove it. Make love to me.' His voice became a silken rasp. 'Pleasure me in the way you want to be pleasured.'

It was a test. But if she didn't do this now, Annis had no idea when she would have another chance. She pressed her palms against her thighs, breathing deeply, trying to think how she would go about it. The first step she had to take.

'Lie back.'

Haakon raised his eyebrows at her tone and lay back on his leather tunic. 'Like this?'

'Exactly.'

'What do you intend?' His voice was a husky whisper.

'You will see. I will take your challenge and prove you wrong. No one is forcing me to do anything.' Annis trailed a hand down his chest. She watched his face change, become hooded with pleasure as her knuckles drew small circles around his nipples.

She bent her head and captured his lips, drinking deep. Her tongue darted forward. His mouth parted, allowing her to enter, and she feasted.

'Is this the sort of thing you had in mind?' she murmured against his lips.

'Hmm, possibly.' His hand came around and cupped her face, holding her there. 'Shall we try it again, just to be sure?'

Warmth began to grow in her body as she felt his hands

slide down her back and pull her on top of him. She could feel the hardness of him, pressing into her. She knew, if she let him, he would take control.

'Can you do better than this?' he whispered, his lip tracing the line along her jaw. 'Exactly how did you intend to seduce me?'

She pushed against his chest. 'I believe we agreed that I was in charge.'

'And so we did.' His hands stopped, fell away. 'What do you want me to do?'

'Enjoy.' She knew suddenly what she had to do. She wanted to prove that she could give as well as receive pleasure. Her late husband had always used her for the briefest of times, asking for nothing and giving very little. She knew she was capable of giving much. She knew she could do to Haakon what he had done to her back at the lake. A surge of power went through her. She was capable. It was her hands, her body that was doing this to him.

She levered her body off his and slowly pulled his undertunic up until his naked chest was revealed. The cuts and bruises from yesterday were not as pronounced, but still clearly visible. She placed her mouth against the hollow of his throat and tasted his skin. Then she took her time, pressing open-mouthed kisses down his body, lingering on his chest.

He groaned in the back of his throat and his pupils darkened to a shining black with pleasure.

Her fingers undid the buttons and hooked the waistband of his trousers and slowly pulled them down. Inch by inch, savouring each bit of skin.

Then the full glory of him was revealed.

She drew in a breath at the sight of him. The old Annis would have been afraid, but the woman she had become wanted more. She put out her finger. Tentatively touched. Hot velvet steel. A sword within a silken sheath. Her hand curled round, holding him. Pulsing in her hand, making her ache inside.

'Annis.'

She put a finger to his lips, quietening him, but he lifted his hands and captured her breasts. She felt the fire grow within her, the overwhelming ache between her legs. She needed him in her, but not yet.

'One of us is overdressed.' His voice held husky laughter.

'I know,' she whispered in his ear but made no move to take off her shift. Instead she trailed her mouth across his jaw where soft bristles were starting to grow, down the line of his neck, his chest, following the faint sprinkling of hair lower still until her lips touched his dark, crisp curls.

His hands buried themselves in her head, holding her there, the heat of him rising up and enveloping her, rousing some deep carnal fire within her.

Then she took the hot tip of him into her mouth, traced the silken head with her tongue. Felt him stiffen further, tasted a drop of him.

'Please.' His hand tore at her shift. 'Take me inside you.'

She lifted her head, rose up, pulled her shift off. His hands grasped her hips, guided her and settled her firmly against him. Her body opened to welcome the full length of him. Deep and deeper. Then she stilled, savouring the sensation.

'You call the time,' he whispered. 'Take control.'

Take control. A great rush of heat went through her, consumed her. She glanced down to where they were joined. Man and woman, but one being.

She lifted her body, felt him slide within her. Then slowly she sank down again, taking all of him within her. His hands tightened on her bottom, caressing her back, urging her on.

She moved her hips, leaning forward so that her nipples rubbed his chest. The points tightened further into a delicious ache. Faster and faster, winding her tighter and tighter until the ache increased beyond all bearing. She wanted this.

He drove deep within her, as a white, hot shuddering engulfed her, engulfed them both. She knew she cried out and heard his answering shout. Then she rested her head on his chest as his arms came around to hold her close.

Later, much later, Annis woke to see Haakon watching her. They were still joined and he had a strange expression in his eyes. A gentle hand smoothed the curls off her forehead.

She breathed his name, tightened her arms about his neck and felt him begin to grow hard again. Haakon desired her for who she was, and not what she could bring to the relationship. Her back arched and she wrapped her legs around him, beckoning him farther in, closing her eyes to deepen the sensation.

'When we return to the hall, I will name you as my concubine,' he said against her ear.

Annis's eyes flew open, widened. She slid away from him and sat up. 'What…what are you asking me?'

'Annis? You do understand what I am offering?' Haakon remained still. 'I want you to be my acknowledged concubine. You will sleep in my bed.'

'I understand,' she said and her breath hissed through her lips. 'It seems so quick, so sudden.'

'Did you think I would simply take my pleasure and go?'

'You did the last time.' Her laugh sounded shaky to her ears.

'Annis, I came after you—not one of my men.'

'I know that. I was pleased.'

'Everyone at the hall will know it as well. It is best to make it official, for me to formally acknowledge you.'

'For me to be called your mistress, your concubine. I hadn't expected it.'

'You seduced me.'

'I did, but…'

'What are you objecting to? You appear to like my touch.' Haakon caught her calf and ran his hand down the skin, sending flames of warmth through her body. 'I spilt my seed inside you, Annis. Twice now. Children are a possibility and I do not run from my responsibilities.'

Her mouth dropped open, but she quickly closed it. Children.

She stood, pulling away from him, fixing her eyes on the side of the hut. She had no thought for the future. This had been all about the moment. 'I understand the honour you do me. Tove and the others explained to me the difference between an acknowledged concubine and a woman a man lies with. I shall sleep in your bed, and any children I bear you, you will recognise as yours.'

'And I will bring them up as befits the son or daughter of an Jaarl. I will not have it said that I do not fulfil my obligations.'

Annis put her hands to her cheeks, tried to ignore the sudden icy cold that swept through her. 'But when my ransom comes, I want to be free to go and I want to take any children with me.'

He dropped his hand, moved away from her, but his eyes blazed with a blue flame. 'We will discuss it then.'

Annis pressed her fingers together. She had to get this right. She knew her future depended on this. If she was going back to the hall, she wanted to be free from the threat of Guthrun.

As Haakon said, they could discuss children if it did happen.

Her womb had not quickened with Selwyn, but she knew of at least three boys and a girl in the village outside the castle who bore his eyes and nose. It was her fault, not his, as he pointed out many times before he died.

She pushed away all thoughts of children.

It was not going to happen. She refused to borrow trouble, but if it did, she knew leaving would be impossible.

'Annis? Your brow is furrowed. And you have not given me an answer.'

'Is it?' She hastily made her lips turn up into a smile. The hardest smile she had ever made. She, the high-born lady, the wronged wife of a persistent philanderer, had become a concubine. She recalled Selwyn's last mistress's words—no man would willingly lie with her. Her only desirability lay in her wealth. Annis knew that for a spiteful lie, but there was a kernel of truth. How long would Haakon's affection last? Selwyn's had changed with the wind.

She couldn't think about that. Her past was past, her future an unknown. The only thing she knew was now. Her ears buzzed and she felt faint. Annis closed her eyes and willed the whole thing to be a dream.

'Annis?'

Her eyes flashed open. Haakon wanted an answer and wanted it now. He deserved an answer.

Whichever way she answered, her position would become more precarious than when she had sat in the sty, not less.

But how could she refuse?

Annis swallowed hard. She had given him every reason to think that she wanted this position. She had seduced him. She had to accept the consequences.

The walls of the hut wavered, pressing in on her. Haakon stared down at her.

'Annis, give me your answer.'

She leant forward, took his face in her hands, refused to think any more. 'Yes, I will be your concubine.'

Chapter Thirteen

'We have company,' Annis said the next morning as she came back from bathing in the stream near the hut. She shielded her eyes. 'Six men on horses.'

Haakon moved to her side. His hand was on the pommel of his sword, ready. He squinted into the sun and his shoulders relaxed. 'Our idyll has ended, Valkyrie. It is time to return to the hall. Thrand has found us.'

Annis thought she detected a note of disappointment in his voice. Or it could be a trick of her mind, reflecting her own mood? Haakon's face showed only hard planes.

Suddenly, everything had changed. She and Haakon had established a fragile truce here. She had to hope it would last. She had to hope his words about her being his concubine until the ransom arrived were not spoken solely in passion. She had seen how quickly passion faded.

All the doubts that she had pushed aside in the past day came rushing back. 'Is that a good thing or a bad thing?'

'It is a necessary thing.'

She watched him walk towards Thrand and his men with a steady, assured gait and without a backward glance. Her throat constricted. She knew it would be very easy to fall in love with this man and love was not part of their bargain. He had not offered to make her his concubine before she had made love to him. She knew that.

She wanted his touch, but more than that she wanted him to feel something for her.

She had to hope that his desire for her lasted. Selwyn had changed his mistresses nearly as often as he bathed. All she knew of Haakon was that he had none besides her—for now.

The six horses covered the distance at an easy pace and Thrand swung off and greeted Haakon with much thumping on his back. Haakon put aside thoughts of Annis and concentrated on his brother. Thrand's face had improved vastly since Haakon had last seen him. All that remained of the burn was a faint red puckering in the middle of his cheek.

'At last, we find you, Haakon. Your horse arrived back at the hall yesterday—bloodied and footsore. Guthrun feared the worst.'

'Has she already lit the funeral pyre for me then?' Haakon gave a short laugh. He could well picture the scene. Guthrun, wringing her hands, declaring what an awful tragedy it was, but in the meantime weighing up the situation to her best advantage.

Thrand put his hands in the air. 'You know my mother. Sometimes I think she will not rest until she has control of the hall and the estate.'

'I believe that she has mourned for my father long enough. A new husband needs to be found.' Haakon gestured towards the sea. 'Let her cause mischief in some other hall. Her ambition has been for you, her only child. She means you no harm.'

'My thoughts exactly, and I have no wish for her to grace my hall when I have acquired it. I intend to take a wife.' Thrand leant forward and gave Haakon another thump on the back. 'I would not wish that fate on any woman.'

Haakon laughed. 'You know your mother well.'

'I see you found what you were searching for.' Thrand nodded towards Annis, who had remained in front of the hut.

'Yes, I found her.' Haakon sobered as he regarded Annis. Her hands were held demurely in front of her and her eyes were downcast. Her hair remained faintly damp from the stream. Haakon remembered the taste of her lips as they stood under the waterfall this morning.

Alive. Vital.

It was not worth thinking about what might have happened had he not found her when he did. More than once in the night, he had woken to her soft whimpers and had held her tight until the dreams passed and her face relaxed into a soft slumber.

'She seems uninjured.'

'Floki found her first, surrounded by wolves.' Haakon gestured to Floki, who limped forward on three legs. 'Thor and Odin were with me yesterday. I don't know how she would have lasted.'

'We saw the wolf carcasses and wondered.' Thrand leant down and stroked Floki's ears. 'Come, I will have more of this tale.'

'It is a tale for another time, Thrand.' Haakon gave an exaggerated stretch.

'Do you mean to claim her as your concubine?' Thrand turned back to him with a serious face. 'You know what will be said, if you don't.'

A faint breeze ruffled Annis's hair. Haakon knew what his half-brother meant. No, Annis was under his protection, and he intended on keeping her there. But he had seen her expression when he had tried to discuss what might happen when she fell pregnant.

'It is my intention. I have informed her of it.'

'You informed her and she has agreed?' Thrand raised both his eyebrows.

'She agreed. She saw the logic of it.'

Thrand put his arm around Haakon's shoulders. 'I have always found women like to be wooed. Should you need any advice…'

'I have seen your wooing and where it leads.' Haakon removed Thrand's arm. He had no wish to confide his inner-most thoughts to Thrand. His half-brother and he had become closer over the past few weeks, but his feelings for Annis were too new, too raw. 'I will woo in my own way. Annis is my concubine. She will have the proper respect in my hall.'

'There will be many who welcome it.'

'Have you discovered the monk's whereabouts?' Haakon asked, changing the subject. His mind shied away from the thought of Annis as the mistress of his hall. It was something he feared that he desired too much. Even now he wanted to hear her sweet laugh. He forced his mind to attend to more pressing issues. 'I must know if you found his body.'

'We have searched and searched, but he has thus far eluded us. You know as well as I the dangers he faces.' Thrand's face grew sober. 'I doubt he survived the first night out in the open. Yesterday we saw a group of ravens circling far to the south and you know that means some large animal has died.'

Haakon regarded Thrand. His brother was probably correct, but there was always a chance the monk had lived and against the odds would get to Thorkell.

What then? How exactly would his tale be received and by whom? Haakon was under no illusion that he had enemies at court and within the Storting. His success with the *felag* would make the other Jaarls jealous. Even last winter Bose, the king's chamberlain, had spread unfounded rumours about his relationship with Asa, Thorkell's queen.

Haakon pressed his lips together. No, Aelfric must be dead. It was all so unnecessary. If Aelfric had done as he was told, he might now be alive, instead of having Odin's ravens circling, picking at his bones. And it all too easily might have been Annis, a thought that made his blood become ice.

'You may be right, but something tells me that we might not have seen the last of this monk. If Annis is to be believed, he has survived much.'

'What would you have me do? Keep searching?'

Haakon regarded the horizon. The monk or his body could be in a hundred ravines.

'No, but keep an eye out as you and the men go about your business. Alert the outlying farms. Your mother will want her oval brooches, if nothing else.'

Haakon waited for Thrand's quick smile, but Thrand's teeth caught up his upper lip and his fists clenched slightly.

'Tell me everything. Leave nothing out, no matter how insignificant it may seem.' Haakon kept his tone measured, but his mind leapt to all the possibilities. Something other than the disappearance of Aelfric had made Thrand ill at ease.

'One of the men saw a sail on the south coast of the fjord,' Thrand said. His words tumbled out in a great torrent, picking up speed as they went on. 'It was only a brief glimpse as the boat was going away from him, catching the wind, but he said that he was sure. Red-and-white checkered, like a Bjornson clan's. It was shortly after we saw the ravens circling in the sky. I would have sent men to investigate, but your horse returned, bloodied, and the hall was in an uproar. It was imperative I find you.'

'You should know I always turn up safe and sound—eventually.' Haakon waved a hand, dismissing Thrand's fear. He wanted to strangle Thrand for finding him before he was certain of Annis, but that was life. He had other responsibilities. Always had. And one of his responsibilities was deciding risks to his people. 'It is the summer. There is nothing strange about boats going south. Not every one stops at our estate. You can remember that nasty business about the fur trader who thought to cheat me. Perhaps he did not get a good look. One boat can seem much like another.'

'I asked Harold about this. He swore it was Sigfrid's boat, taking off from the shore.'

Haakon tapped his fingers against his thighs. A chill went over him. 'Sigfrid should be many miles to the north of here. Unless…'

'Unless what? I told Harold that he was seeing things and should stop drinking so much ale.'

Haakon regarded the woods, seemingly peaceful, but hiding predators seeking to take advantage of the unwary. The Viken court had certain parallels. It was only the force of Thorkell's personality and his strong fighting arm that ensured the fragile truce between the Jaarls held.

'I believe we should prepare for a summons from Thorkell, sooner rather than later,' Haakon stated. 'If it was Sigfrid, he has gone to demand that the Storting be assembled. He will want all the nobles and freedmen to investigate Bjorn's death.'

'What are you saying—Sigfrid did not go back to the clan to mourn Bjorn? He must have done. They were very close and there is the widow to think of.' Thrand looked genuinely shocked.

'Sigfrid likes to weigh the odds. He is a born politician. He might see there is more advantage to be gained by putting his side of the story to Thorkell and asking for the Storting to assemble and judge.'

'How long until we know?' Lines of worry appeared across Thrand's face. 'A blood-feud with that clan. We would win in the end, of course, but at what cost?'

Haakon gritted his teeth. He should have thought of the consequences when Sigfrid left and prepared to go to Thorkell, despite Thorkell's request that Jaarls wait for an invitation.

'A week, ten days at most. You know as well as I do how

long it takes a boat to sail from Kaupang to here, even with a fair wind.' Haakon regarded the hut. Already the time he spent here in the hut with Annis seemed like a dream, the calm before the storm. 'We shall have to be ready to move quickly.'

'It will take at least a week to outfit a boat properly.'

'Then we do it. We shall have to hope to get to Thorkell before Sigfrid can pour poison in his ears.'

'But Thorkell will have to believe you. You made a fair offer for Bjorn's life when you sent the message stick.'

'Sigfrid has yet to reveal why he was here,' Haakon reminded his brother. 'I suspect he will not wish to settle. He will want to try to force a blood-feud, believing that he can win, but he wants to do it with the backing of Thorkell and the assembled nobles.'

'Do you think he had planned to move against you when he sailed down the fjord?'

'I no longer know what I believe any more.'

'Haakon, is there trouble?' Annis laid her hand on his arm. Her warm fingers curled slightly around his upper arm. Haakon patted them, held them against him. 'Your face has darkened like a thundercloud. Has Aelfric's body been found?'

'Nothing that need concern you.' He gave her hand one last squeeze. It was important to keep Annis safe. If Sigfrid ever discovered who had actually killed his brother, Annis's life would be in danger. She had enough to face without worrying about something that might never happen. He had made a vow to protect her until he returned her to her people. 'We need to return to the hall as soon as possible.'

Haakon issued orders to the men to make a dragging sledge for Floki as well as skin the carcasses of the wolves, then he turned to Annis. 'It is time to go. We need to leave this place while the sun is high in the sky. We have many miles to travel.'

Her eyes showed her surprise as her fingers clutched at the collar that she wore around her neck. Haakon winced when he saw the action, but she was safer if her status as a captive was known. 'There are not enough horses.'

'No, you shall ride with me.' Haakon swung himself on to a brown horse with a blond mane, then reached down and picked Annis up, settling her in front of him. She held her body stiffly upright, away from his.

Already the doubts had begun to crowd into her mind and she was pulling away. He refused to allow the whispers from Aelfric and others to return. He wanted her as she had been here, close and intimate. Haakon ran a hand down her back, saw her involuntary shiver. This passion between them would last as long as he decreed.

'Put your arms about my waist, and it will give better balance.' Haakon turned her so that his arm came either side of her and her mouth was mere inches from his. He gave Baldur a kick. The movement of the horse sent her jolting into him, her soft breasts colliding with his chest. Her arms came up and tightly clasped around his waist, hanging on as Baldur thundered through the forest.

'Why did you do that?' she said in a furious whisper as her face went a dark red, but she made no move to reposition her hips. 'What they will all think!'

'They will know when we return to the hall. I told you I intend to formally take you as my concubine. Those words were not idle after passion. I keep my promises, Annis.'

His concubine. His concubine. The words echoed in Annis's brain. She had to accept what she had become. She had been the one to seduce him. No one had held a sword to her back and forced her.

She had to live with the fact that she knew nothing about seduction and a concubine was supposed to know everything.

She should have thought, but what did she have to bargain with except her body? Once he had asked, how could she refuse? She had not wanted to refuse. It was only now, clasped in his arms as the horse's hooves thundered beneath them, that the doubt started to creep and eat away at her. What would happen to her once his passion started to fade? Would he pass her to another and, once started on this slippery slope, would she indeed become like the women she had seen at the feast—wanton and desperate?

Haakon's large body pressed against her so that with each movement of the horse she felt him move against her, his chest meeting hers, his thighs shifting under her. Annis tried to concentrate on the low rise ahead, instead of the way his body felt every time it rose to meet her. A pleasant ache was already developing in her body, an ache she knew only he could assuage.

When they returned to the hall, what would happen?

Did she dare start to care for Haakon, knowing that he might turn against her? She had nothing to bind him to her.

To start to care for him?

Her cheek scraped his linen shirt as the horse surged forward. Haakon's arm tightened around her, holding her, protecting her.

She already cared for him.

She was rapidly coming to need him, wanting to see his smile, and the way his eyes mirrored his moods. She had hated Thrand as he rode up, breaking their idyll.

She wanted Haakon, not only his body, but also his mind. He was pleasant to talk to. But was that enough? She had seen how many mistresses Selwyn had possessed in their marriage. Why should Haakon be any different? And the worst thing was that she wanted him to be different. She wanted him to care for her. But she knew she had to hide her feelings. He had enough power over her already.

* * *

All too soon, the large wooden building appeared on the other side of the lake. She had not thought to see it again, but a lump came into her throat.

Guthrun's eyes narrowed appreciably when she saw who was in Haakon's arms and she made a clucking noise in the back of her throat.

'I recovered our missing captive,' Haakon said. He allowed her to slip from his arms without even a reassuring squeeze of his hand.

Annis hastily tried to pull the skirt of her torn shift lower. She was aware that it revealed far more of her calf than strictly necessary. She forced her hands to still and faced Guthrun with her head held high.

'Indeed.' Guthrun made a clicking noise of disapproval. 'At least this one is alive. I suppose it is too much to ask that she return the oval brooches.'

'You know who took the oval brooches, Guthrun. You are attempting to cause trouble. I will not have my hall disrupted in this way.'

'I have done nothing of the sort.' Guthrun's voice rose to a high-pitched squeak of indignation. 'I merely wanted to remind you of what I have lost. And your horse returned all bloodied. We had no idea what had happened to you! The trouble this woman has caused. Ingrid has had to leave in tears.'

'Enough!'

'But I have much more to say.' Guthrun released a stream of complaints—both real and imagined.

Haakon tapped his fingers against his thigh during the speech, allowed Guthrun to finish. Then he cleared his throat, and spoke slowly and clearly like one might to a child or someone very hard of hearing.

'This woman is my concubine, Guthrun, and I will have

you treat her well. I wish her to be shown the respect she is due. Is that understood?'

Guthrun gave the tiniest of nods.

He turned to Thrand and started discussing farm matters as if Guthrun mattered very little in the grand scheme of things.

Guthrun blanched slightly, and Annis heard the excited whispering of the women behind Guthrun. Tove, in particular, wore a very smug expression.

'I must congratulate you, Annis.' Guthrun came over to her with a sickly sweet smile. 'It would seem that you offer my stepson something that the Viken women do not. A touch of the exotic. I am sure not one of my maids had ever thought to play the runaway slave before. You are riding high, but how quickly men can change.'

Annis flinched as if her face had been slapped, but she held her head high. She refused to allow Guthrun to see how deeply the remark had cut her soul. She glanced at Haakon, hoping for a quick and easy denial to fall from his mouth, but he was engrossed in a conversation with Thrand.

She tightened her jaw. The last thing she wanted was a fight with Guthrun. It would allow the woman to win. It would be far better if she ignored her, pretended that she wasn't there.

'I wish to see the monks, Haakon,' she said, pulling on his tunic until he looked at her. 'To tell them Aelfric has not been found and of his probable demise.'

'If you wish....' Haakon put a hand under her elbow. 'There is no need for you to do this. Nothing is certain.'

'There is every need. I wish to. I have to. I heard Thrand tell you about the ravens.' She clasped her hands together to stop them trembling. Above all she wanted to be the one to tell them of her new position. It was better if it came from her. She wanted to make them see that she was not ashamed. 'Remember, I have faced a wolf pack. The monks are hardly that.'

'Very well, if you feel you must, but afterwards I wish to show you your new quarters.'

Her new quarters. She pressed her lips together. She had not really considered that. Instead of whispers, everyone would know when Haakon had had enough of her company, every quarrel would be dissected. Very few secrets remained so for long in this hall. She wondered what the monks would make of it. Would they, like Aelfric, condemn her? Or would they understand?

She stood still, waiting. A little breeze ruffled her hair, making it stand on end. She had to admit that this style was much cooler than her previous long hair. The monks were brought out. Like her, they all wore collars, but they appeared no worse for their ordeal. They marched forward with their heads held high and their step firm.

'You have returned,' the eldest monk said.

'Haakon Haroldson saved me from a pack of wolves.'

'It is good that you have returned. We prayed you would be safe, as we continue to pray for our lost brother.'

'There is no news of Aelfric.'

The monks bowed their heads. 'We still hope that our brother may be returned to us, but he chose his own path. He has become one of the *gyrovagi,* the lost ones.'

'Haakon has made me his concubine.' She waited for the word of condemnation, the sharp intakes of breath and pursing of lips. The monks stood and regarded her, their faces sorrowful if anything.

'We will pray for you.' The monk put out his hand. 'My sister, it is for God to judge and not us. You have power. Use it wisely.'

Annis nodded as her throat closed tightly. She had not expected that. And now it would seem that the monks were counting on her to use her position. But how? She had no power to change their lot.

The monks were led away, out to work again.

'I cannot have idle hands,' Haakon said, putting his hand about her waist. 'They have had a fright. I expect them to work hard until their ransom arrives.'

Annis pressed her hands together. She had expected the monks to react as Aelfric had, but they hadn't. The monk had implied that she might be able to do good in her position.

'But is it necessary for them to wear their collars?' Annis asked.

'I have already lost one.' A muscle in Haakon's jaw jumped. 'These men are valuable to me. I have no wish to lose another. I had no wish to put them in collars. Aelfric forced my hand.'

'You will sleep here now,' Haakon said, gesturing to the raised nook behind the high table. 'Where I sleep.'

Annis entered, pausing on the threshold, her feet dragging slightly. Tove had always forbidden her to go in, but now it would be her home for as long as Haakon decided to keep her. She wanted to hate it, but found it charming, full of unexpected sophistication.

Unlike her old sleeping area, which she had shared with Ingrid and Tove, the nook was wide and sumptuously furnished. Tapestries depicting Viken legends hung on the walls. A carved bed stood in the centre, piled high with furs and pillows. It was so easy to imagine falling back against the fur, Haakon leaning over her. Her cheeks grew hot. Even her thoughts were becoming wanton. The old Annis, the one who existed back in Northumbria, would not have dared think such a thing. She had vowed once never to become like Selwyn's many mistresses—all doe-eyes and sensual gestures—but it appeared her body had other ideas.

At the side of the bed stood a chest with Haakon's *tafl* board on top. A tub of steaming water stood at the foot of the bed. There were even curtains to draw across the entrance, so that the Jaarl could be private, if he desired. Privacy. Until the attack on Lindisfarne, she had not realised what a precious commodity it was.

She breathed in, savouring each piece of furniture, each small luxury.

'Do you like it?' Haakon's hands were behind his back and he looked very much like a young boy showing off his favourite toy.

'Yes, I like it very much.' Annis answered his smile with one of her own. She hoped life would not be so cruel as to take this away from her suddenly. 'And you even have a tub to wash in.'

'For those times when I do not wish to take a sweat-bath.'

Haakon lit a torchlight and then drew the curtain across the entrance. Annis stood in the centre of the room, uncertain of how to proceed. She knew she should do something, but her fingers were clumsy and awkward.

Haakon rummaged in the carved chest and pulled out the little silver cross and a thin silver chain.

'Allow me.' He slipped it over her head and it hung between her breasts. 'I believe you would like to wear this. Much better than keeping it locked away.'

Her hand curled around it and she hardly dared breathe. He had returned it. Without her asking.

'Thank you,' she breathed. 'It was a gift from my mother.'

'I had wondered about its importance.' His voice was soft, lulling her, sending tingles along her skin.

She trailed her fingers through the warm water and allowed the droplets to fall back into the wooden tub. She had seen the looks and knew what was expected of her. But here it was very different from the hut. There it had been just the two of them, but now, everyone knew that she shared Haakon's bed.

If she retained Haakon's favour, she might do much for the monks and others. But what if she failed? She had failed to retain Selwyn's favour beyond a few days. Failed miserably.

'We have had a long ride.' Haakon reached over and poured mead into a goblet, but his eyes watched her. 'You are dusty.'

'As are you.' She ran her tongue over her lips. Haakon appeared tense, ready to spring. She felt as if they were engaged in some of sort of game. It was her move, but she had no idea of the rules.

'There is a bath. Tove and the others have filled it.'

'It is not big enough for two.'

His lips twitched upwards. 'You do have a point.'

'You may go first.' Annis smoothed her hands against her shift. 'Shall I leave you to it? There is sure to be something for me to do in the kitchen.'

'Very well.' Haakon slowly shed his garments, allowing them to fall to the floor. Annis sucked in her breath at the sight of his naked body. He strode over to the tub, seemingly unconcerned at the effect it was having on her. 'Your duties are here now. Attending to me.'

'What do you mean?' Her mouth became parched.

Haakon gave a stretch. 'You may wash my back. The linen cloths are over there.'

He settled in the tub, his knees drawn up to his chin. Annis did not move from where she was standing. The torch shone golden shadows over his skin.

'Annis?' he asked softly. 'What's wrong?'

'Nothing.' Annis walked briskly over to the tub. She opted for the quick approach, splashing the warm water on his body, and washing as rapidly as possible.

His hand caught hers. 'What are you nervous about?'

'I am not,' Annis lied.

'Ever since the monks spoke with you, I have sensed a change.'

'They said nothing. They approve in a way, I think.' She dipped the cloth into the water, then wrung it out. She concentrated on making circles on his skin.

'They do?'

'I think they are expecting to get better treatment.'

He pulled her hand so she overbalanced and lay sprawled against him, half in and half out of the water.

'My shift is getting wet.' She tried to push against his chest, but his mouth was so close. Her lips tingled. He cupped the back of her head.

'You should wear something else,' he said, against her mouth. 'I will not have my woman dressed in rags.'

'Then what will you have me wear?' She lifted her chin. 'I am not a Viken woman.'

'No, you are not that.' His hands roamed down her back, pulling her towards him. Then he stopped and his eyes searched her face with a quizzical expression.

'What are you doing?'

'Making a memory, Valkyrie. When we are old and grey, I want to be able to close my eyes and think of you like this.' His voice lapped at her senses, lulling her.

'Like what—damp around the edges?' Annis gave a slight laugh, but her heart started to race. She kept her mind away from his words— she had to concentrate on the now. There would be time enough for memories later.

Haakon's finger traced a small circle around her breasts. 'Only a little damp.'

'Haakon! Haakon! A ship has been sighted!' Thrand's voice resounded in the hall as a horn was blown.

Haakon let his arms drop and Annis put her hand on the bed post to steady her legs. He reached for a cloth and quickly dried his body. He pulled on his trousers and a linen tunic. 'Alas, my lovely, my duty calls.'

'Thorkell has recalled the Storting,' Vikar said without preamble after he had disembarked. In the few days that he had been gone, the other Jaarl's features had become more careworn, harder. Haakon knew his news was not good. Thorkell had not called an assembly simply to celebrate the success of the *felag*.

'I had anticipated he would call such an assembly once he received my message stick.' Haakon clasped his friend's forearm in greeting. He'd allow Vikar to deliver his news in his own time. 'But since when does a Viken Jaarl act as a messenger boy?'

'Since Asa asked me to. She wants you there before the Storting is fully assembled. She says it may be in your best interest.'

Haakon stared out to the fjord. 'It is good that she still remembers me with fondness. It is many years since we journeyed from Denmark together, I to rejoin my family and Asa to be married.'

'She does, with great affection.' Vikar put his hand on Haakon's arm. 'She remembers your friendship when she had none to turn to. And Thorkell values her counsel.'

'Why does Asa believe I need to be there? My estate needs me as much as, if not more than, my queen. I have no wish to seem the supplicant by arriving too early.'

'Sigfrid sailed south. He arrived a day after me.'

'I had heard rumours.' Haakon gave a shrug. 'I am not his keeper. It would appear his grievance with me means more to him than securing Hilde's dowry.'

'Maybe he does not want Hilde's considerable assets that quickly. His concubines have always been petite and no one could call Hilde that. After all, she is at the family's hall and hardly going anywhere.' Vikar's eyes grew serious. 'It was after Sigfrid arrived that Thorkell called for the Storting to be assembled. Before then, he seemed content with his share of the bounty and your explanation of the fight. He knows, they all know, what Bjorn could be like.'

'Has he summoned me? Or was it Asa?' Haakon kept his

voice expressionless. What was between Asa and him faded many years ago, but the friendship remained. He knew the gossip.

'It was Thorkell. He wanted to send someone who was not a member of the *felag*, but Asa insisted I come. I left that very night. And, thank Odin, the winds were in my favour.'

'I do appreciate it.' Haakon stared out at the fjord where the white-capped waves moved. This morning, when he saw Thrand, the feeling that everything was too perfect had washed over him.

'Which warriors will you bring?' Vikar's voice was low and urgent.

'Are you asking me who do I think will be loyal?'

'I am asking you to consider very carefully. You will want ones who are discreet and not hot-headed. I heard about what Thrand did. You cannot risk a repeat.'

'I will bring enough men to guard my lodgings. It is still the raiding season. Having had a visit from Sigfrid, I have no wish to experience another one.'

Vikar pursed his lips. 'How long will it take you to fit out a boat?'

'A week, two at the outside.' Haakon thought about Annis. What was between them was too new. He would use every instant they had together to enjoy her.

'It is too long.' Vikar slammed his fist into his palm. 'Whispers fly around Kaupang that you are an oath-breaker, that you attacked Bjorn in cold blood. Mention has been made of your quarrel the night before the raid. Your desire for wealth and fame.'

'Bjorn expressed an opinion. I disagreed. He chose not to challenge for the leadership. There the matter ended.' Haakon tightened his jaw. 'Bjorn was too far gone in his blood-lust. It is the price berserkers sometimes pay.'

'Bose and Sigfrid were observed together. The combination fills both Asa and me with dread. Having been married to Bose's daughter until we divorced, I know what the man is capable of. If something should happen to Thorkell, Asa's son is not old enough to rule. I have my orders, Haakon. You must be there quickly to counterbalance. Asa commands it.'

Haakon stared at Vikar as the implications started to sink in. Sigfrid was determined to undermine him. An oath-breaker! Bjorn had attacked first, but such an accusation, if proved, could put his entire estate in jeopardy. An oath-breaker had no status, nothing. 'I shall leave at once. We depart in the morning.'

Vikar paused, drew a line in the dirt with the toe of his boot. 'I thought you should know Sigfrid mentioned your captive to Thorkell.'

Haakon felt a cold pricking at the back of his neck. He had planned to take Annis, but would he be putting her in danger by doing so? She could stay here where she was safe. 'It is good to know that.'

Chapter Fourteen

'Have you heard Haakon is leaving for Thorkell's court? On Vikar's boat?' Tove rushed into the bedchamber, her kerchief and apron slightly askew. 'They depart as soon as the wind changes.'

Annis finished fastening the small oval brooches at the top of the apron-dress. The fine linen shift and heavily embroidered apron-dress were lovely, but between the shorn hair and the clothes, she did not recognise herself in Haakon's small mirror.

'I had expected he would. He is a Jaarl and does have a duty to the king.' Annis kept her voice calm, but she could not prevent a hollow from appearing in the middle of her stomach. Haakon had not come to tell her. She had heard the sound of his voice in the hall, shouting for his men, but he had made no move to re-enter the chamber.

It had started, much in the same manner as Selwyn after their wedding night. Already thoughts of court and court life occupied Haakon. He would go, and when he returned, would he remember what they had shared?

'You might be right, and I admire you for taking the news with dignity.' Tove made a little moue with her mouth.

'Is there any other way?'

'I would have been wild. He had just declared you his concubine and he is leaving.' Tove shook her head. 'I don't understand it.'

'Perhaps that is the difference between you and me.' Annis kept her shoulders square and stared back at the woman.

'Perhaps.'

Annis willed Tove to leave, but the other woman sauntered about the chamber, opening pots of scents and peering into the chest.

'Out with it, Tove.' Annis crossed her arms. 'What is it that you want to tell me?'

'Most Jaarls take their wives and concubines with them when they go to court.' Tove batted her eyelashes, the very picture of innocence.

'And your point is?' Annis tapped her foot. The beginning of a headache gathered between her eyes.

'Why isn't Haakon? I heard him tell Thrand that he was to look after you and not to let Guthrun bully you. He intends on leaving you here.' A look of genuine concern crossed Tove's face. 'I like you, Annis. We have had our differences, but you know I really hold you in great respect. Anything you tell me will stay confidential.'

'No doubt he has his reasons.' Annis drew on all her training and kept her face bland. Despite Tove's assurances and concerned face, if Annis showed the slightest flicker of emotion, Tove would pounce and the tale would spread around the kitchen quicker than Fress or Kisa lapped up their afternoon milk.

'It is a mystery,' Tove continued, in a speculative fashion. 'I mean, he only formally declared you his concubine when you returned earlier. There is always Thorkell's queen to consider. Maybe Haakon does not wish to offend her. They were quite close once, if the stories are to be believed.'

'I have other things to do, Tove.' Annis pointedly turned

her back and closed the chest. 'I promised Haakon that I would make some ointment. He wants plenty in case someone is burnt again.'

'I only wanted to help. If I were a Jaarl's concubine, I would make sure I went. The feasts are legendary. You should ask, rather than accepting the dictates. I know that is what I do—twist him around my little finger.'

'But you are not Haakon's concubine, nor are you ever likely to be.' Annis crossed her arms. She could well remember Aelfric's words—Thorkell might be sympathetic to her and the monk's plight. She had to go. If not for her own sake, for the monks'. It was possible that Charlemagne did have a representative there and she might get word to the Northumbrian king that way.

Tove's face flushed scarlet and she tossed her head. 'Guthrun says that you look like a thrall, and she for one is glad you are not going.'

'She was the one who cut my hair,' Annis said lightly. She needed to keep Tove as an ally. The woman had a different sort of ambition than she, but she did understand how the household was run. She needed friends, not enemies, particularly with Guthrun waiting to exert her power. 'There is no love lost between us, but Haakon has declared me his concubine. She will not be able to boss any of the women around as much, I promise you that.'

Tove laughed. 'I had not thought of it in that way. Perhaps it is good that you are staying—to counterbalance Guthrun.'

Annis forced her lips to smile. She had to think about the future and the time when Haakon might not be enamoured of her. She could well remember the number of mistresses Selwyn had gone through during their five-year marriage. Absence had never made his heart grow fonder.

Why would Haakon be any different?

Even that thought made her want to curl up in a small ball.

She had vowed back on Lindisfarne that she would never make herself vulnerable as she had done. She knew her happiness depended on this man. She wanted him to care for her in the way she was beginning to care for him.

'You are leaving tomorrow.' Annis stared at Haakon, who concentrated on making a fuss of Floki.

'That is correct.' Haakon stood up, but made no move to take her into his arms. 'Guthrun will be staying here as well. She dislikes sea voyages. You need not fear anything from her. Thrand will be in charge while I am gone. He is under strict orders not to allow his mother to harm you. I would like you to have a look at the herbs, see if there is anything the hall needs. I have no wish for my estate to be without your ointment again.'

'How long do you expect to be gone?' Annis forced her hands to stay at her sides. She wanted to twine them around his neck and press her face close to his, to beg him to take her with him because she needed to be near him, but she had some pride.

He gave a half-shrug. 'It all depends on the king.'

'Then why are you not taking me with you?' Annis rushed the words. She had to say them before her nerve gave out. She wanted to fling herself into Haakon's arms and demand to know why. It made no sense. Before Vikar had arrived, he had not seemed able to keep his hands off her and now he wanted to abandon her. He did not even have the courtesy to come and tell her first. Her body moved slowly as if she were made of ice. She refused to cry, but found it impossible to deny the hurt.

'I have been summoned. I have to go immediately. There is much going on. It is only through good fortune that Vikar heard of the plotting.' Haakon reached out and pulled her to him. Her body collided with the hardness of his. He ran his hands down her back and his lips pressed against her temple. 'I will miss you, but you will be safer here.'

'You did think about taking me.' She breathed in sharply as the world that had appeared so black became suddenly infused with colour.

'Thorkell mentioned your name. He wanted to know about you and why I had taken you as a captive, but no other women.' Haakon smoothed her hair back from her forehead, making a heat grow inside Annis as surely as the fire which burnt in the central hearth. 'I want to be cautious. You do understand.'

'Cautious is not keeping me here, while you put yourself in danger.' Annis pulled away and tried to think. If she was close, she'd agree to anything he said simply to keep his lips near her.

'I never said that I was in danger.' His eyes blazed with an intense blue flame. 'I can handle any man with a sword in a fair fight.'

'Then there is no reason not to take me…if there is no danger.' She gave a little laugh.

'I have been summoned and I have no desire to leave you here, but it will be for the best. Rumours fly around.' Haakon raked his hand through his hair. He explained about the Storting, Thorkell's assembly of nobles who helped him judge difficult cases.

'Has Thorkell requested to see me?' Annis tilted her head to one side. She had not considered the possibility. Her heart beat faster. 'Then you must take me with you.'

'It is not that simple.' Haakon's hands were like hard vices around her upper arms. 'If anyone ever knows the full truth of what happened in that upper room, your life will be in danger. Thorkell may forgive me, but you are not a Viken.'

Annis closed her eyes. She could clearly see that upstairs room and the shaggy beast-man. A violent shiver came over her. Even after all these weeks, the sights and sounds of that day were clearly imprinted on her brain.

'Are you trying to protect me?'

'Yes,' came the terse answer. 'I told the story my way.'

Annis went over to him and laid her hand on top of his. 'I can look after myself, Haakon Haroldson. It would seem to me that if Thorkell knows about me and I do not appear, questions will be asked.'

Haakon withdrew his hand.

'Questions I can answer. You are in no danger here. Thrand and Guthrun—after her fashion—will look after you until I return. This will not take long.' Haakon cupped her chin with featherlike fingers. 'There, let me have a smile from you. Something to carry in my heart.'

His eyes became a midnight blue, a blue so deep that it threatened to swallow all of Annis's protests and leave her weak at the knees and unable to think clearly. She forced her gaze elsewhere.

'Haakon, I want to go. I want to be with you.'

'Why?' His hands dropped to his sides and his smile faded. 'Why, Annis, after all that I have told you?'

Because you are going. Because I fear your passion waning if I am not there. Because I will miss you, she longed to whisper, but the words stuck in her throat. To say them would leave her utterly vulnerable to him. She prided herself on being self-contained.

Annis wrapped her hands around her middle and forced her voice to sound decisive. She had to concentrate on the practical.

'Because if you fail to produce me, Thorkell might take offence, if he is anything like my king in Northumbria. I would hate to be the cause of your downfall.'

'It is a risk I am prepared to take.' Haakon hooked his thumbs around his sword belt, and stood there, feet planted firmly.

The tiniest of sighs escaped her lips. She had tried and failed. Annis bowed her head slightly.

His gaze became as soft as the furs on his bed. 'I do want you with me, but I also want you safe. I know what a snake pit Thorkell's court can be and I made a vow to protect you.'

'I have survived the court life in Northumbria. York can be a dangerous place. I dare say that I can survive the Viken court as well.' Annis raised her head and forced her lips to smile. She had to take a risk. 'I want to go. Please take me with you, Haakon.'

'Are you insisting on going?'

'Yes.' Annis knew here was the point that she should seduce him, but Haakon had to allow her to go of his own will. 'I will not disgrace you.'

'Who told you that?' Haakon's eyes blazed. 'I never said anything about you disgracing me.'

'My hair is short. I wear a collar.' Annis held out her hands. 'Guthrun says that I look like a thrall and it would never do for a Jaarl to have a thrall for a concubine.'

Haakon's eyes narrowed. A muscle in his jaw twitched and Annis took a step backwards. Had she said too much? Then she lifted her head defiantly. She had nothing to be ashamed of. She knew that she, despite everything, remained the Eorl of Birdoswald's daughter.

Her eyes clashed with his.

'Hold still.' Haakon withdrew his dagger from his waistband. His fingers caught her collar, and with one decisive stroke Annis was free. 'Your hair will grow back in time.'

Annis's fingers explored the skin. 'Why did you do that?'

'Guthrun was correct—if you went as you were, you would be considered a disgrace to me and my house. I should be able to bind my concubine to me with something other than a collar,' he said, his voice slipping into a husky rasp that played along Annis's skin, sending out the silken lure of promised pleasure.

She knew what bound her to him and the links were not forged from steel, but from his touch and his manner.

He opened the chest and pulled out a heavy silver torc, engraved with highly stylised serpents. 'However, there are others who need to see to believe my claim. Know you belong to me.'

He slipped the torc around Annis's neck and fastened it. The metal felt cool against her skin, but rapidly warmed. Annis hooked her fingers around it. It weighed much more than her old collar, but it was a collar, a symbol of her captivity.

'And if you wear your old gown, no one will remark on your short hair. They will all think it is a strange barbarian custom.' A smile touched his lips. 'You will not disgrace me or my house.'

Annis stood still. He meant her to go! He wanted her to go! She pressed her hands together in case she had heard and reacted in the wrong way. 'Are you saying that I am to come with you?'

'As you appear determined to see what the Viken court is like.' He drew her into his arms. 'And you are correct, I will sleep better knowing that you are there with me, rather than busy trying to escape. Now you may thank me.'

'I am done with escaping.' Annis gave in to her feelings and laid her head against his chest. His hand stroked her hair.

He raised her chin and his deep blue eyes peered into hers. 'Promise you will stay in the background, Annis. Promise you keep our secret about Bjorn's death, no matter the provocation.'

'Yes, I promise.' She raised herself on to her toes and kissed his warm lips, feasted on his mouth.

'I will hold you to that promise.' Haakon released his arms and Annis stumbled backwards, her senses tingling. 'We leave as soon as the boat is packed.'

* * *

'Haakon Haroldson, come and greet me!' Thorkell's deep voice boomed out from where he sat on his stool, receiving petitions. 'I had not thought to see you so soon. The messenger left two, three days ago.'

'I understand you have called for the Storting to assemble.' Haakon pushed forward in Thorkell's crowded hall and started to kneel in front of his king and queen. He carefully watched Thorkell's face for any sign of favour. Since they had last met, Thorkell's blond mane had become streaked with silver. He thanked the gods that his trip had been swift and that he had arrived before the main body of Jaarls.

Thorkell rose from his stool, came forward and kissed him on his cheek, as a father would do a son. Haakon's shoulder muscles relaxed slightly. Perhaps it would not be as bad as Vikar feared. Vikar sometimes let his dealings with his former father-in-law, Bose, colour his otherwise sound judgement.

Behind Thorkell, the shadows parted and Sigfrid and Bose appeared. They stopped their conversation and stared at him in amazement. Sigfrid cupped his mouth with his hand and urgently whispered to Bose, who nodded.

A sense of grim satisfaction filled Haakon. He had disrupted their plotting. He had arrived before Sigfrid had planned. He nodded to Asa, who permitted a small smile to cross her sculpted features. Once Haakon had thought her the most beautiful woman in the world, but now he knew her outward beauty could not compare with Annis's inner glow. The difference between stone and living flesh.

'We have heard of your adventures. It is good that you have come in peace,' Thorkell continued as if he were unaware of the urgent discussion behind him.

'I sent messengers as soon as I arrived back in Viken.' Haakon regarded Thorkell's watery blue eyes.

'Quite, quite, but it is not the same.' The querulous note in

Thorkell's voice was clearly evident and not what Haakon expected. He and the king had parted on amicable terms—Thorkell had to understand that he had stayed away, and not landed with his warriors, since he had no wish or intention of usurping the kingship.

Haakon gave a quick glance to Asa, who shook her head almost imperceptibly—a warning, if he needed it to hold his temper.

'I wait until I am invited,' Haakon responded carefully. He glanced over towards where Sigfrid stood in all his finery with a hard expression on his face. Exactly what sort of mischief was Sigfrid intent on? 'I sent Vikar and Ivar with the rings and gold. Far more use to my king than my body. I had been away from my estate for many months. How many Jaarls do you want to see?'

Thorkell's laugh held echoes of the man Haakon remembered. 'The rings are appreciated, and now I call the Storting, to honour you and the rest of the *felag*. You are too modest, Haakon. Vikar and Ivar have told me all that you did. We must have much feasting and merriment. Thor and Odin have given us a great victory.'

'It is better to let another praise a man,' Haakon replied. 'It is a lesson I believe you taught me.'

The muscle in Thorkell's cheek twitched. Haakon gritted his teeth. Even though he had arrived earlier than anticipated, his enemies had done their groundwork well, sown doubts in Thorkell's mind. Did he really consider Haakon to be an oath-breaker, after all they had been through together?

'Come, let us speak of other things.' Thorkell raised his hands in an expansive gesture. 'I understand Bjorn perished in the raid on Lindisfarne. How did that come about? Those monks spend too much time praying to their God to be good fighters.'

Haakon forced his eyes frontward and did not gaze at Annis, who stood behind him. He had taken responsibility for the death and he had no intention of putting Annis in danger, particularly not here. Thorkell had to believe his explanation. He knew what sort of man Bjorn was. 'He was killed during a fight with me. He was too far gone in his berserker madness to know me as a blood-brother. I look to your Majesty's guidance on how best to recompense his family.'

'I will give the matter my careful consideration, but word has reached me that you quarrelled the night before.'

'True, but the quarrel ended before we reached Lindisfarne.'

Annis watched Haakon. She heard his easy words about Bjorn's death, but a cold shiver went over her. Exactly what was he going to have to give up? She had been the one to strike the fatal blow. But here was not the place to explain. The undercurrent of menace was so high she could taste it in the air. Haakon had been right to be concerned. Perhaps she should have stayed back on the estate, but then he would have faced his enemies alone.

'You brought your captive with you?'

Haakon's hand was at her back, propelling her forward, so she received her first proper look at the Viken king—tall, rangy with fair hair, but his skin had an unhealthy glow. Annis detected a slight tremor in his hand as he lifted it to acknowledge her presence.

'My concubine.'

Thorkell raised an eyebrow. 'She must be special, for I cannot remember you ever formally having one.'

'I have acquired one.' Haakon's jaw twitched. 'She suits my needs at the present time.'

'Indeed.' Thorkell stroked his beard.

Annis remembered the story of Haakon and the queen. Was it true? She stole a glance at the woman sitting serenely next to Thorkell. Her head was covered with an elaborately embroidered kerchief, and she wore gold about her neck and on her fingers. Her dress shimmered. Her face was serene, calm, beautiful. Annis ignored the trappings and concentrated on Asa's eyes—determined but wary.

She tore her gaze away and looked about her at the rest of the courtiers gathered around the king.

The unguarded expression on Sigfrid's face when Haakon looked away made her shiver. Sigfrid whispered again to the hatchet-faced man standing next to him.

Annis swallowed hard, thinking she should say something, issue a veiled warning, but her mind was a blank. She watched as Thorkell's eyes slowly closed and his head touched his chest—only for him to jerk awake and look around him in an agitated fashion. The hatchet-faced man whispered in his ear and Thorkell nodded.

'We need to greet the next noble! So many are here. So many people to see. People who keep their sacred oaths.' Thorkell gestured to someone behind Haakon. Annis did not miss the slight audible gasp that echoed around the room.

'The king is tired, Haakon Haroldson. Last night's feast went on a long time. He retired to bed quite late,' the Queen said, her low voice resounding throughout the hall.

'I have no wish to tire him further. We will speak another time.'

'We will speak before the Storting and then your loyalty will be decided.' Thorkell's voice sounded old and trembling. 'You may go now and wait for my next summons.'

An audible gasp filled the hall.

Annis saw Sigfrid's smirk increase as Haakon stood there, a disbelieving expression on his face. He had been dismissed like a naughty boy, rather than with dignity.

Haakon's fingers grasped her elbow, led her out of the chamber. Back in the open air, Annis drew a breath. The king's actions made no sense. Unless…

'Your king is ill,' Annis said with sudden insight.

'He is merely tired.'

'His skin is not the right colour, and there were beads of perspiration on his forehead.' Annis ticked the symptoms off her hand. 'He should be seen and his illness looked into.'

'What would you do have me do, Annis? I have been dismissed. Bose and Sigfrid are in the ascendancy. I will speak with Ivar and Vikar, but I am not a rebel.' Haakon put his hand to Annis's waist and propelled her forward. 'Remember, this is not Northumbria. Life is different here.'

'I never forget it.'

'But I don't understand.' Annis tried again once Haakon had returned from his meeting. The air of gloom settled around him like a cloak. 'Your king's life may be in danger if you do nothing.'

Haakon pressed his palms against his eyes. 'I have to respect Thorkell's wishes. To act against them would be to declare myself in opposition. Thorkell could proclaim me an outlaw.'

'Even if you are trying to save his life?'

'Hush, Annis, someone is coming.' Haakon held up his hand and his entire body tensed.

A small tap at the door and a hooded figure was ushered into the rooms. The woman looked around. When she saw the room was empty except for Haakon and Annis, she allowed her hood to drop, revealing her silver hair and unlined face—Asa, Thorkell's queen. She went over to Annis and imprisoned her hand between hers.

'You are a healer,' Asa said without preamble in a low, musical voice.

'I have some small skill,' Annis admitted.

'I had heard that it was more than a small skill.' A tiny frown appeared between the woman's perfect eyebrows as she released Annis's hand. 'It does not signify. I must have help,

Haakon. Our healer departed for Trondeheim on a mission for Bose. And your concubine will have to do.'

'Once I know what is required of Annis, *I* will make the decision.' A tiny smile that did not reach Haakon's eyes played on his mouth. He held out a glass goblet of mead that Asa accepted, delicately tasting the amber liquid. 'I have been expecting you, Asa.'

Annis put her hands on the table and tried to control the jealous surge that coursed through her body. And it hurt far more than she thought it could to see Haakon and this woman together. 'Would it not be better if I made the decision? I am the one she came to visit.'

Haakon reached out and caught her hand, imprisoning it between his. Annis forced her hand to stay limp and unresponsive.

'You made a promise, Annis.'

'Let her hear me out, Haakon, for the sake of our long friendship. I come not for myself, but for my husband and my young son.' Asa's pale blue eyes were wide and frightened. Her hand shook. 'I have never seen Thorkell like this. He has become worse through the day and there is nothing the soothsayers can do. Please help me. They will accuse me and say that I am responsible. Me, the foreign queen. You are my only hope.'

Annis gave a wild glance at Haakon. His mouth had tightened to a thin white line. What was he thinking?

'Thorkell does not want help from me or any of my household. He said as much in our interview.'

'You know that is unlike him.' Asa held out both her bejewelled hands. 'Hear beyond your hurt pride, Haakon Haroldson.'

'If he is truly ill…' Annis began. The fear and concern were clearly etched in Asa's face. She knew what had happened this afternoon, but it could be that she had the power to help. She was certain she had seen symptoms like that before, but her head pounded and her mind went blank.

Haakon held up a hand, silencing her. 'Annis, before you speak, you must know the ways of my people. Do not allow Asa's soft words and honeyed manner to blind you. If Thorkell dies in your care, your life will not survive the length of a torchlight.'

Annis started to pace the room, ignoring the pair of eyes on her. Deep inside she knew she might be able to help. If Thorkell perished, Haakon and his friends would face a struggle. Sigfrid was in opposition to him, she knew that. The hatred on Sigfrid's face was clear this afternoon. Where would she be safer—in a world ruled by Thorkell or one by Sigfrid and his cronies? Where would Haakon?

'I cannot sit idly by, doing my spinning, while a man lies possibly dying.' Annis clapped her hands together, giving in to her instincts. 'It is against my nature.'

'For once, Annis, will you listen and believe me? I am concerned about your safety!' Haakon's roar filled the room. Annis saw Asa wince and turn her face away, but Annis lifted her chin and stared directly back at him.

'And I am interested in saving you.'

'Know that the reward will be great if you succeed.' Asa's low voice filled the lull. 'My and my son's gratitude will be as nothing compared to my husband's.'

'Royal favour is a fleeting thing.' A small, sad smile touched the corners of Haakon's mouth. And Annis wondered again how close he had been to Thorkell. Or did he speak of his time in Charlemagne's court?

'I have never wavered in my affections,' Asa replied. She turned and her shoulders crumpled slightly. Annis went forward and put her arm about the slender queen's shoulders. She could understand the need that drove her. She would do the same for Haakon. Instinctively she knew that, if Thorkell died, things would be much worse for Haakon, for the monks, for all of them. She had seen what Bjorn was capable of and she knew his brother would be the same, if not worse. She had to try.

'My lady, if you will allow me to get my cloak, I will come with you,' Annis said, and Asa smiled through a sparkle of tears.

Haakon reached out and grabbed her arm, his strong hand pinning her to her place. 'Annis, I forbid it. You are still my captive. Obey me.'

Annis moved her arm sharply and he let go. But he continued to block her path. When he was angry like this, he was easier to fight. Annis knew if he asked her softly, she would be unable to refuse him anything. 'Haakon, I will not do anything rash. I shall only look at him and see what I can do. I told you before, there was something about him, something that I could not put my finger on.'

She held out her hands and willed him to take her in his arms. She wanted the reassurance his embrace brought, but he simply looked at her, then at Asa.

'We will speak alone, Annis.' Haakon's knuckles shone white against the red of his tunic.

'It is what I must do.' Annis reached up and pressed her lips to his cool cheek, 'Earlier you complained Thorkell was not himself. Once he has been returned to full health, he can make the right decision. He will back in your fight with Sigfrid.'

'Annis…' Haakon gave a strangled sigh.

'You must trust my skill, Haakon. I saved Thrand and Floki. I will do what I can. Allow me to examine him.'

She wanted to ask Haakon to come with her, but it would be too much. She knew she would have to stand alone. If Thorkell did die and she was blamed, he should be held to be innocent.

'She wants to try, Haakon. For the sake of our long friendship, let your concubine try. I will do all I can to protect her.'

'Asa, you do not know my concubine very well. Protecting her is a full occupation.' A quick smile flitted across Haakon's face.

'Thank you, Haakon. I will see her safely home.'

Annis turned to go, but Haakon blocked her path. His blue eyes became unfathomable pools. 'Not so fast. I am coming with you. Asa, you return to your husband, and we shall follow afterwards, first to your chambers and then to the king's. I will hold you to your promise of protection.'

Asa's lips parted as if she wanted to say something. She glanced from Haakon to Annis, then gave a brief nod of understanding. 'Come to the south gate and I will be there.'

Chapter Fifteen

After Asa had departed, leaving only a trail of expensive scent in her wake, Haakon barred the door. He had to make one more attempt to save her life.

'You do not have to go. This is not your fight. In due course, the ransom will arrive and you will be free to go.'

'I am going to see him, your king. I have given my word.' Annis leant forward, her hands clasped under her chin, her eyes burning with a deep intensity. 'Asa is frantic with worry, desperate enough to come here and ask a stranger for help.'

'I have known her for a long while,' Haakon replied, looking at the fire. 'She is a strong and determined woman who loves her husband, but she is also an accomplished politician. She plays her own game. She fears for her own life—not mine and certainly not yours. Everything she does, she does for her own benefit.'

'How long have you known her?'

'When I travelled back from Charlemagne's court, she and her courtiers were also travelling to Thorkell's court—a young Danish princess to appease and quiet the northern border.' He smiled, remembering those long-ago days when he had been young and brash, more likely than not to pick a fight. It had been through first Asa's influence and then Thorkell that he learnt the hard lessons of diplomacy and tact. 'Like you, she is a survivor. But she is ruthless, much more ruthless, Annis.'

'Do you love her?' Annis asked softly, the words slipping out and then hanging between them. She wanted to tell him that it did not matter, but she also knew it would be a lie. His response mattered very much.

'She was a bright shining star in an otherwise gloomy night.' Haakon threaded his fingers through hers. The lines on his face smoothed and his eyes took on a faraway look. 'Once I very much envied Thorkell his choice of bride.'

'And now?' Annis prompted. She had to know. Her heart had nearly stopped beating. She needed to know that he cared a little for her. Her soul cried out for the answer.

'I was very young, and it was a long time ago. She was more a young man's dream than anything else.' Haakon gave Annis's hand a pat and strode over to the fire. 'We are friends after a fashion. We both want peace in this kingdom.'

Annis regarded the glowing embers of the fire. A small bubble of happiness grew inside her. His feelings for Asa were friendship. It did not matter what he had once felt for the woman—that had been many years before they had met. It mattered to her what his feelings were now. She and Haakon had shared passion, but could they become friends? She knew with each passing day that her life in Northumbria seemed ever more distant, almost a dream. 'What will happen if Thorkell dies?'

'Who knows?' Haakon held up both his hands in an exaggerated shrug. 'Politics is the same around the world. What will happen when any strong king dies, particularly if he leaves a very young son? I need no soothsayer to tell me the outcome. Do you?'

Annis shook her head. 'I know the answer.'

'As do I. Utterly predictable, utterly boring, but very bloody. My country does not need that. Its people are poor enough as is. It is why we take to the boats and hope to find Njordr the sea god in a favourable mood.'

'But if he survives, it will be good for you. Thorkell dismissed you and has called the Storting to discuss your future,' Annis pressed. She had to know the answer. She had to know exactly the danger Haakon faced.

'If he dies, there is more of a chance that I will become involved in a blood-feud—yes, but such a thing does not worry me.' Haakon's eyes crinkled. 'I am a fighter. My sword arm is strong. It will be a good while before I see the portals of Valhalla. Do not put your life in danger on my account.'

Annis hid her face. She knew if she looked him in the eye, she'd reveal her heart. 'And I am a healer.'

The silence in the room grew to a breaking point. Finally Haakon gave a sigh and folded her into his arms.

'You are determined to go, then.' He kissed the top of her head. 'Here I thought I could persuade you to stay once Asa had gone.'

'If I stayed away, I would not be me.'

His eyes narrowed and became inscrutable. 'You speak a certain truth, Annis. And I am rapidly discovering that I like you the way you are.'

He leant forward and their lips touched, clung. Annis brought her hands up and held on to the material of his red tunic. Her body tried to tell him all the things her lips would not. Then she freed her mouth and stood a little way from him, and concentrated on her breathing. She reached for a cloak and with trembling fingers fastened the trefoil brooch. 'I am ready to go now.'

'We go together.' Haakon strapped on his sword. 'You will need a protector tonight.'

* * *

Annis wiped the perspiration from the back of her neck as she lowered her hood. After they had arrived back at the great hall, Haakon had proceeded quickly to the queen's chamber, keeping his hand on his dagger in case of any opposition.

'Are you ready, Valkyrie?'

'As ready as I will ever be.' Annis took some comfort from Haakon's use of his pet name for her. He believed in her and was willing to support her. She hoped her knowledge would save Thorkell's life. 'And I promise not to do anything unless I am positive.'

'I know that.'

'I do have some small skill, Haakon. You must believe that. Floki believes.'

There was no answering smile back. His face had become etched with heavy lines. The news of Thorkell's illness had aged him. Annis knew he must be thinking about what might happen if Thorkell did not live. The thought sent a shiver down her spine. As long as she looked, did not actually do anything, no one could accuse her of murdering the king.

Haakon put a hand on her shoulder, steadying her. She looked up at him and gave a watery smile. He smiled back and his hand tightened for a brief instant.

'Here we go. Stay close to me and the queen. Keep your hood up until we are inside the chamber.'

Annis nodded, marvelling that the simple touch should steady her. The trembling in her stomach subsided to a dull ache.

Asa was waiting for them in her chamber with torch bearers and her women clustered around. She held out her hands. Annis grasped them.

'I knew you would come…in the end.'

'I must see Thorkell to decide what is to be done. And if I can help. I make no promises.'

'I have thought of that. You and your bodyguard.' She gave a nod to Haakon. 'You both come with me.'

Asa swept through the guards, silencing them with a quick haughty stare. Then they were there, standing near the fallen king.

The king's chamber was overly hot and full of strange odours that stung Annis's eyes and hurt her nostrils. Six torches burnt golden orange around the fur-piled bed.

Several soothsayers were huddled in the corner, mumbling to their beads, the horned headpieces glowing with a faint light from the fire. On the bed, the king lay. His greenish pallor was much worse than this afternoon, and his breathing laboured. With each breath, he appeared to be fighting the spectre of death.

'Where are the other Jaarls?' Annis asked quietly, surprised that the hatchet-faced thug and Sigfrid were nowhere to be seen.

'They will be waiting to see what happens.' Haakon's face was grim. 'If the king lives, much will go on as before. If not, it will be who controls the most men. The vast majority of the Jaarls have yet to arrive and none wants to be accused of hastening the king's death.'

Thorkell began to splutter and cough. His body went rigid, his eyes rolled back, then without warning he shook. The spasm went on for only a few breaths, but while it was happening, it lasted a lifetime.

Asa gave a cry and rushed to the king. His hand lifted slightly and tried to stroke her head before falling back on to the bed. The queen gave Annis an anguished look.

Please help him, she mouthed, before turning back to press her face against his throat, murmuring his name over and over again.

Annis's heart turned over. Asa's actions weren't all for show; there had to be genuine affection there. She could understand the love that drove Asa to ask a stranger, a potential enemy, for help. She knew if Haakon was in similar need, she would not hesitate to go on her knees and beg for his life. The thought stunned her.

A soothsayer came forward and rattled bones in her face. Annis attempted to brush past, but the soothsayer persisted, mumbling incantations and placing evil-smelling sticks on the fire. The heavy scent made thinking difficult.

Asa started to beat her breast and wail along with the soothsayer. Annis scrunched up her eyes, tried to concentrate, but the pounding filled her brain, numbing it. If she was going to do anything, she had to have silence. She needed to be able to examine the king.

'Haakon,' she whispered.

He seemed to understand. He went forward and put his arm around Asa, taking her to one of her women. Asa gave a great gulping sob and tears sparkled like diamonds in her eyes. With one last reluctant kiss to Thorkell's forehead, she went and sat in a corner. Haakon snapped his fingers and issued orders. The soothsayers looked at each other, but did not move. Haakon started to unsheathe his sword. He drew it out halfway and the soothsayers rushed for the entrance, pushing and shoving to get out of the way.

Asa motioned to her guards. 'No one will disturb you now.'

Annis stirred the fire to make it burn hot and clear instead of smouldering. Within a few breaths, cleaner, fresher air entered the chamber. Annis tried to concentrate. She was looking for the smallest sign, something that would give a clue as to the cause of his sudden collapse.

She walked over to the king and took a closer look. A sheen of sweat covered his pale green skin. Now that the smoke had cleared, the scent of vomit assaulted her nose. He opened his eyes and stared directly into hers. He tugged at her hand. Annis knelt down.

'You have a yellow light around you,' he whispered. 'You all do.'

Annis stared at him, trying to think. She should know what was causing this. The answer was somewhere on the edge of her brain. Her head pounded from the smoke and her stomach wanted to revolt. She forced her attention to stay on Thorkell. 'Remain calm. Breathe deeply.'

Thorkell suddenly grabbed his middle and started moaning again. 'The pain, the pain.'

'Annis, do you have any solution?' Haakon put his hand about her waist. 'Thorkell looks far worse than he did this afternoon. Death stands in this room.'

Annis's hands shook and the pain in her head increased to breaking point. She walked away from the bed and forced breath into her lungs.

'It is on the tip of my tongue. He reminds me of …of someone my uncle told me about…that last night at Lindisfarne.' Annis looked at Haakon. She had it. Poison. 'Mushrooms. Or some other dried herb. Foxglove, maybe. A little at a time and the victim becomes worse and worse until death comes as a blessed relief. Someone has poisoned him.'

'What are you saying, Annis?' Haakon's brows drew together. 'The only person who knows about herbs is you.'

'It will have to be mushrooms, then. The cure is the same.'

'Mushrooms?' Asa tilted her head. She freed herself from her women. All her grief and hysteria was gone in an instant. Her eyes glittered dangerously. 'What are you saying about mushrooms? My husband lies dying and you are speaking of food. Are you accusing *me* of poisoning him?'

'Has Thorkell eaten any mushrooms?' Annis fought to keep her voice calm. 'It is quite possible that he ate something accidentally, something that made him sick.'

'It is not the right season for mushrooms,' Haakon said.

'I would expect to find them in the autumn, but not now in the summer.'

'But you do dry mushrooms. You have touchwood, for example,' Annis persisted.

'We do, but I don't see it.' Haakon shook his head. 'Thorkell would not knowingly eat touchwood. He knows what is good for him.'

Annis turned to Asa. 'What has Thorkell eaten recently?'

'Nothing very much. His appetite has decreased markedly over the past few days. He is worried about Haakon's intentions. I told him that it was nonsense, but he persists. I made him eat some stew this afternoon. Spooned it into his mouth myself. Surely you are not suggesting…' Asa stuffed her hand into her mouth. Tears trembled on the brink of her eyelids. 'That is an infamous suggestion. I have never wanted to cause my husband harm. Without him, my son will never reach manhood.'

'We believe you.' Haakon's voice came calm and steady. Asa gave a tremulous nod. 'Annis did not mean to accuse you. Did you, Annis?'

Annis shook her head. She wanted to believe it wasn't Queen Asa, but it had to be poisoning.

'Could anyone get to it, change it? Perhaps sprinkle something on the top? Your stews are quite heavy.'

Asa's brow furrowed. 'They could, but who would dare? Who would know about such things? As I said before, only healers know about herbs and ours has left for the time being.'

'When did Thorkell first start feeling ill?' Annis asked.

'Shortly after Sigfrid arrived. Three days after the healer departed.' She pressed her lips together. 'They had gone out on a hunt and when they came back Thorkell complained of stomach pains. That was the first time, I am sure of it, because I begged him not to go to the feast and to rest. Like a man, he would hear none of it.'

'We need to make him sick until whatever is in his stomach

is gone. Then I will give him ground-up charcoal. It will absorb any of the poison left in him.' Annis placed her hands on her hips. 'Get me a feather to stick down his throat.'

Both Haakon and Asa stood looking at her, incredulous expressions on their faces.

'A feather? Charcoal?' Haakon questioned. 'Annis, are you sure?'

'If you want to save his life.'

'I will get them,' Asa said, hurrying from the room.

'I cured Floki with touchwood.' Annis ran her hand through her hair. 'I can save Thorkell, but I need those things now.'

Haakon stood still, glaring at her.

'Annis, I warned you. If you get this wrong, you will be held accountable for his murder.'

'If I get this wrong, he will die. Bose and Sigfrid will take power. Sigfrid will declare a blood-feud and have the other Jaarls support him.' She placed her hands on her hips. 'The blood-feud will be against everyone in your household. Sigfrid and his clan will not spare me simply because I am a captive. They are looking for an excuse.'

'Are you positive it was mushrooms?' Haakon asked quietly.

Annis shook her head slowly. There were many things that could have caused the poisoning. She had to try. 'I feel certain that it was poisoning, but what exactly caused it I don't know.'

'Then you don't know if it was accidental or on purpose.'

'No,' Annis breathed. To accuse someone of deliberately poisoning the king would be to openly accuse that person of treason. She had no proof and Asa said that she had personally spooned the poisoned food into Thorkell's mouth. Asa's distress was real. She had no reason to poison to the king. 'No, there is no proof, but he was poisoned.'

'I trust your judgement, Annis. You knew what was right for Thrand and for Floki. I will get you your charcoal and stand guard at the door until Thorkell recovers….'

Haakon's quiet words filled the room and her heart. Annis knew that she would not betray that trust.

Asa hurried back into the room as Haakon bid the rest of Asa's women to depart. She held a long white feather in her hands. 'How a simple thing like this can help I have no idea. Are you going to wave it over him and mutter an incantation?'

Annis took the feather from Asa, went forward. Her mouth felt dry. Thorkell's eyes were open, but she knew he did not see her as he kept muttering incoherent words and phrases. She whispered a prayer and then set to work.

Once she had done everything she could, she stepped back and wiped the sweat from her brow. It had taken all her ingenuity to get the charcoal down his throat. Thorkell's breathing was even and his colour was less pale.

'How is he?' Asa leant over her. Despite Haakon's urging, she had remained in the room while Annis worked, obeying Annis's requests for bowls and cloths without a murmur.

'He is sleeping peacefully.' Annis pressed her hands together. 'I have done everything I can think of. The crisis is past. Now it is a matter of time. Hopefully he will sleep for a long time. If he survives the night, he will survive.'

'He is a fighter, my husband.'

'I can see that.'

At that, Thorkell opened his eyes and looked directly at Asa. 'It is you, my wife. The light has gone from around you.' His voice sounded tired, but held an inner strength.

Asa gave a cry and put her face on Thorkell's chest. Gently, Annis took the queen from his bed.

'Let him sleep. All will be well, you shall see.'

Asa's cold hand tightened around Annis's, squeezing tight.

'Thank you, Annis. I can look after him now. We are safe, the both of us.'

A great wave of weariness washed over Annis. All she wanted to do was to stumble back to Haakon's rooms and sleep. But she did not dare leave her patient yet. She glanced around her, but Haakon had departed, gone without saying goodbye. She sighed, but what had she really expected? Haakon had other problems to solve. He had kept his promise.

'You are looking for Haakon. You are in love with him.'

Annis's stomach clenched. She thought for a moment that it was a voice inside her head speaking. Annis put a hand to her forehead and tried to think what she could say. She ought to deny it, but she found it impossible to lie.

Annis turned back to Asa, startled. The queen's eyes held a knowing look. 'Is it that obvious? I thought I had concealed it well.'

'To one who knows the signs.' Asa held out her hands. 'Come, let us be friends. You have saved my husband. We both owe you a life-debt. Speak a while with me. It has been a long time since I have able to be frank. Haakon will not have guessed. Men are often blind in these matters.'

Annis nodded slightly. She had no idea what to say. If Asa had guessed, it was only a matter of time before Haakon guessed. Then their relationship would change. Emotions were not supposed to be part of the arrangement. 'It will be pleasant to speak with you.'

Annis withdrew her hands, but sat down on the bench next to the queen and watched the glowing embers of the fire.

'I know you saved my husband because you feared for Haakon's life.'

'I did it because I dislike seeing anyone in pain.'

'But you did it, knowing that it might cost your own life. You could have kept quiet. Had Haakon's own life not been in danger, I doubt I could have prevailed on you. You did not care about my life.'

Annis gave a tiny shrug. 'I did it because it was the only way. You must not think I am totally naïve.'

'I never said you were.' Asa's eyes held a hard glint. She tapped a finger against her mouth. 'I think you know very well what you are about. You and I are two of a kind.'

Annis found it difficult to sit still under Asa's gaze. Asa was quiet as Annis moved around the chamber, tidying, keeping her hands busy, picking up goblets and bowls, then placing them down again. All the time, she felt the queen's eyes on her. It unnerved her that her feelings were that easy to discern. Haakon had not guessed, but how many others would? She had prided herself on her ability to conceal her emotions, yet, within hours, this woman had guessed her deepest feelings.

'Jaarls can never marry captives,' Asa said smoothly as her words echoed around the room and resounded in Annis's brain like the tolling of a bell. 'They are important men and marry for reasons other than pleasure.'

Annis's hand trembled as she set down the goblet. 'Nobody has ever mentioned marriage. Certainly not Haakon, and never me.'

'But surely you understand that Haakon must marry.' Asa stood up with a smooth, fluid movement. She came over to Annis, taking the goblet and placing it down. 'Thorkell will insist he marries. And he will have to marry well as he is now the richest Jaarl in the land. You must impress this on him. If he survives the Storting and I have reason to believe he will, he must do as Thorkell requests…for his own safety.'

'I have no influence with Haakon over whom he marries.' Annis forced her voice to be steady. Her stomach ached. She had no desire to have this conversation. She wanted to run and hide. She also wanted to scream, to fight back.

Annis clenched her fists. She had to control her temper.

How dare Asa, queen or not, ask her to help with Haakon's choice of wife?

'You think not?' Asa's eyes narrowed and her voice became cold. She drew herself up to her full height. 'You will not be able to hold him for ever.'

'I know.' Annis hated the fact that her voice was small. 'You tell me nothing I have not thought of.'

'There again, it may take longer. Haakon cannot afford to defy Thorkell, you must understand that. He must listen to wiser counsel.'

'I do not believe, with all due respect, that his intention is to disobey his king, but I am *only* a captive.'

Asa paced around the room, quick, decisive steps that sent her skirt swirling about her ankles. She tapped a finger against her mouth.

'Do you expect your ransom to arrive soon?'

Annis shrugged her shoulders and attempted an unconcerned air. Where was this conversation leading? Was she now going to have to confess her fears about that as well? 'It depends on how long it takes for the news to reach Northumbria. I am not without dower lands.'

'Then it depends on what happens there.' Asa inclined her head. 'Will whoever is in charge of your dowry *actually* send the money?'

Annis started. She had never said or given any indication about the ransom. How had Asa guessed? 'Are you a witch?'

'I have survived for a long time. The ways of women and politics are the same all over the world.' Asa leant forward. 'Tell me. Why were you at Lindisfarne? You are not a nun.'

'I went to see my uncle, the Prior, and ask his advice… about something, a betrothal.'

'And his advice?'

'To join a convent,' Annis spat out the words.

'Something you have no intention of doing.' Asa's laugh

was a silver trill. 'Just as you have no intention of marrying this man your family wants you to.'

Annis regarded her hands. 'I have no idea what I shall do when I return home…if I return home.'

'But you would like to go there.' Asa pinched Annis's chin between her fingers, forced her head up and then released her. 'There is nothing for you here but heartache. Trust me on this. I have known Haakon for a long time.'

Annis gave a desolate nod as a wave of homesickness swept over her. It would be far worse to stay here and see Haakon's affection slowly fade. She could never be a rival to a wife. She knew what sort of special pain it caused. Even though the woman was unknown, she felt sorry for her. She would come to the marriage with high hopes and discover her husband preferred another woman's bed.

How could she ask another to suffer as she had suffered? 'What should I do?'

'Leave me to think on it.' Asa laid a cool hand on Annis's sleeve. 'This conversation shall be a secret between us two, I think. Remember, the king and I owe you a life-debt.'

Annis nodded. She had no wish to repeat the conversation to Haakon. The thought was too humiliating. But she knew Asa's intention was to warn her and the queen meant well with her words. But sometimes the kindest words cut the deepest.

'Thorkell is over his worst,' Haakon said as the faint streaks of dawn appeared in the sky. 'Asa will be relieved you saved her slender neck.'

Annis turned from where she looked out to sea. She had come here after her conversation with Asa, to think and to decide what to do next. Asa had promised to keep her secret, but did her feelings for him shine too clearly in her face?

How was she going to guard her heart?

'His colour is much better and his breathing is back to normal,' she said, keeping her voice neutral.

'But you are exhausted. You can barely stand.' Haakon put a hand on the back of her neck and kneaded her flesh. Annis wanted to lean into him and draw the strength from him. 'Let the queen and her women nurse Thorkell. I am taking you back.'

'To sleep?' Annis's eyes fluttered.

'Sleep definitely.' Haakon regarded the black smudges around her eyes. He knew what she had done for him, and the cost to her. 'After you are rested, we shall see if I may join you.'

Her lips turned up in a sad smile. Haakon frowned. He had expected her to be a bit more enthusiastic.

'Is there something wrong, Annis?'

'No, no, I am tired. It takes longer for my brain to work. It would be lovely to go back and go to sleep.' She reached up and touched his cheek. 'With or without you in the bed.'

'Afterwards, we speak.' Haakon resisted the temptation to hold her hand to his face, to hang on to her.

She had saved Thorkell's life, at real danger to her own. With each passing day, Haakon knew she was becoming as necessary to him as breathing. He wanted her in his life—for ever. By the time the ransom arrived, he hoped she would see reason and stay.

'Yes, talk. You make a nice pillow.' She leant her head against his shoulder. Her body was infused with a warmth. How long did she have left before Haakon wearied of her? Or a suitable bride was found? However long it was, it would be too short. 'Make love to me like you mean it.'

'You are too sleepy for that.' Haakon gave a soft laugh as he felt his body respond to her nearness. Even that simple request had desire flooding through him.

Haakon put his arm about her waist and led her very gently back to where they were staying. The fire in the hearth had long since smouldered down into cinders, but the heat in his body burnt brightly. But he hesitated. She needed to rest.

She lay back amongst the furs and lifted her arms to him.

'You promised.' Her voice was a sleepy slur, but her lashes fluttered closed, followed by a soft snore.

Haakon cradled her in his arms. 'Sleep well, my Valkyrie.'

Chapter Sixteen

$\mathcal{A}$nnis remembered little of the next day and night, sleeping in Haakon's bed, soft fur cocooning her. She vaguely recollected Haakon taking off her clothes, but after that it was a blank. She woke once to find Haakon gone with only the imprint of his warm body and his faint masculine scent to comfort her. But the next time she opened her eyes, he was there, standing at the foot of the bed.

'You should dress.' He held out her gown. 'Time is wasting.'

'How is Thorkell?' Annis levered herself up on her elbows. The gold and silver chains hung off Haakon. It would be hard to think of a Northumbrian wearing such clothing or as many rings, but it suited him. 'He hasn't had a relapse, has he?'

'Recovering, thanks to you and your methods. No one would ever have dared to use ground-up charcoal.' Haakon's eyes were soft. 'He begins to issue orders, and speaks of the day that he will wrestle and fight again. He finds the confines of his bed difficult.'

'Can I go and see for myself?' Annis tried to ignore her pounding heart. She had thought Asa's words would fade over time but she kept hearing them—*Haakon must marry soon.... He needs a wife and sons.... He cannot marry a captive.* Was this one of Thorkell's orders? She understood the political necessity. And yet, she had no desire to give him up. She prayed that some miracle would take place and she'd be gone before the marriage happened. To see Haakon with another—unbearable.

'That was my intention. You need to see what your skill has done. Thorkell wanted to thank you immediately, but I insisted you needed your rest.'

Haakon ran a hand down her bare shoulder. She shivered slightly as her body responded.

'It would never do to keep a king waiting,' Annis said, catching his hand as it trailed towards her breasts.

'Unfortunately, you are right, but your body is temptation.' Haakon gave a husky laugh. 'If we stayed here much longer, we would risk the king's displeasure and he has yet to rule on the *wergild*.'

Annis rose and began to dress quickly. Her hand snagged on the silver chain as she tugged her gown into place. She felt the chain give, then break. She caught the little silver cross as it fell. She placed it on the chest by the bed. Her fingers lingered a little. 'I will have to leave it here. I have no desire to lose it.'

'I can send the chain to the silversmith.'

'It is not important. I know where it is.' Annis said the words and was amazed that it was true. The cross had ceased to be a symbol of what she had lost. She could leave it behind, knowing that she would return to it.

'As you wish…' Haakon's lips brushed the top of her head. 'But I will get the chain repaired.'

'Haakon, Annis, at last.' Asa came out of the chamber shortly after they arrived at Thorkell's hall. Her hair was intricately arranged, and her make-up perfect, but it was the liveliness in her eyes that held Annis's attention. She held out both hands to them. Haakon lifted one to his lips. 'Thorkell is awake and he wishes to speak with you both. I thought I might have to send guards to fetch you.'

'There is no need for that, surely.' Haakon's hand touched his sword belt.

'No, no.' Asa's twinkling laugh rang out. She linked arms with Haakon and started to lead him towards the chamber, leaving Annis to trail in their wake. 'You are here now, Haakon.'

'But he is better,' Annis said, moving quickly towards the chamber. 'Haakon should have awakened me before now. I did want to know if there was the slightest change.'

'Even a healer needs rest,' Haakon said, discreetly disentangling his arm from Asa's. 'And it is up to me to see that you take care of yourself.'

Annis saw Asa's eyes narrow, but then a bright smile lit her face. She turned towards Annis. 'Thorkell is well recovered. As you suggested, he has been only eating simple things like coddled eggs and wheat bread.'

'It is good to know.'

Thorkell was sitting up in bed, a fur draped about his shoulders. His colour had returned and his eyes were bright and lively.

'Haakon Haroldson, I believe I owe you my gratitude and thanks.' His voice boomed out as Annis approached the bed.

Haakon inclined his head. 'It is my concubine, Annis, who is deserving of your thanks.'

Thorkell's eyes fell upon her. 'My wife and queen has much good to say about you, Annis of Northumbria. Your knowledge has proved a great boon to me. We are grateful.'

'I am pleased my skill has been put to good use.' Annis tilted her head, subtly trying to see if there was any lasting damage from his fit.

Asa leant over Thorkell and whispered in his ear. His face turned grave and he gave a nod.

'Haakon has made an interesting choice for his concubine. My wife informs me you are highly born and are waiting for your ransom.'

'She speaks the truth.' Annis saw Haakon's neck muscles grow taut. She found it difficult to breathe. Thorkell had a hidden meaning to his words. She made sure her shoulders were upright and dignified. Asa's words about her not being good enough for Haakon still rankled. She was not an ordinary concubine who had few prospects of her own.

'My uncle was Prior of Lindisfarne. My father and late husband were Eorls,' she said. 'The same rank as Jaarl in your kingdom, I believe.'

Thorkell nodded. 'I have lain here, pondering my reward to you. It took me a long time to think of an appropriate one, but finally it came to me. You gave me my life. I give you your freedom.'

'My freedom?' Annis stared him, trying to comprehend his words. What sort of freedom did he mean? She had no expectations, no warning. To be free to do what? She had no means of support or transport.

'You are no longer a captive,' Asa said firmly.

Thorkell made a gesture, and one of the guards came forward to take off her silver neck-ring. She had grown used to the weight. Suddenly her neck and shoulders felt light, but naked, exposed. All the outward signs of her captivity were gone.

Haakon's face had become thunderous as his brows drew together in a straight line. Annis realised that he had had no idea of Thorkell's intentions.

'Stop glowering at me, Haakon. You will be recompensed. The treasury is full, and we can afford the price of a captive.'

'You should have spoken to me first.'

'And allowed you to spirit her away?' Thorkell shook his head. 'It is the woman I need to think about. What would Asa long for if she were in similar circumstances? It is the right and correct thing to do. Asa and I discussed this point in depth. The Northumbrian should return to her home, her life.'

Haakon's tone held menace. 'It is well that you are my king.'

'I call on you now to remember your oath to obey me.'

'You leave me little choice.' Haakon bowed his head, but his voice was cold. 'I am not an oath-breaker. I have never broken a vow and I do not intend to begin.'

'It is good to hear.'

'What…what is to happen to me?' Annis did not dare look at Haakon. To break with him now was far better than later. With each day that she spent with him, her ties to him grew. When the time for him to put her aside came, as it must, it would be far worse. But if he took one step towards her, gave any indication that he wanted her, she'd be in his arms.

'You are under the queen's protection,' Asa's voice rang out, strong and assured. 'You will have a place with my women, and when the next boat leaves for the Holy Roman Empire, you will go, with enough money to buy passage to Northumbria.'

Annis stared at the queen, disbelieving. She wanted to scream that this was not what she wanted. It was not a reward, but a sentence.

'And the monks?' Annis asked. 'They were captured at the same time.'

'The Pope will send their ransom in due course,' Thorkell said. 'Charlemagne's representative has left to secure it.'

'It appears everything has been decided for me,' Haakon said. A winter had descended on his features, making him seem remote and stern, very different from the lover of early this morning.

A shudder ran down Annis's back. He was angry with her for escaping. She had found a way to leave, instead of him leaving her.

'What is the problem, Annis?' Asa asked. 'Don't you want to be free?'

Annis looked at Haakon. If he made one move towards her, she knew she'd run and cling to him. But he didn't. He stood there, angry and aloof.

She gave a small nod. She had to be practical and pragmatic. Their affair could not last for ever, as much as her heart might desire it. She would leave with dignity.

'Of course I want to be free. Returning to my home is the most important thing to me.'

She knew she lied. She had to. Better to suffer now, than slow death later. Her whole being was infused with pain.

Thorkell said something that she did not catch. He held out a ring and Annis saw Asa give a small nod, indicating that she should go forward and receive it.

'If you ever have need of it, know that this ring will allow you access to me.'

Annis's fingers closed around the ring. She'd treasure it—a reminder of where her heart was. 'I know the honour you do me.'

Thorkell waved his hand, dismissing her as Asa escorted her out. Annis gave one last backward glance, but Haakon had turned resolutely away.

'A boat leaves on the next tide,' Asa said, bustling into the chamber where Annis had spent the night.

Annis turned from the slit where she had watched the courtyard. She had hoped Haakon might appear and demand that she stay. But he had not. He had not even had the courtesy to say goodbye. She heard he had left the hall and nobody knew where he had gone. Nothing but that last terrible look. And now this, the offer of a boat.

'Where is it going?' Annis attempted to inject enthusiasm into her voice. She had thought an offer to leave Viken and go back to Northumbria would have filled her with joy.

'Bose is sending a trading mission to Charlemagne's court. I have spoken with Bose and he has agreed that his captain should take you. There is a purse of money and a letter of introduction for you. All is in order.'

'I don't understand why you are doing this for me.'

'You saved my husband's life, and I know if I were a captive, my dearest wish would be to return to my old life.'

Return to her old life? But what about if there were parts of her new life that she cared about? Annis caught her lip between her teeth. She wanted more time. 'How long until another boat leaves?'

'It could be weeks, maybe months. It depends on the Jaarls and their requirements. Do not think to stay, Annis. My help is offered but the once.'

Annis stared at the gold ring on her right hand. Weeks. She could not face weeks of possibly meeting Haakon in the corridor. Or even seeing Haakon with someone else. No, it was better to go now, before the torment really started. It was better to begin her life again as quickly as possible. She had no real excuse to remain. She had to do it. She had to begin to live her future.

'Yes, I'll go. I have nothing but my clothes.' Annis thought of the little cross, but she had left that in Haakon's chamber. The thought of the interview to retrieve it was too much. She'd mourn for the loss later.

Asa's face turned grave. Her bejewelled fingers pushed back a curtain of silver hair. 'It is better this way, Annis, truly. A fast break and soon this whole episode will be but a distant memory.'

Annis gave a brief nod. 'I have no wish to remember my time here.'

As she said the words, she knew she would never forget Haakon. Always somewhere in her life, there would be a question. It did not matter now. Perhaps she would do as her uncle and stepfather wanted—marry Eadgar. Nothing mattered now. She would only be existing.

'As Thorkell said yesterday, if you ever have need of our help, send word with the ring, and we will do what we can.'

'I shall remember.' Annis knew she would never do that. She would keep the ring, the one last connection to her time here.

'Shall we go, then?' Asa lifted the hood of her cloak and motioned to her women and guards. 'We will see you to the ship. To make sure you are safe and properly treated.'

The hall held an expectant air as they passed through. Various thralls were busy laying tables and hanging richly embroidered tapestries on the walls.

'The Storting meets today,' Asa said in answer to Annis's look. 'After the business is completed, they will come back here and feast. All will be friends again. As a precaution, though, Thorkell has decreed no one is to bring weapons.'

'Is this usual?'

'My husband is a cautious man, Annis.' Asa's lips turned up into a smile. 'He knows what Viken nobles are like, particularly when their king has been ill. All too easily a minor quarrel can turn into a blood-feud. Come, let us hurry. Bose said that the boat would leave on the tide.'

Annis took one last glimpse of the hall. Where would Haakon sit? At Thorkell's right hand or farther down the table? She did not believe that his differences with Sigfrid were settled. Then she forced her mind away. Haakon's problems were no longer hers. She was a free woman.

All the way to the harbour, she kept looking for Haakon or one of his household. She wanted to say farewell, even if it was from a distance, but no one appeared. And her pride would not let her ask for the chance to find him. A soft sigh escaped her lips as she gave one last backward glance.

'Remember it is for the best, Annis.' Asa's cool lips brushed her cheek. 'One day you will have a child from your husband, and Haakon will have the sort of wife that Thorkell intends him to have. One who befits the leading Jaarl of the land. You have no wish to see another woman suffer.'

'Tell Haakon…' Annis tried to speak around the blockage

in her throat. She swallowed several times and the world blurred. 'Tell him farewell.'

'I will.' Asa squeezed her hand. 'You have done the right thing.'

'It was the only thing.'

Annis mounted the gangplank, forcing her head to remain towards the red-and-white checked sails. Her feet felt like lead. She greeted the surly captain. Then she moved towards the back of the hold where she would not have to see any more. She wanted to lay her head against her knees and weep for what might have been.

A pair of outstretched legs caused her to trip. She put out a hand, grabbed the side of the boat and then righted herself.

'Hello, Annis. Fancy meeting you here.'

The menace of the Latin words sent a shiver down her back. Annis forced her face to remain expressionless. She turned slowly to the figure lounging against the hull.

'Aelfric, what are you doing on this ship?'

Haakon stared at the silver cross. It was all he had left of her. He had found it when he returned to his lodgings, discarded on the chest.

The fact that she had not had it made him believe that perhaps he had been mistaken—she had not intended to be freed in that way.

He gave a wry smile. He had thought yesterday would end in a very different fashion. But the first chance she had, Annis had opted for freedom. And he found it impossible to blame her.

He didn't know whom he was more angry at—Annis for accepting the offer of freedom without a backward glance, or himself for not fighting for her.

He would see her, and… Haakon's fingers curled around the cross, felt it bite into his palm. Was he prepared to reveal his heart to a woman who wanted to leave? Who cared little for him? All he knew was that life was bleak without her. There had to be a way.

'Haakon, the Storting has begun to assemble.' Vikar came into the chamber. 'I have assessed the mood and we may be able to carry the day. We know you are not an oath-breaker as some have whispered. But others from the *felag* have come forward. They will testify that you and Bjorn had never fully reconciled.'

'I will get there on time.'

Vikar paused, and rubbed the back of his neck. His countenance took on a sheepish look. 'There are no weapons allowed.'

Haakon nodded. 'I had expected it. Tempers are bound to run high. Thorkell has always been cautious. It is why he has retained his kingship these past ten years.'

Vikar shifted on his feet, started to say something and paused.

'Out with it, man! What news is so dreadful that you hardly dare speak it? We have been friends long enough, Vikar, if you must say something, say it!'

'One other matter—Sigfrid and Bose are sending a trading vessel to Charlemagne. Your former concubine left on it.'

A huge hollow place opened up within Haakon, a deep sense of betrayal. Annis had not even bothered to say goodbye. He and their time together meant that little to her. All her soft cries… No, he was sure he had given her pleasure. Vikar had to be mistaken. 'When did this happen?'

'This morning. I just heard about it. I thought you would want to know.' Vikar gestured with his hand. 'This trading journey is too pat, too easy. Since when did he trade with Charlemagne? Most of his business had been to the east, not to the south. Bose is up to something. I know my former father-in-law well.'

Haakon nodded. Vikar was correct. Something did not

ring true. The boat journey was far too quick. He could not believe that Annis would leave without saying goodbye. There had to be an explanation and he intended to discover it. He had not given her a choice. It was time she had one.

'I have her cross.'

'And are you going to keep it?' Vikar raised an eyebrow. 'It is a paltry thing and not worth very much.'

It is worth more than you will ever know. Haakon held the words back. There was no point in explaining. Vikar would fail to understand. For Vikar, women were to be used and discarded. They came a distant second to fighting.

'I shall return it, Vikar…personally.' Haakon tucked the cross into his pouch, nestled it next to his fire-steel. 'We failed to say goodbye.'

'And saying goodbye is that important.'

'To my mind, yes.'

'When do you leave?' Vikar dropped his gaze. 'You cannot abandon the *felag*. Besides, it will take time to outfit a boat. You will catch up with her at Charlemagne's court. Do not let Sigfrid destroy your reputation like this.'

Haakon gritted his teeth. Vikar was right. He had duties and obligations. He could not concede the floor to Sigfrid and be declared an oath-breaker. For all he knew, given Sigfrid's devious mind, it could be the course of action that he counted on Haakon taking. Annis would have to wait until he could devote the proper attention to her, until he assured that she was safe from reprisal.

'After the Storting meets, I go. There is a score to settle with Sigfrid first.'

Chapter Seventeen

Annis stared at Aelfric. The monk was dressed in Viken clothes, much finer than she thought possible. He appeared well fed and groomed, but his eyes held a superior look.

'Did you weep a few tears at my demise, Annis?'

'How did you get here?' Annis put her hand to her throat. He had to be real. 'We were all sure you were dead.'

'You need not fear.' Aelfric's air of superiority increased. 'I am very much alive. The captain knows about me. Sigfrid paid for my passage.'

'Sigfrid?' Annis did not bother to hide her astonishment. The head of the Bjornson clan had given this escaped captive passage. It made little sense—or did it?

'His boat discovered me after I escaped from that hell hole. I had fallen down several ravines. That witch Ingrid had no idea about the terrain. After his sailors captured me, Sigfrid was uncertain about what to do with me and, more than once, I felt my life hung in the balance.' Aelfric tapped the side of his nose. 'But my knowledge about herbs proved invaluable to him, and he is allowing me to leave.'

Annis stared at him, lounging against the side of the boat, mystified. Then comprehension dawned. He was speaking of the king's mysterious illness. He had to be. She had been right in her assumption that it was not accidental.

'It was foxgloves. You put foxgloves into Thorkell's food. The symptoms were correct. And you dined with my uncle and me that night…'

'God put tools at my disposal.' Aelfric placed his hands together and adopted a pious expression. 'I wanted to bring down his enemies. Even now, your lover will be punished. Think on that, Annis. Weep and repent. Weep and repent, and you may yet be saved.'

'You are mad!'

Aelfric frowned.

'Of course, Sigfrid was irritated at my failure to dispose of the king, but with my help, he has devised a new plan. After today, he will have everything he requires and your precious Haakon will be destroyed.'

'What did you tell him?'

'Haakon is an oath-breaker. You only have to look into his eyes to know he is not telling the full truth about the fight with Bjorn.'

'What have you done?'

'I told the truth—Haakon attacked Bjorn. After I did, Sigfrid listened to me.'

'But you weren't there. I was!'

'I know. Why do you think you are here?'

Annis went cold, seeing all too clearly the future. Haakon was about to lose everything. She had fallen very neatly into the trap that Sigfrid had laid.

Only she could stop this. The king had to believe her. She had his ring. She paused, trembling. And if she told the truth, she'd lose her life. She had killed in self-defence, but was that enough to save her?

If Haakon lost everything, would her life be worth living, knowing she could have prevented it?

Annis drew a breath. She had to think, but there was no time. She had to bring Aelfric with her, to expose the plot. Without him, it would be only the word of a concubine trying to protect her former lover.

How to do it? Annis tapped her mouth.

'You are a fool, Aelfric, to think the world would be a better place if Sigfrid was in charge. You will have caused more raids on Northumbria, not fewer.'

'You are a feeble woman, and understand little of these matters. Soon you will be home and safe. You should be on your knees, thanking me.'

Annis pressed her lips together. They were alone in the hold. Aelfric was not much bigger than Ingrid. She had brought down one; she could bring down the other. She sprang forward, sending Aelfric to the ground. He put out his hands to protect himself, but Annis used the momentum of her fall to force him over on to his stomach. She planted her knees firmly in his back and prevented him from rising. Then she grabbed his arms and forced them upwards. Time for a bit of plain speaking.

'This is what a poor, feeble woman like me can do, Aelfric!'

'Let go of me! You are hurting me!' Aelfric's voice rose to a nasal, self-pitying whine. 'You know I dislike violence.'

'You foolish, foolish monk, God hates a coward. And you are one,' Annis said in Aelfric's ear. 'You listen to me. Sigfrid is not going to let you live. Your days are numbered. You are coming with me.'

'Not let me live? He promised.' The nasal whine grew ever louder.

Annis was tempted to throttle the monk. Only he could be that arrogant and short sighted. He had caused untold misery and still he persisted in believing.

'You know too much. You are a danger to him.' Annis did

not attempt to hide her growing exasperation. Time was slipping through her fingers. The shouts of the sailors were growing ever louder. Soon the boat would move and Haakon would be gone—for ever. 'How many people simply disappear when they are out at sea, and nobody knows what happens to them? Do you think a man who is willing to poison his king will really think about the niceties? Think on that and tell me who is feeble-minded.'

Aelfric went still and appeared to consider her words. 'What you say has a certain ring of truth. What do you propose?'

'Getting off this boat before it starts moving. This boat stinks of death.'

'Can I come as well…please?'

'You are a coward, a cheat, a thief and a liar, Aelfric. I want you to know that. But I have need of you.' Annis loosened her grip slightly. 'You may come with me and I will try to protect you. Do as I say *now*— Or die a watery death.'

'Protect me?' His voice squeaked slightly. 'You are only a woman, even if you did knock me down.'

'I fought a pack of wolves and survived, Aelfric. Nothing frightens me any more.' Annis knew it was a lie—losing Haakon frightened her to the very core of her being. But she was not going to think about that. She had the power to save Haakon. 'We need to go now.'

'All right, I will go with you. I have no liking for your alternative.' Aelfric stood up reluctantly, but Annis held on to one of his arms, twisting it behind him. 'What are you doing?'

'March.' Annis put her knee against his back and propelled him forward. 'We leave now or not at all.'

'You don't trust me.'

'You are correct in that. Now keep quiet…if you wish to get off this boat.'

They moved up and out of the hold. The seamen, unaware of their intentions, had not bothered to guard the gangplank.

Annis glanced over her shoulder, not quite able to believe the laxity. A seaman coiled a piece of rope, while two others moved a chest. They could do it. Annis forced Aelfric down from the ship at such a fast pace that she nearly stumbled.

'This is where you and I part company,' Aelfric said as soon as they were on dry land. 'You may let go of me now. I am safe.'

'I think you are mistaken. You are coming with me. For once, you are going to face up to the damage you have wrought.' Annis tightened her grip on his arm, and propelled him forward, towards Thorkell's great hall.

As they got closer, Aelfric tried to twist and turn but Annis counterbalanced him, proving more than equal to the monk. She gritted her teeth and wished for her dagger.

'Why are we going here? I never agreed to this!' Aelfric made self-pitying noises. 'Annis, please have mercy! I am not a violent man.'

'And I never agreed to your escaping and putting the lives of everyone at risk! Did you ever think about your fellow monks when you were busy helping out Sigfrid?'

'Ah, yes, I can explain that.' Aelfric stopped in the middle of the street and threw what he must have considered a winning smile over his shoulder.

'The time for explanation is over,' Annis said, squaring her shoulders and pushing against his back again. Her muscles screamed at her, but she paid no attention. She had to warn Haakon and Thorkell.

They approached the hall and two guards stepped in front of them. Annis held up her free hand so that the ring gleamed in the sunlight. 'I am on a mission from the king. This man is an escaped captive. Admit me to Thorkell's presence at once!'

She held her breath while they conferred.

'You may pass.'

Annis quickened her steps towards the hall where the Storting was assembled.

'You cannot go in there. Women are not allowed.'

Annis held up her ring again. 'Thorkell promised me aid if I ever required it. I require it now! Will you make your king a liar?'

'No, I… The Storting is in session. All the nobles are there.'

'Then take me there and we can consult your king.'

'Annis, what are you doing? You don't want to go in there!'

Annis tightened her grip, and Aelfric squeaked.

'It would give me the greatest pleasure to slit your throat. Your only hope of survival is to throw yourself on the king's mercy.'

The guard shrugged and discussed it with another one. Their discussion was too low and rapid for Annis to completely follow.

Sweat began to trickle down her forehead, making her eyes sting. Was she too late?

Annis tried to control the feelings of panic rising within her. She had never had Haakon's love, she knew that, but she might still save his life and his estate.

'We cannot take you there. We will take you to Bose, the king's adviser.'

'Where is he?' Annis asked, trying to remember which of the Viken Bose was. By the sudden brightening of Aelfric's features, she suspected that he would not be sympathetic to her story.

'In the Storting. You will have to wait.'

'What I have to say concerns the king's life! Do you want to be held responsible?' Annis revised her plan. She'd tell the assembled nobles of the plot on Thorkell's life and then her part in Bjorn's death.

The men glanced uneasily at each other.

'Take me to Queen Asa.'

'She is sitting with the king.'

'Then take me there! What I have to say is of the utmost urgency. Are you going to make your king break his oath to me?'

The men shuffled their feet and regarded the ring again. Annis held her breath.

'All right, you may come with us,' the first one said, 'but if you lie…your life will be forfeit.'

'I understand,' Annis said and concentrated on forcing the increasingly reluctant Aelfric to move forward.

The hall was crowded with a sea of men who all appeared to be talking at once. The sea parted as the guards led Annis and Aelfric forward. And like a tide, as they passed, each man fell silent until Annis and Aelfric came to stand in front of Thorkell and Asa and the rest. Haakon stood off to one side. His eyes widened as he saw her. Beyond a glance, Annis forced her body to ignore him, instead concentrating on Thorkell.

Thorkell had to listen, had to understand the danger. Asa frowned at the intrusion, her lips forming a thin line.

'This man is an escaped captive, one of the monks from Lindisfarne.' Annis forced her voice to sound strong. She heard its echoes in the hall. 'I discovered him on Bose and Sigfrid's boat. Sigfrid promised him safe passage to Charlemagne's court.'

'Sigfrid?' Thorkell turned towards the Viken, whose face had gone pale, then a purplish colour as his eyes bulged out and his hands became massive clenched fists. Then, suddenly, he appeared to take control of himself, and the colour subsided.

'I have no idea what this woman is talking about. How could such a person get on the boat? She is the concubine of a known oath-breaker.' His lip curled back.

'Let me speak, and then judge my words for the truth they are!' Annis held up her hand. He had to listen. 'I ask you on the promise you gave me with this ring to listen to my tale and judge it on its merits.'

Thorkell leant forward, eyes bright. 'Go on. I am interested in what you say.'

'When you were ill, I suspected you had been poisoned

from foxgloves. But no one here had the knowledge. Your healer had left on sudden business to the North.'

'It is correct. We leave such things to healers and I have none at court. What happened to me was an act of the gods. My soothsayer confirmed it this morning.'

'This man had the knowledge!' Annis pushed Aelfric forward so he went prostrate before the king.

'How does he know about herbs?'

'He is a monk and was a member of my uncle's order. My uncle, like the rest of my family, was very knowledgeable about the power of herbs. Aelfric was there when my uncle described how foxgloves can be used to induce melancholy.'

'Interesting.' Thorkell stroked his beard. 'And to whom did this monk impart his knowledge? I have not seen him around. My food is guarded very well, tasted. Did he hang from the rafters?'

The Storting gave a general burst of laughter.

'I think we can leave such fantasies where they belong—in the women's chambers,' the hatchet-face chamberlain said. 'And our next order of business is—the application by Sigfrid for *wergild* from the oath-breaker, Haakon Haroldson.'

Cries from the benches of 'No! No! Let him be judged.'

The man held up his hand. 'The alleged oath-breaker.'

Annis's heart sank. The guards were starting to come up and pull her away. Nobody believed her. She gave a despairing glance at Haakon, but he had not moved and sat stony faced.

'Why are they crying no? Annis, I was mad to follow you!'

'Tell them who forced you to give the king poison,' Annis said in an undertone. He had to believe her words. 'Tell him now in Northumbrian or all will be lost!'

Aelfric eluded the guards' arms and raced forward. 'It was Sigfrid and your chamberlain, Bose, the man who even now stands at your side.' He screamed the words in Northumbrian. 'They made me. Bose put the herbs into the king's stew after the taster had tasted it and before he gave it to the queen.'

He dug his hand into his pouch and pulled out some dried leaves. 'See, I have the remainder here!'

Thorkell went still. Annis sent a silent prayer upwards.

'The man is clearly deranged,' Bose said, but his eyes flicked from Thorkell back to Aelfric, never stopping.

'You might be interested to know how this man came to be here,' Annis said conversationally. She quickly related the story Aelfric had told her.

'Thorkell, this is a blatant attempt by Haakon to disrupt the proceedings,' Sigfrid roared. 'He is using his concubine to cause mischief and sow doubt in your brain. When have I been anything but a loyal servant?'

'Let Annis speak.' Haakon's face was stern and unyielding. 'Your Majesty knows I have had no contact with Annis since he freed her. I have no power over her.'

'Because you saved my life, I will overlook this interruption, but I will hear no more preposterous tales.' Thorkell gave a little cough. 'Bose, indeed. He'd sooner poison his own mother.'

'This man has been sheltered by Sigfrid.' Annis made one final attempt. 'It was on his boat that I discovered him. Has anyone asked why Sigfrid and Bose suddenly need to make a trading mission to Charlemagne? Why the healer suddenly and conveniently left?'

'One of my men saw a sail stop at the inlet on the south of my lands,' Haakon said quietly. 'Sigfrid, you went south, instead of north, after you visited my hall for reasons you never fully explained.'

'The monk lies!' Sigfrid advanced towards Annis and Aelfric, his large hands outstretched, his face contorted with fury. 'I never wanted to poison Thorkell, only control him! I must have justice for my brother!'

'Remember your oath, Sigfrid! Harm none in this room!' Thorkell thundered.

A gasp went around the room as Sigfrid continued to advance.

This is it, Annis thought. This is truly the end. She had lived all this time, only to be killed by Bjorn's brother.

'You offered me gold if I got rid of your king! As much gold as I could stand up in!' Aelfric tried to scramble away from Sigfrid, but tripped and fell sprawling to his knees.

Sigfrid caught Aelfric by the neck and twisted. The monk gave a choked, inhuman sound and fell to his knees. Sigfrid turned towards Annis. His countenance had changed. His nostrils flared; his eyes were ringed in white. The berserker had returned.

Annis started to run, but his hand grabbed her arm, held her fast. The other hand caught her throat, pressed. Annis gasped for air, saw the edges of the world darken. This was it. She attempted to scream, but no sound issued forth, and all the while Sigfrid's grip tightened.

'This is what I think of oath-breaking!' Haakon's fist slammed into Sigfrid and sent him backwards into Bose. Annis gulped air into her lungs, felt Haakon's arm go around her waist.

She looked towards where Sigfrid had gone. Sigfrid's eyes had widened into a surprised expression. He fell forwards, a knife sticking in his back.

All colour drained from Bose's face. He pointed to the prone figure. 'That man was a traitor. An oath-breaker. The king had to be protected.'

'Thorkell ordered everyone to give up their weapons. How is it that you retained yours?' Haakon's voice was as cold as the sea in winter.

'It was an oversight. I feared an attack on my lord….' Bose's voice trailed away as he saw Thorkell's expression.

'Seize him!' Thorkell thundered to the guards. 'For Odin's sake, do something right today!'

'Bose is the only one who had access to your food,' Haakon said quietly as the uproar subsided.

'Can you believe the word of a man who attacked and killed a member of his own *felag* in cold blood? Do not let us forget why we are here today,' Bose said in a bored tone, as if his arms were not being held by two guards. 'Haakon disliked Bjorn's challenge and took it upon himself to rid the *felag* of such a man. He is an oath-breaker and his lands should be forfeit.'

'The Jaarl, Haakon Haroldson, did not kill the berserker, Bjorn Bjornson—I did,' Annis said. 'I was there and I know what happened. The soothsayer was correct. No man killed him. It was my dagger.'

'Annis!'

Annis paid no attention to Haakon's furious tone of voice. She stood there with her head up, glad to be telling the truth about that day. They had to listen and understand Haakon had broken no oaths. 'I am no longer under your protection, Haakon Haroldson. I may speak my mind and tell what truly happened.'

'I am intrigued. Is this tale as enlightening as the last?' Thorkell whispered something to Asa, who gave a tiny shrug. 'How did you kill him?'

'I thought my time had come, then Haakon appeared. The beast-man…Bjorn…attacked him without provocation. Haakon's shield was down. My maid took the opportunity to run. She tripped Haakon and he lay on the floor.' Annis very slowly and clearly related the remainder of what happened.

'Why was Haakon fighting Bjorn?' Thorkell asked when she had finished.

'In self-defence. Bjorn raised his sword first, struck the first blow.'

'Self-defence? It strikes me as odd that a berserker, even one such as Bjorn, should not recognize a member of his own *felag*.'

'I can answer that,' Bose called. 'Let me speak. Now that I know the truth about this sorry business.'

'If you can shed some light…things may go easier for you.'

'Sigfrid came to me with his tale. Like everyone assembled here, I had heard the soothsayer. It did not strike me as right. Why should Haakon attack? He convinced me to help him. I thought only to persuade you to listen. I never intended harm.'

'What did Sigfrid confide in you?'

'Before the *felag* left on its voyage, Guthrun rained down curses on Haakon's head for taking her only son, and it is no secret that Guthrun coveted Haakon's estates.'

'Go on.'

'Last night when I was too far in, Sigfrid confided the rest of the story. Guthrun approached Bjorn before they left to kill Haakon if ever they two should be in battle. Bjorn sent a message stick to his brother.'

'Sigfrid saw his chance,' Haakon broke in. 'The reason for his visit now makes sense. He thought to marry Guthrun when she was minimally protected, take control of the estate and kill Thrand if he returned. All my wealth would have been his.'

The entire Storting fell silent as they regarded Sigfrid's body. Thorkell motioned to the guards and they led Bose away.

'Will Annis have to pay *wergild?*' Haakon's voice rumbled in her ears. Annis lifted her head and moved away from Haakon's sheltering arms.

'As Bjorn was the aggressor and as I owe you a greater debt than I can ever repay, I absolve Annis of any need to pay *wergild* to the Bjornson clan.'

'It's over, Annis.' Haakon put a hand on her shoulder. 'Time to take you home.'

Home—a word that had had one meaning, but its meaning had changed for ever.

'I am not going back to Northumbria, Haakon.' Annis looked up at him, directly into his deep, unfathomable blue eyes. She had to take a risk. If today had taught her anything, it was how fragile and precious life was. If he chose to reject her, then she'd know. It would not be a question to ponder the rest of her life. 'My life would have no meaning there. I would only exist.'

'What are you saying, Annis?' His voice was no more than a breath.

'I want to stay here…as your concubine…if you will have me.'

Haakon's eyes grew an even blue. 'Not as my concubine.'

Annis stared him. Her stomach plunged downwards He did not care about her She had tried and failed. She gave a small nod, tasted the tears in the back of her throat. She would go with the last few remaining shreds of her dignity.

His hand caught hers and held it to his heart.

'I want you here as my wife.' He paused. 'Please, Annis, say you will marry me. I give you that choice.'

'Your wife?' A light-headed wonderment filled Annis. 'But…but…'

She tried to think of all the reasons why he would never say such a thing, but her mind failed her. It kept going back to the word *wife*. Haakon wanted her as his wife.

'What possible objection could you have?' Haakon threaded his fingers through hers. 'It is the only way that I can ensure you are with me for the rest of my days, Valkyrie.'

'Asa said—'

Haakon put a finger to her lips, stopping her words. 'It does not matter what other people think or say. The only thing that matters is you and your feelings. You captured my heart that day at Lindisfarne. I want to share my life with you. I want you beside me in all that I do and most definitely I want you in my bed.'

'Yes! Yes, I will marry you!' Annis threw her arms about his neck and their lips met.

Haakon reached into his tunic. 'After the Storting was over, I intended to come and find you. I wanted to give you this.'

He pressed the silver cross into her hands. She turned it over.

'You were coming to find me?' Annis found it hard to credit.

'Having guarded my heart so long, it came as a surprise when it was stolen by a Valkyrie.'

'But you hold my heart instead. And I have discovered that where my heart is, that is where I find my place of refuge.' Annis reached up and touched Haakon's face, her fingers tracing its familiar contours. 'Let's go home together, Haakon, you and I.'

Epilogue

Ten months later

'I have had a reply from your stepfather.' Haakon strode into the bedchamber where Annis lay resting with their new-born son. Floki the elkhound raised his head from his paws, but stayed guarding the entrance to the chamber.

'Hush, you will wake Harold.' Annis nodded towards the sleeping bundle she held in her arms. 'It has taken me for ever to get him to sleep.'

'My nurse always told me that I was a poor sleeper.' Haakon put a finger on his son's head. 'The world is a very new place for my son.'

'What were you saying about my stepfather?'

'Now the monks have returned to Northumbria, they have shamed him in front of the king. Your stepfather sends a letter of contrition.'

'It was a wonderful wedding present you gave me—freeing them without waiting for the ransom money, then sending them back, giving them protection.'

'It took a while for them to make it overland from Charlemagne's court.'

Annis gave a smile. 'Guthrun would have been furious if she had known that you had given away so much money.'

They were both silent, remembering the terrible news they had returned to discover. Guthrun, on hearing of Sigfrid's death and Bose's confession, had suffered a stroke and died. Bose had accepted banishment to his estate.

'She was a good mother to Thrand,' Haakon said quietly. 'She had never intended him harm, I am sure of that.'

'If Thorkell had not been insistent on us staying at court, we could have delivered the news in person. Maybe then it would not have come as such a shock.'

'There is no point in going over past regrets. We can only go forward.'

Annis shifted the baby to her other side. 'I am so glad that Thrand had no part in the plot.'

Haakon squeezed her hand. 'Now, do you want to read what your stepfather says?'

Haakon held out the piece of vellum to Annis. Annis quickly read the words. 'He has sold my dower lands to Eadgar! And hopes it will be enough to pay for my ransom if I desire it! He is sorry it has taken so long to raise the funds, but gold is hard to come by in Northumbria after the raid on Lindisfarne.'

She started to laugh. Her stepfather had managed to secure the land for Eadgar after all.

'You are not upset?'

Annis smiled at her husband. Once she would have been furious, but those lands were meaningless to her now. 'I could never go back to Northumbria. My home is here with you and our son, our children. I shall always remember it with great fondness, but it is where I grew up. It is here that I became my own woman. Why would I want to be anywhere where the love of my life is not?'

'Thank you, my Valkyrie.'

'Your tamed Valkyrie.'

'The heart of my home and the mother of my child.' Haakon put his arm about her shoulders and they sat listening to the soft gurgling sound their son made. A family together.

Author's Note

On 8 June 793 AD, according to the Anglo-Saxon Chronicles, *the harrying of the heathen miserably destroyed God's church on Lindisfarne by rapine and slaughter*. Exactly who these "heathen" were and which part of modern day Scandinavia they came from has been lost in the mists. Modern day historians' best guess is the raiders came from somewhere in southern Norway, possibly with a stop-over in the Shetland Islands. And other than the understandable wrath of the monks, we have no independent primary source that gives the reason for the raid. Why did it happen? And more importantly, was it planned?

The raid and its aftermath traditionally marks the beginning of the Viking age. The word *Viking* comes from West Norway—a verb meaning to raid, rob or plunder. Again, historians are divided as to its exact origins. Several sources do think it might be derived ultimately from the Viken who inhabited part of Norway, but it is open to question. Unfortunately the written record of the Viking people is sparse, and consists mainly of short runes.

Vikings have been much romanticised, particularly by the Victorians, and many legends, including wearing horns on their helmets, are simply untrue.

The vast majority of written evidence comes from the Icelandic Medieval Manuscripts, in particular the Poetic and Prose Eddas. These sagas were based on oral tradition which does in some cases date back to the Viking Age. The sagas are clearly fictionalised history but throughout time, they have captured the imagination. JRR Tolkien and Wagner both drew inspiration from them.

The best and most complete physical evidence for the age, thus far, was found in Oseberg in the late nineteenth century. The Oseberg ship grave yielded up a number of objects including buckets, several beds, a sleigh, a piece of tapestry and a cart. The ship dates from the time of the Lindisfarne raid and was only used in the later part of its lifespan as a royal barge. Was it actually used on the raid? Again, one can only speculate. There is also speculation that it was the final resting place for Queen Asa, one of the founders of the Yngling dynasty. Whatever the truth, the ship and its contents, which are on display in the Viking Ship Museum on Bigdoy, Oslo, Norway, makes for an impressive reminder of a bygone era.

I have used the modern Norwegian word for their parliament—*Storting*, which literally means the big assembly, rather than the more probable *Ting* or *Thing*, simply because I did not want to affect the reader's enjoyment of the story. I hope that this excuses my anachronism!

I found Magnus Magnusson's book *The Vikings* gave an excellent overview of the period. If you are interested in reading the Icelandic sagas, *Seven Viking Romances* is a good place to start.

Books I found useful include:

Jesch, Judith. *Women in the Viking Age*. Woodbridge, Suffolk: The Boydell Press, 1991.

Magnusson, Magnus. *The Vikings*. Stroud, Gloucestershire: Tempus Publishing, 2003.

Magnusson, Magnus and Hermann Palsson. Trans. *Laxdaela Saga*. Harmondsworth: Penguin, 1969.

Palsson, Hermann and Paul Edwards. Trans. *Seven Viking Romances*. Harmondsworth: Penguin, 1985.

Rosedahl, Else. *The Vikings*. Trans. Susan Margeson and Kirsten Williams. Revised ed. Harmondsworth: Penguin, 1998.

Woods, Michael. *In Search of the Dark Ages*. 2nd ed. London: BBC Books, 2005.

THOROUGHBRED LEGACY
*The stakes are high when it comes to love,
horse racing, family secrets
and broken promises.*

A new exciting Harlequin continuity series coming soon!
Led by **New York Times** *bestselling author Elizabeth Bevarly*
FLIRTING WITH TROUBLE

Here's a preview!

THE DOOR CLOSED behind them, throwing them into darkness and leaving them utterly alone. And the next thing Daniel knew, he heard himself saying, "Marnie, I'm sorry about the way things turned out in Del Mar."

She said nothing at first, only strode across the room and stared out the window beside him. Although he couldn't see her well in the darkness—he still hadn't switched on a light...but then, neither had she—he imagined her expression was a little preoccupied, a little anxious, a little confused.

Finally, very softly, she said, "Are you?"

He nodded, then, worried she wouldn't be able to see the gesture, added, "Yeah. I am. I should have said goodbye to you."

"Yes, you should have."

Actually, he thought, there were a lot of things he should have done in Del Mar. He'd had *a lot* riding on the Pacific Classic, and even more on his entry, Little Joe, but after meeting Marnie, the Pacific Classic had been the last thing on Daniel's mind. His loss at Del Mar had pretty much ended his career before it had even begun, and he'd had to start all over again, rebuilding from nothing.

He simply had not then and did not now have room in his life for a woman as potent as Marnie Roberts. He was a horseman first and foremost. From the time he was a schoolboy, he'd known what he wanted to do with his life—be the best possible trainer he could be.

He had to make sure Marnie understood—and he understood, too—why things had ended the way they had eight years ago. He just wished he could find the words to do that. Hell, he wished he could find the *thoughts* to do that.

"You made me forget things, Marnie, things that I really needed to remember. And that scared the hell out of me. Little Joe should have won the Classic. He was by far the best horse entered in that race. But I didn't give him the attention he needed and deserved that week, because all I could think about was you. Hell, when I woke up that morning all I wanted to do was lie there and look at you, and then wake you up and make love to you again. If I hadn't left when I did—the way I did—I might still be lying there in that bed with you, thinking about nothing else."

"And would that be so terrible?" she asked.

"Of course not," he told her. "But that wasn't why I was in Del Mar," he repeated. "I was in Del Mar to win a race. That was my job. And my work was the most important thing to me."

She said nothing for a moment, only studied his face in the darkness as if looking for the answer to a very important question. Finally she asked, "And what's the most important thing to you now, Daniel?"

Wasn't the answer to that obvious? "My work," he answered automatically.

She nodded slowly. "Of course," she said softly. "That is, after all, what you do best."

Her comment, too, puzzled him. She made it sound as if being good at what he did was a bad thing.

She bit her lip thoughtfully, her eyes fixed on his, glimmering in the scant moonlight that was filtering through the window. And damned if Daniel didn't find himself wanting to pull her into his arms and kiss her. But as much as it might have felt as if no time had passed since Del Mar, there were eight years between now and then. And eight years was a long time in the best of circumstances. For Daniel and Marnie, it was virtually a lifetime.

So Daniel turned and started for the door, then halted. He couldn't just walk away and leave things as they were, unsettled. He'd done that eight years ago and regretted it.

"It *was* good to see you again, Marnie," he said softly. And since he was being honest, he added, "I hope we see each other again."

She didn't say anything in response, only stood silhouetted against the window with her arms wrapped around her in a way that made him wonder whether she was doing it because she was cold, or if she just needed something—someone—to hold on to. In either case, Daniel understood. There was an emptiness clinging to him that he suspected would be there for a long time.

* * * * *

THOROUGHBRED LEGACY
coming soon wherever books are sold!

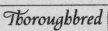 

Cole's Red-Hot Pursuit

Cole Westmoreland is a man who gets what he wants. And he wants independent and sultry Patrina Forman! She resists him—until a Montana blizzard traps them together. For three delicious nights, Cole indulges Patrina with his brand of seduction. When the sun comes out, Cole and Patrina are left to wonder—will this be the end of the passion that storms between them?

Look for

COLE'S RED-HOT PURSUIT

by USA TODAY bestselling author

BRENDA JACKSON

Available in June 2008 wherever you buy books.

Always Powerful, Passionate and Provocative.

REQUEST YOUR FREE BOOKS!

Harlequin® Historical
Historical Romantic Adventure!

2 FREE NOVELS PLUS 2 FREE GIFTS!

YES! Please send me 2 FREE Harlequin® Historical novels and my 2 FREE gifts (gifts are worth about $10). After receiving them, if I don't wish to receive any more books, I can return the shipping statement marked "cancel". If I don't cancel, I will receive 6 brand-new novels every month and be billed just $4.94 per book in the U.S. or $5.49 per book in Canada, plus 25¢ shipping and handling per book and applicable taxes, if any*. That's a savings of 20% off the cover price! I understand that accepting the 2 free books and gifts places me under no obligation to buy anything. I can always return a shipment and cancel at any time. Even if I never buy another book, the two free books and gifts are mine to keep forever.

246 HDN ERUM   349 HDN ERUA

Name	(PLEASE PRINT)
Address	Apt. #
City	State/Prov.	Zip/Postal Code

Signature (if under 18, a parent or guardian must sign)

Mail to the **Harlequin Reader Service:**
IN U.S.A.: P.O. Box 1867, Buffalo, NY 14240-1867
IN CANADA: P.O. Box 609, Fort Erie, Ontario L2A 5X3

Not valid to current subscribers of Harlequin Historical books.

Want to try two free books from another line?
Call 1-800-873-8635 or visit www.morefreebooks.com.

* Terms and prices subject to change without notice. N.Y. residents add applicable sales tax. Canadian residents will be charged applicable provincial taxes and GST. This offer is limited to one order per household. All orders subject to approval. Credit or debit balances in a customer's account(s) may be offset by any other outstanding balance owed by or to the customer. Please allow 4 to 6 weeks for delivery. Offer available while quantities last.

Your Privacy: Harlequin Books is committed to protecting your privacy. Our Privacy Policy is available online at www.eHarlequin.com or upon request from the Reader Service. From time to time we make our lists of customers available to reputable third parties who may have a product or service of interest to you. If you would prefer we not share your name and address, please check here. ☐

HH08

Romantic
SUSPENSE

Sparked *by* Danger,
Fueled *by* Passion.

Seduction Summer:
Seduction in the sand...and a killer on the beach.

Silhouette Romantic Suspense invites you to the hottest
summer yet with three connected stories from some
of our steamiest storytellers! Get ready for...

Killer Temptation
by Nina Bruhns;
a millionaire this tempting is worth a little danger.

Killer Passion
by Sheri WhiteFeather;
an FBI profiler's forbidden passion incites a
killer's rage,

and

Killer Affair
by Cindy Dees;
this affair with a mystery man is to die for.

Look for
KILLER TEMPTATION by Nina Bruhns in June 2008
KILLER PASSION by Sheri WhiteFeather in July 2008
and
KILLER AFFAIR by Cindy Dees in August 2008.

Available wherever you buy books!

Visit Silhouette Books at www.eHarlequin.com   SRS27586

Royal Seductions

Michelle Celmer delivers a powerful miniseries in
Royal Seductions; where two brothers fight for the
crown and discover love. In *The King's Convenient Bride*,
the king discovers his marriage of convenience to the
woman he's been promised to wed is turning all too
real. The playboy prince proposes a mock engagement
to defuse rumors circulating about him and restore
order to the kingdom…until his pretend fiancée
becomes pregnant in *The Illegitimate Prince's Baby*.

Look for

THE KING'S CONVENIENT BRIDE
&
THE ILLEGITIMATE PRINCE'S BABY

BY MICHELLE CELMER

Available in June 2008 wherever you buy books.

Always Powerful, Passionate and Provocative.

COMING NEXT MONTH FROM

HARLEQUIN®
HISTORICAL

- **THE LAST RAKE IN LONDON**
  by **Nicola Cornick**
  (Edwardian)
  Dangerous Jack Kestrel was the most sinfully sensual rogue she'd
  ever met, and the wicked glint in his eyes promised he'd take care of
  satisfying Sally's every need....
  Watch as the last rake in London meets his match!

- **AN IMPETUOUS ABDUCTION**
  by **Patricia Frances Rowell**
  (Regency)
  Persephone had stumbled into danger, and the only way to protect her
  was to abduct her! But what would Leo's beautiful prisoner do when he
  revealed his true identity?
  *Don't miss Patricia Frances Rowell's unique blend of passion spiced
  with danger!*

- **KIDNAPPED BY THE COWBOY**
  by **Pam Crooks**
  (Western)
  TJ Grier was determined to clear his name, even if his actions might
  cost him the woman he loved!
  Fall in love with Pam Crooks's honorable cowboy!

- **INNOCENCE UNVEILED**
  by **Blythe Gifford**
  (Medieval)
  With her flaming red hair, Katrine knew no man would be tempted
  by her. But Renard, a man of secrets, intended to break through her
  defenses....
  *Innocence and passion are an intoxicating mix in this emotional
  medieval tale.*